SO
WELL
AS
YOU

SO WELL AS YOU

LYNN GALLI

PENIKILA PRESS

Synopsis

Running a horse ranch is all Nora Cleary needs to be happy. She's spent her life working on her family's ranch and competing to showcase their training program. When the opportunity to start a new ranching operation abroad comes up, she jumps at the offer. Scotland will be her chance at happiness after suffering some disappointments at home.

Once, Damisi Dalziel reached for happiness only to have it slip away. Today, she's content with her work as a professor and her wonderful circle of friends. Everything is just right in her life, until a certain American cowgirl saunters through the door of her home with an outrageous declaration.

Will their forced cohabitation lead to a constant battle of wills, or will it prove that differences can sometimes lead to fiery connections?

BENEDICK. I do love nothing in the world so well as you—is not that strange?

BEATRICE. As strange as the thing I know not. It were as possible for me to say I lov'd nothing so well as you, but believe me not; and yet I lie not: I confess nothing, nor I deny nothing.

> —Shakespeare, *Much Ado About Nothing* (4.1.267-272)

CHAPTER 1

WHEN THE LOOMING shadow of the gigantic structure came into view, I gulped audibly. My new employer was rich. Filthy, inconceivably, tech billionaire rich. I knew that before taking this job. Google gave me a lot of information about Hearn Ogilvie and his not one, not two, but three mega successful apps. He'd sold his first two for an eye-blinding amount of money. The chief software architect on all of them, and now the CEO of his latest, he'd also founded an admirable charitable foundation. Rich didn't seem a significant enough label for his level of affluence. The grand scale of this country home was the embodiment of showing versus telling on that score.

"The castle is a replica, actually," the driver told me when he noticed my wide eyes in the rearview mirror of the Rolls Royce Phantom. "Sir had it built from the ground up, stone by stone, precisely as it was when first constructed. Historians, archeologists, and architects from area universities gave their input to ensure everything was done correctly."

Sir? He really called his boss that? Hearn better not expect the same from me. When we'd met a few years ago, he was like any typical first-time visitor at a horse competition, hiding the fascination while trying to act as if he'd seen everything before. When he opened his mouth and a Scottish lilt spilled forth, a few of my fellow competitors laughed. Because I'd stayed to answer his questions, he'd sought me out at more competitions over the years. When his niece joined him, she couldn't contain her fascination with the horses and my competition in particular. Based on the number of times he'd attended and brought his sister's family with him, the designer clothes, the caliber of ultra-luxury cars, the offer of dinners at the best restaurants in whatever town we were competing, I'd guessed he was well off. It wasn't until his first offer of a job that I'd run a cursory search on him. The geeky, family guy I'd pegged him to be turned out to be Airbnb-rich. Still a sweet guy, earnest in his admiration for horses and making his niece's wishes come true, but wow, knowing he could buy and sell my home town of Pocatello, Idaho many times over was a little intimidating.

"Ms. Cleary?" the driver asked as if he'd been calling my name a few times.

"Yes, sorry, I was still marveling." I didn't bother asking him to call me by my first name again after refusing two times already.

"Quite. As I was saying, Sir plans to build out the estate over the next few years. Currently, there is only one other completed building on the grounds. A guest cottage for now, but it will eventually be the permanent home of the stables manager."

It was one of the best reasons for taking this job. I'd been operating my own small ranch for four years now. The last thing I wanted to do was shove myself into a tiny apartment somewhere to take this job, even if it was just temporary.

We kept driving about a half mile past the castle. Dark tree-shaped forms lined the drive as we meandered farther into the darkness. He could probably drive the road without lights, but they helped me see the façade of my temporary residence. The "guest cottage" looked larger than the three-bedroom house on my ranch. In daylight, it might appear even larger.

As I stepped out of the car, the driver said, "I'll get that, miss." His hand gripped the handle of the door after I'd already started to close it. Oops, blunder number six since I'd stepped foot on foreign soil. I could only imagine how many more I'd cause before dropping off to sleep tonight.

I reached into the trunk to grab my luggage before he could. "Thanks. I appreciate you making a special trip to pick me up at the airport tonight."

His distinguished look could pass for anywhere from forty to sixty. Silver threads glittered in his light-colored hair. Crow lines weren't too deep, but they were present. He had a formal air about him, but I wasn't sure if it was due to his job or his age. "You're quite welcome."

"I can take it from here," I said as he moved to pick up my bags.

He looked down at the two rolling suitcases, carryon duffle, and backpack with the barest hint of doubt, but he didn't voice it, which I appreciated even more. "Very good, miss."

Very good? This guy was a living PBS Masterpiece Special. "Good night, then. Thanks again for the ride."

"My pleasure." He seemed to float back to the car.

On the flights over to Edinburgh, I'd gone over the details of Hearn's offer. The estate would be part vacation home for him, part public tour to benefit the country's historical society, and part horse training stables. The horse stables were always going to be part of the grounds, but after his niece's fascination with my competition specialty, Hearn decided to add a training and breeding facility. He asked me to get it up and running, but my career path and future were already set. Or so I thought. When that changed unexpectedly, I called to see if the offer still stood. Hearn was so pleased he put a rush on my visa application, and being a well-known billionaire, the app was expedited. Almost before I was ready, I found myself on flights to New York, then London, then Edinburgh, and finally, a fifteen-minute drive to Bathgate in the most expensive vehicle I'd ever seen.

The only caveat, besides traveling out of North America for the first time in my life, was the housemate situation. Hearn had offered to make one of the rooms in the family wing of the castle open to me, but then I'd be sharing a home with my boss and his family whenever they visited the estate. Not to mention, the other areas of the structure were going to be used for public tours to showcase the architecture and period pieces acquired. The guesthouse would be closer to the stables than the main house, but currently, one of his friends from college was staying there. That was also temporary, but for a few months, we'd be sharing the cottage, unless I wanted to stay in a hotel for months. I'd had several roommates in college and my best friend as a periodic roommate at home, but it would be a completely new experience sharing a house with a stranger.

When the code for the spiffy door lock worked, I breathed a sigh of relief. On the ride from the airport, I'd been worried this might have been an elaborate practical joke. Get the hick from Idaho on several planes, crossing international borders, with the promise of an exciting job and a place to live, only to have her turned away at the door an hour shy of midnight. But, it worked, which meant, this was no joke. I was in Scotland, starting a horse training and breeding business from the jump, running it how I wanted without interference from anyone. If I weren't so exhausted from all the traveling, I'd be too excited to sleep.

As the door swung open, faint music could be heard from inside. The housemate was up or fell asleep to music. I should have pushed for more information on her or him. I had a name, but I'd never heard it before and couldn't tell if it was feminine or masculine. Not that names were one or the other anymore. Or people for that matter. But it would be nice to know if I'd be sharing a home with a man, woman, or nonbinary, or gender fluid, or crap, I'm a bad lesbian because I don't know all the terms for everyone on the gender spectrum when I probably should.

I set my suitcases by the door, not wanting to meet this person with arms full of luggage that would look like an invasion of her temporary homestead. I was, in fact, invading, but presentation was key upon a first meeting.

A stairway rose up to the right of the foyer. The music seemed to be coming from down the hallway straight ahead, so I kicked off my shoes and went toward it. The hall opened up into a spacious living room with modern furniture, a stone fireplace, and a massive television mounted above it. A dining area sat just beyond with the kitchen to the left. A popular R&B song came from built-in speakers, but there was no sign of the housemate. There were two doorways on the other side of the living room. I didn't want to barge into what might be a bedroom, but I couldn't just stake a claim to a bedroom without first meeting the housemate who'd been living here for a few months already.

Before deciding how best to announce myself, I heard a sound from one of the rooms across from me. A singing voice, higher pitched than most men's, but still not a conclusive fact. It sounded lovely, as good as the professional singer on the track. Heat built up in my chest and spread to my neck and face. I was never comfortable with people singing around me.

For some odd reason, it embarrassed me. Karaoke bars were my living nightmare.

I blew out a breath and sucked in another, rubbing a hand over my stomach to keep from getting too knotted up at this already odd circumstance. So, she—likely she not he—sang. So what? It was her house; she could sing along to music. It was going to be my house, too, and I could draw or read or play Xbox all I wanted. There, good. Fleeting embarrassment over with. I was ready to meet whoever liked singing in her home.

The voice got louder just before the person it belonged to slid through the doorway in a slick dance move. Her shoulder length black curls flicked aside for a glimpse of the most beautiful face I'd ever seen in person or on screen in my entire life.

Her eyes caught mine and widened in shock. Her perfectly proportioned mouth opened, and instead of more of her admittedly good singing voice, she screamed. Loudly. The scream should have been what startled me, but really, it was how gorgeous she was. So gorgeous, I almost didn't notice she was stark naked.

Holy hell and all things magnificently naked. Welcome to Scotland.

CHAPTER 2

REFLEXIVELY, I WHIRLED and faced the hallway. We were both women. Seeing one naked wasn't a big deal. Yet, I was honorable. I had no right to see her naked without her permission.

"Who the fuck are you?" she yelled after she finished her scream, and I had to stop from laughing because her accent made "fuck" sound more like "feck."

But this wasn't a laughing matter. She was terrified and I couldn't blame her. Someone pops into her living room as she's dancing naked in private, of course, she's scared.

"I'm Nora. Nora Cleary. Your new housemate," I tried in a calm voice.

"My what? No. That's not possible."

"It is, though," I relayed, losing some patience. After all the traveling, my back ached, my feet felt numb, and my head, which had started pounding while waiting in line at passport control, was flaring to a raging headache right about now. "Are you decent?"

"Of course, I'm decent. What sort of question is that? Are you American?"

I wasn't sure if they used "decent" here the way we did, so I clarified. "I meant, are you clothed? Can I turn around now?"

"As much as possible without going to my room. I spilled something on my dress and went to put it in the laund—why am I explaining myself to you?"

"I know this must be a shock, but didn't Hearn let you know I'd be arriving late tonight?" I took a quick peek over my shoulder to make sure she wasn't still naked, not that I'd mind another glimpse of her stunning body. She'd wrapped a bath towel around herself, probably having ducked into the laundry room where she'd dropped her dress to be cleaned. Slowly, I twisted back around to face her.

"Hearn?" She shook her head, those loose curls dancing as wonderfully as she'd been. "He didn't tell me anything. Why are you here?"

I started rubbing my temples. "For the horses."

"What horses? There aren't any horses here. Certainly not in my home. Why are you in my home, specifically?"

I sighed, the knots of embarrassment from earlier turned into twisted snarls of aggravation. She wasn't getting it, and I was really, really tired. "Didn't Hearn tell you I would be sharing this house with you? If you're, uh, crap, I can't remem—oh, Damisi." I snapped my fingers upon remembering her name.

She even frowned beautifully. A single crease formed on her forehead while her lips pressed into a brief straight line. My attention immediately went to her shapely mouth. Full, dusky red lips chiseled with precise arches and sweeping curves stood out on her gorgeous oval face.

Her reply snatched my attention from the catalog of her features. "He did not, which isn't like him at all." Uh-oh, Hearn must have forgotten to mention our living arrangement in the haste to get me a visa and the preparations for the horse stables. "I'm going to call him. Stay right where you are."

I lifted my hands, giving her a posture of surrender. Didn't matter how gorgeous she was; her attitude was a little grating, and yet, understandable. If someone just showed up in the middle of my living room, with me naked or not, I'd probably be going to my shotgun locker. If she were a man, I wouldn't hesitate to draw down, but a woman, I'd hear her out first. Still, it wasn't my fault she was so damn unprepared for me. I was clearly nonthreatening. I'd introduced myself and nobly turned around to preserve her modesty. She couldn't give me a sliver of a break?

Her footsteps sounded on the stairwell. Minutes passed as I looked around the space, taking in more of the details on this sweep. It was decorated in a comfortable modern style. The couch looked especially comfy after my extended day of travel, but I didn't dare move to show her she could trust me.

Finally, her voice could be heard again. "...believe you did this and didn't tell me. Hearn, that's not like you. Have I overstayed my welcome?" She paused at the top of the stairwell. "Then why here?" After another moment, she started down the stairwell. "I understand. Describe her, please." She stepped onto the landing in the foyer, bare feet still, but the rest of her was clothed. She walked with a sexy swing to her hips, and it totally wasn't on purpose, not if the scowl she wore was to be believed. "This woman's hair isn't long or even chin-length. It's short, very short."

My hand ran over my new haircut. A close cut up to chopped chunks at varying lengths on top. An inch here, an inch and a half there, add some paste and it was a chic choppy pixie that was so much easier to care for than my previous shoulder-length locks. The haircut symbolized part of my newfound freedom. I absolutely loved it and how easy it was to take care of. Also, how it represented the exact opposite of what had been pounded into me from birth about the acceptable length of women's hair.

I reached out. "May I speak with him, please?"

Her dark eyes narrowed. If she could have used an apparatus to extend the phone to me without getting closer, she would have. She stopped murmuring into the phone and tentatively reached it toward me.

"Hi, Hearn. I've managed to scare the living daylights out of your friend here. How's your evening going?"

He chuckled as if this was all a funny mix-up. "I'm glad you're there. Can't wait for you to get started."

"Hearn," I borrowed some of the tone usually reserved for my irritating brothers. "Why didn't you tell Damisi I would be arriving tonight? And why didn't she know I would be sharing this house with her?"

"Aye, well, to tell the truth, I forgot. I've been so busy with work it slipped my mind. You understand. Damisi understands. She'll be grand in no time."

I flicked my eyes back to the supposedly understanding woman, who stood several arm lengths away. She didn't look like she'd be grand any time soon, but at least she wasn't about to call the police and seemed resigned to the idea of me being in her home. "You might want to apologize to her. My appearance really did give her a fright."

"Sure, sure. Pass me over. And, Nora, glad to have you on board. We'll have a chinwag tomorrow after you've had time to look at the progress we've made with the stables."

"Thank you, Hearn. Talk to you tomorrow." I handed the phone back.

She turned around and murmured more into the phone. Her shoulders rounded and a noticeable breath left her lungs. "It's your home, Hearn. I'm grateful you've let me stay." She listened and said, "It was a bit of a shock. Sorry for the panicked call. Yes, chat tomorrow."

When she faced me again, her shoulders straightened, expression composed, hair fabulous, mouth sensational. "It seems we're to be flatmates."

I refrained from a sarcastic retort. My head still pounded and my patience was on its last legs. If I couldn't understand how she must have felt in that first moment of seeing me, I would have adopted the same reticent attitude she had.

She held out her hand and introduced herself. I had to step forward into the greeting. A complete power play on her part. If not for my exhaustion, I'd have gotten more annoyed. But that was no way to start a cohabitation.

"D-e-E-l-l-e as it sounds, or is it spelled like the Dalziel character in those novels?" I asked of her last name.

Her eyebrows shot up. "Not the character on the telly?"

"I do read," I shot back.

"Quite." A slight dip of her head acknowledged my protest. "You're correct. It's Dalziel like the character, both literary and on television. Or perhaps you Yanks never got to see the series."

My shoulders hitched. I hadn't seen it on television and didn't know if one of our networks had picked it up. The books were pretty good, not my favorite of British police procedurals, but good. The most memorable part for me had been the pronunciation of the lead detective's last name. Completely different from how it was spelled.

"Why does Hearn think you have long hair?"

I just stared at her, my head pounding too hard for me to bother responding to the obvious question. I glanced around the space, hoping to get past this and settled soon.

"I should have asked when you got it cut?"

"Recently." So recently I'd forgotten why the TSA and customs agents had reason to stare so intensely at me, then at my passport. It didn't occur to me that I no longer looked like the woman in my passport photo because I'd always looked like her. The haircut was so drastically different it warranted more than just a long look. Each agent had held up my passport next to my face to compare the features.

Her eyes examined my hair, which did not in any way look its blond shiny best after twenty-two hours of travel and hat wearing. Her own hair with its perfectly shaped curls and rich black tones put mine to shame, even as much as I loved this new cut.

"How did you meet Hearn?"

"At a horse-riding competition a few years ago. We've seen each other several times since. His niece loves horses."

"She does. I didn't realize she loved them enough for Hearn to bring over a teacher from America."

"I'll be getting the stables up and running. Training the horses and helping his niece find a suitable coach."

Her head nodded, poker face in place. Perhaps she thought she'd be rid of me after a two-week training session while his niece visited over a school break. Hearn really needed to do a better job communicating with his friend.

"My rooms are upstairs. There's a suite here on the ground floor. Perhaps that will suit? It should maintain the civility, don't you agree?"

I hadn't planned on anything less than civil. Friendship would be great, but I could tell she felt backed into a corner and our less than stellar meeting—for her—probably added to her reticence. "Certainly, ma'am," I agreed because polite never hurt anyone

"Ma'am?" she repeated, then a small smile tugged at those beautiful lips. "Don't call me ma'am. I'm not the bloody queen."

I matched her smile. "Now that's a show I have seen. The books were great, too."

She gave another nod, more definitive this time. Perhaps she'd decided she could trust me not to sneak upstairs and murder her in her sleep due to my appreciation of Jane Tennison. "The bedroom's just through there." Her hand gestured to the door past the one she'd danced out of earlier.

Heat touched my cheeks again as I remembered the briefest flash of her sleek naked body swiveling in time to the music. I really shouldn't have turned away. Her frosty reception told me it would be the last chance I'd get to see her naked.

CHAPTER 3

AT QUARTER TO six in the morning, I stepped lightly out of my bedroom, listening for any signs my new "flatmate" was awake. No sounds drifted downstairs, but this looked like a well-built home. I went to the kitchen and checked the narrow refrigerator, hoping there would be space in there for me to place food after a shopping trip later. That was always a tricky part when moving in with a roommate. Add to that, this woman apparently had no idea I'd be sharing this space with her. I really had to get the whole story on that. Hearn had done a primo recruiting job, always assuring me how welcome and necessary I'd be. Clearly, he hadn't informed his current temporary resident about his newest temporary resident.

After checking the refrigerator, cabinets, and pantry, I mentally rearranged what was there to accommodate my additions without poking the tiger upstairs. The mudroom held a tankless water heater, utility panel, and a combo washer/dryer unit. Back in the living room, my eyes roamed the space again. It felt comfortable with nice quality furniture. My fingers crossed in hope that Damisi would be open to letting me test the comfort of the fixtures without the massive tension from last night.

Grabbing my boots and hat from my room, I headed outside for my first daylight glimpse of the grounds. A half-circle, paving stone driveway cut around a nice planting area. Green stretched over rolling hills along the driveway that must lead up to the main house. With the leafy trees and bends in the road, the castle was not visible from the front stoop. I tried to remember if the driver told me how big the estate grounds were. Several hundred acres at least, and Hearn was still buying up any available property in the vicinity to add back to the original estate grounds.

I took one of the pathways off to the side of the house. A walled cottage garden surrounded the back of the house. That would make for a nice breakfast spot when the weather warmed up a bit. Various vegetation surrounded the pathway I followed and led to wide open green spaces. Fenced paddocks should already be spread out here. Before I took this job, Hearn had a project manager send me an update on the progress of the ranch buildout. Fencing was listed as done. Only so far, there was no fencing.

Stepping off the pathway, I ventured into the pasture area to take a better look at the state of the grazing grass. A hundred feet in, ATV tracks ate up the ground, carving deep muddy ruts that crisscrossed the pasture as far as the eye could see. From the walking trail, this wouldn't have been visible. Someone was using this land as a dirt bike and ATV track. That would have to stop. Since it was so far away from the main house, no one would have heard the riders. I'd have to ask Damisi if she was around during the day and heard any engine noise.

Up ahead, the stable barn came into view. Modern amenities and high security would be in place from the start. It was so amazing to be heard about what needed to be done for the horses. Having grown up on a horse ranch, working it day and night, I'd made endless suggestions to my father about improvements and necessities only to have them brushed aside. Not so with Hearn. At first, I thought it was a way to recruit me, make empty promises, anything to get me to take the job he'd been offering for two years. He was happy enough to have me work as a consultant from afar as soon as construction began, but he really wanted me here to run things because he knew farm business was my passion. Born into it, studied it, and currently living it. Hearn was a business tycoon, a coding wizard, but didn't have any ranching experience. We couldn't be more different, and yet, when he decided to move on an idea, he went all out.

The stable barn was still under construction. Not a surprise, but I'd been led to believe it would be ninety percent done, ready for horses in early May. It wasn't. It was fifty percent done. Construction always ran into problems, sure, but there's a difference between three more weeks of work and what looked like seven. One more thing not going as planned.

I shook my head. We were supposed to have horses here in a few weeks. Their passage was booked already, which was another quirk of Hearn's. When he found out I rode American Quarter Horses, worked on them, trained them for other cutting competitors, Hearn decided those were the horses he'd want on his ranch. It didn't seem to matter they were native to the US and only one other rancher in all of Scotland had them available on his ranch.

As I walked the length of the barn, I took notes on what still needed to be done. The construction manager probably had the same list, but if I was going to do this, it would be done right. Using a discarded tape measure, I took down the measurements and did some math. On this side of the H-shaped barn, there'd be room for twenty horses in large stalls with a twenty-four-foot aisle, an equipment room, and a wash stall. The crossway would hold restrooms, a tack room, feed room, and the stable office. If the business grew according to plan, Hearn would greenlight building the other side of the H with the same amenities and connect it to the crossway. Exponential growth could warrant even more wings added. All lessons I'd learned over the years of working on my dad's farm. His original small barn had been replaced four times over to include everything but well-placed equipment rooms, which I'd been hounding him about for years. To have everything in place and a plan to expand without need for replacement on day one would be a blessing.

A look at my watch said I'd been out here for more than two hours. The construction crew should be here by now. So should the three guys Hearn hired to prep the grounds, put in the fencing, and be ranch hands once the horses arrived. Maybe they had different work hours in Scotland.

My stomach growled. Breakfast time, but I needed to go shopping first. Hearn had a truck purchased for my use, but I hadn't seen a garage on my way over. Perhaps it was on the other side of the cottage. A granola bar would have to tide me over until the workers arrived and I could introduce myself and get them started on the day's tasks.

My walk back through the pastures on a different route showed the same torn up conditions, making the grounds look more like a dirt bike track than a pasture. Everything would need to be regraded and reseeded. Closer to the cottage, a road came into view. The start of a fence bordered the road. At least they'd gotten something started. Close up, I realized I'd spoken too soon. A dozen thin rail posts stretched along the pasture with chicken wire attached, which was wholly unsuitable for horses. The road bent back inland, away from the pasture area dividing the trees hiding the cottage from the stable barn. I stood on the road and glanced left and right along the pasture. From the road, it looked like the pasture was fenced, an illusion of completed work.

Following the road, I stopped off at the detached garage, eager to see what kind of truck Hearn had purchased. The entry door was locked, and without a remote, I couldn't get inside. Hopefully Damisi would know where the remote or key was. I drew in a deep breath and turned back to the cottage.

Unlacing my ropers, I left them near the front door. Sounds came from the kitchen area. Seems Damisi was awake.

"Good morning," I called softly.

She jerked in place, her back to me, the cup she'd been about to set down clattered against the saucer. She twisted to face me. Her eyes narrowed slightly before a forced smile graced her beautiful mouth. She was put together for work. A fitted skirt and wrap blouse gave her a comfortable dressy look. Bare feet looked as good as her heels would. In the morning light spilling through the windows, she appeared even more gorgeous than she had last night. How that was possible, I didn't know, especially with a slight scowl on her symmetrical face.

"Morning," she replied. "You've been out already?"

"Habit. I usually have horses to feed first thing in the morning before breakfast." From the moment I was old enough to help feed the horses, all the way up to yesterday, my routine was to get up early, feed the horses, attend to any unignorable issues in the stalls, then come back to help my mom make breakfast for the family, and after, off to school. When I moved out of the house, the routine altered to make breakfast for myself, then off to work or back to farm duties, depending on the day and year.

Her dark brown eyes flicked to the refrigerator. She was probably trying to come up with a semi-polite way of telling me I couldn't eat her food.

"I have to go shopping. You wouldn't happen to know where the remote for the garage is or the keys to the farm truck?"

Another frown pulled her skin tight momentarily. "The other door remote is in the sideboard in the foyer. I don't know anything about keys or another vehicle."

Hearn hadn't told her about me, she probably didn't know about anything going on with his ranch. His assistant assured me one of the workers had purchased a truck for the farm's use. If Damisi didn't know about it, perhaps the worker had been taking it home at night. That would make for an awkward first day conversation when I had to tell him he'd need to leave it here from now on.

"Hearn said the furniture and appliances are available for my use, but I don't want to overstep with something of yours. He might have told you something different, seeing as he forgot to tell you about me."

She let out a breath and took a sip from her teacup. "The cottage has everything you'll need. I've brought a few personal pieces for my space upstairs, but everything else belongs to the cottage. It's for our use."

"Thank you." I reached up and opened three cabinets before I found the glasses. Pulling one down, I filled it with water and took a drink. The granola bars were in my backpack, but I didn't want to leave her presence when we were talking. "You look nice. Are you off to work?"

She glanced down at her outfit and rolled the gaze over me. "I am."

"Do you enjoy it?"

Her head tilted, brushing perfectly twisted curls over one shoulder. "You're not a typical Yank, are you?"

"Are you a typical Scot?"

She snorted, surprising both of us in its indelicateness. "Hardly." She waved a hand in a ta-da gesture near her face.

Was she pointing out how gorgeous she was? Was she one of those people who knew just how good she looked and tied every ounce of her self-worth to it? She had perfect skin, too, absolutely no marks or wrinkles, and a warm hue to the fair coloring. The flash of her flawless skin from last night told me she wasn't sporting a farmer's tan. The warm tone reached everywhere. Perhaps that's what she meant by not being typical.

"What do you mean?" I had to ask.

"Yanks are quite concerned with what people do for a living. It's often your first question for someone."

Hmm. So, she wasn't going to answer the question I really wanted her to answer. In what way was she the non-typical Scot. She focused on me being an atypical Yank. Her repeated use of the term meant she was trying to get a rise out of me. "I guess we do." I'd held my tongue for most of my life; no reason I couldn't keep doing it here for a little while.

"You told me what you did within moments of meeting you."

"That I did. Of course, you were thinking I was an axe murderer. Pretty much had to explain why I was here."

She nodded in acknowledgement, a small smile ghosting over her expression. "It was nice to find out you're a cowgirl and not an axe murderer."

"Safer, anyway. And you? Any axe murdering in your previous work experience?"

A full-blown smile bloomed on her face. "Knife throwing is more my style. Comes in handy at work."

"Chef? Magician? Carney?"

She gave a breathy chuckle that was as sexy as everything else about her. "Professor." Surprise must have shown on my face. "At Edinburgh, and temporarily, Glasgow."

"A guest lecturer?"

"Something like that."

"You must be in high demand to work two universities."

She shrugged and turned to set her cup and saucer in the sink. On bare feet, she came in around five-seven with toned calves, a slender frame, and shapely arms that showed she had a regular exercise regimen. Not ranch-work toned like most of the people I knew back home, but still, damn fine.

To keep from obsessing about her fit body, I continued, "I met someone in the vet school from Edinburgh when she was giving a lecture back in the States. It's a prestigious university." My mind took a moment to mark that as a reminder to get in touch with Dr. Luskin. She'd been my first call to learn more about the area when I was considering taking this job. "You never answered my original question. Do you enjoy it?"

Damisi's eyes flared. "I do, and I'm guessing you love your work or you wouldn't have traveled so far to carry on doing it."

"You'd be correct."

"Well," she paused, glancing around to check the counters were clear. "I should be off. I'll be chatting to Hearn later. Do you need me to pass anything along?"

"No, thank you." I planned to call him myself as soon as I could get into town for some supplies and a UK sim card.

"Farewell, then," she said, waving her fingers before turning and heading for the front door. She stopped at the closet, opened it, pulled out her heels, a lightweight jacket, and her purse. With ease, she slipped on her heels, shouldered into the coat, and was out the door in seconds.

A professor, gorgeous, and determined to give me a hard time. A tantalizing triple threat. This could be a long spring and summer.

CHAPTER 4

BY NOON, NEITHER the workers nor the construction crew had shown up. I'd planned to wait until after the workday to go into town, but I needed real food and a way to contact Hearn. He'd said the staff at the main house would be available if I needed anything, but so far, his belief about how things would go weren't proving true.

If I remembered from the drive last night, the town center wasn't in realistic walking distance loaded down with groceries. Without knowing where the truck was, I'd have to call a cab. Not a big deal, except I hadn't gotten an international calling plan on my phone because everyone told me it would be idiotic to pay those charges when I could get a local sim card and use Skype to call home. My only option was to walk up to the main house and see if I could borrow a landline or someone's cellphone.

The lavish landscaped grounds surrounding the castle came into view after a quarter mile of walking. I stopped to take in what I couldn't make out in the floodlights on our drive past last night. The architecture wasn't the typical rounded wall, drawbridge type castle. It looked more like a large manor house with subtle turrets. A palace by most standards, it could have been used in any of the period movies set in the UK.

It didn't take long before I ran into the first landscaper. He did a double take when he saw me waltzing up the road from the back of the property. I waved and took off my hat to greet him. "Hi, I'm Nora. Just started out at the stables."

His concern eased as his head bobbed. "Aye, Gresham mentioned you."

I wasn't going to ask what he mentioned about me. The morning already had enough surprises. "Could you tell me where to find him?" If anyone knew where the farm truck might be kept, it would be the driver from last night.

I followed his directions to the pathway through the elaborate flower garden, past the sweeping fountain, across the croquet field, and over to the multi-car detached garage. Hearn had left nothing undone on this property. Hopefully, the stables would be similarly detailed.

"Hello? Mr. Gresham?"

He came out of a doorway to my left. "Ms. Cleary, good afternoon."

My eyes snagged on the car collection. Exactly what you'd expect of a billionaire. Actually, a little modest for a billionaire. Eight cars were set out in angled rows, gleaming and aching to be driven. All were ultra-luxury or rare classics. Given Hearn's wealth, he could easily have five times the number and more expensive models. Still, Gresham must love his job.

"May I assist you with something, miss?"

"Please call me Nora," I asked him again. It seemed like we might be pushed together more often than I originally thought. "I was hoping you would know where the truck Hearn had purchased for use at the stables was located? I checked the cottage garage, but no luck."

His brow furrowed. "I'm not aware of any lorries on the grounds."

Lorries? Right. I was going to have to study up on these word differences. "No, this would be a passenger vehicle, not a parcel truck. I'll be using it to tow horse trailers, carry feed and hay, and as a personal vehicle to go into town for supplies. A pickup truck?"

"Of course, miss—Nora." He leaned back into his office for a quick perusal. "There are no new keys here, and I've not been told about another personal vehicle."

"His assistant told me one of the stable workers made the purchase. None of them have shown up yet, and I didn't have the foresight to get a sim card for my phone at the airport before you picked me up. I don't have any way to check in with Hearn or call a cab for a ride into town to get some food and other supplies."

"You don't need a cab. I'll be happy to carry you into town."

"I couldn't trouble you." But the idea of riding in another of these amazing cars had its appeal.

"I'm here for the estate. You're part of the estate now. I'll check to see if the housekeeper needs anything and we'll be on our way." He watched my gaze move back to the cars. "Any one you like, except the Lamborghini. That's for Sir's driving pleasure, only."

After a quick phone call from his office, Gresham was back and standing beside me, surveying the cars. "Did you decide?"

"They're all quite beautiful. Which is your favorite to drive?"

He smiled, which made him look younger than the wide age range I'd given him last night. "They're all fun, but I don't get to drive the GranTurismo very often."

"If you're sure Hearn won't mind us taking it to run errands." I waved toward the exit.

"I had to get used to tooling around in such luxury myself." He reached back and fished the keys to the car from a locked cabinet.

In no time, we were back out on the drive, and I could see the grounds in the daylight. It really was impressive. From the bits and pieces Hearn had told me, he'd wanted to do something to honor his Scottish heritage and found a property that had once been a castle with thousands of acres of tenant farmers and a small independent village. The surrounding land had been sold off over the years, but the still standing castle had been bombed during World War II and left in ruins. The previous owner, a millionaire from England had purchased the property thirty years ago and taken down the ruins to replace it with a mansion that he used for vacation purposes. Hearn made him an offer and razed the nondescript thirty-year-old mansion to rebuild the original caste and grounds.

"Are these neighbors?" I pointed to a stone cottage with a detached garage and animal pen.

"Aye. That was the site of the original gatekeeper's home. We've relocated the main entrance to the castle grounds to spare these neighbors the traffic past their home. Beside them is a fifty-acre sheep farm. Both properties would have been part of the original estate grounds, but Sir is quite happy to have them as neighbors. He has several other bordering neighbors with farms."

Gresham provided a brief overview of the town of Bathgate as we drove. About twenty miles west of Edinburgh, it was originally an industrial town but now had all the amenities of towns its size elsewhere in the world. Efficiently, Gresham took us to a shop where I could get a sim pack for my phone, then onto a market for groceries. On our last stop, I convinced him to let me spring for a latte when he wouldn't accept my offer to take him to lunch. I grabbed a sandwich to go while waiting for the lattes, and we were back at the estate in less than an hour. All while riding in a beautiful car.

Quickly, I put away the groceries, shifting Damisi's food to the other shelves in the refrigerator and staking claim to only one. Same with the pantry. Hopefully it wouldn't spark another scream from Damisi, but I needed to move in here, too.

I wolfed down my sandwich, having not had anything more than a granola bar since the sandwich I'd grabbed at Heathrow before jumping onto the last flight yesterday. Placing my plate into the dishwasher, I added the tea cup and saucer Damisi left in the sink this morning. I wasn't a neat freak, just trained well by my mother.

Back outside, I headed toward the stables, happy to hear the sounds of construction in the distance. At least some of the people who were supposed to be working were. Four guys were scattered around the work tables when three times as many should be working on a structure this size.

"Help you, sir?" one of the guys at the work table asked as I approached.

Admittedly, with hat hair, I wasn't much to look at, but this was one of the side effects of going so short with my hair. Add my five-foot-nine-and-a-half-inch frame, and from a distance, most would assume I was a man. "Hi, I'm Nora. I'll be getting the stables up and running over the next few months."

"Oh, excuse me, miss." He looked around hastily for someone else to deal with me.

The guy to his left stepped forward but looked back at the embarrassed one. "It was a Mr. Clary or something, wasn't it?"

"Cleary," I corrected. "And it's Ms."

"Ah." He digested the information slowly.

Too slowly, so I jumped right in. "Isn't this a full-time project for your crew?"

He blinked and rubbed his chin. "Aye, it is."

If we'd been back on my father's ranch, or my own for that matter, I would have bitten his head off for showing up after lunch to start his day, but I really needed to check with Hearn to make sure he hadn't exaggerated the authority he was granting me. He promised one hundred percent, but again, he'd been wrong about other things so far. And no reason to start off my relationship with the construction crew on a snippy note.

"I've made some notes on elements for the stables. I was hoping to go over them with you."

"Right, well, we've got a lot of work going right now. Perhaps in a few days we can have a bit of a natter."

I swallowed the rising anger at being treated as if I were a silly little woman. I'd been swallowing my anger at the unfairness of gender dynamics for three decades; this should be no different. I'd just hoped to have a clean slate here. "I see. Then, if you'll provide me with a copy of your latest building plans, I can check them on my own."

His eyes slit in suspicion. "As I said, we'll have that chat in a few days."

"I have a call scheduled with Hearn later this afternoon. I can bother him to get the plans he'll make you deliver to me, or we can save each other the extra travel, and you can just hand over a copy of the plans now."

He took a long time to weigh his response. Reluctantly, he went to his work table and rummaged around, pulling a set of plans from beneath the ones he had spread out. He didn't look happy about turning them over, but if I was who I said I was, he knew he'd be getting a call from Hearn or an assistant anyway.

I walked them over to the barn entrance. The plans showed smaller measurements for the stalls, but that was an easy fix. At the rate they were going, it would be a while before they started on the interior dimensions. They hadn't put in the windows at the apex of the roofline either. That could be a budget issue, but I made a note.

"When do you pour the floor?" I asked the guy who'd gone back to looking like he was busy.

"Lass, the floor's already there."

My eyes took in the natural earth floor. "You were told to keep a dirt floor?"

"Aye."

We'd have to see about that as well. For cleaning and health purposes, I preferred a concrete floor pad with drainage and a specialized antimicrobial crumbled-rubber coating for extra cushion and ease of cleaning. In the stalls, padded stall liners kept bedding costs down. A dirt floor had to have significant natural drainage, and even then, it was hardest to keep sanitary. Cheap, definitely, but I doubted Hearn would go all out on his estate, and then suddenly cheap out on a few high-dollar amounts in the barn.

"Thanks. I'll take these with me to check over, and we can have that status chat tomorrow morning first thing." I nodded my head and left before anyone could protest my taking the plans offsite.

Yesterday's travel day was rapidly catching up and wearing me down. I sent a text to Hearn's assistant asking for some time to chat with him as I made my way back to the cottage. I was knocking off early, but after only four hours of sleep, I was ready to relax for a while, cook some dinner, and read a bit before bed.

The cottage was still quiet, but again, Damisi could be very quiet or the sound insulation between floors excellent. It would keep me from dancing naked in the house until I learned whether or not I was truly alone. Well, the naked part of the dancing would keep me from dancing naked, but holding back on any other embarrassing behavior would be in effect until I was certain I was alone.

My cell rang and I looked at the display. Not Hearn's assistant, but Hearn himself. My eyebrows rose. For a tech CEO, he sure made time for all of his employees, not just the people in his London office.

"How're you going, Nora? Settling in well enough?"

"Hard to say, Hearn. Have you talked to Damisi today? She wasn't happy to have someone standing in her living room last night, nor did she look like she was prepared for a housemate."

He chuckled as if it were no big deal. "Damisi's not bothered. My fault for not telling her, but she knows the situation now. She's a wonderful friend. I'm certain you'll get on."

Satisfied he'd done enough to smooth things over with her, I moved on to the next issue. "You did say you hired three ranch hands, didn't you? Are they part-time?"

"No, full-time. Great lads. Dunbar's a mate from college. Did they show you around?"

"They didn't show up. Maybe they got my arrival date wrong." I offered an excuse since they were his friends. "What about the construction crew? Are they full-time as well?"

"Don't tell me they weren't there either?" His voice rose in concern. Working in software, he was used to people who plugged in and didn't leave until a project was done. Having someone not show wasn't typical in his line of work.

"Not till after lunch. It also looks like they're way behind schedule. I was supposed to have the horses on a plane soon."

"Yes," he drew the word out. "Will it not be ready in time?"

"Not unless they have superpowers I don't know about."

He gave a nervous chuckle this time. "I haven't been up there in six weeks. I thought they were on track. I know the fencing is in, and the pastures are seeded."

"About that," I broke in. "The fencing is not in, and the pastures have been torn up by some people on motorcycles and ATVs. Those areas will need to be regraded and reseeded, which is something I can handle if you okay the equipment rental."

"Dunbar told me the fencing was done. He sent in the invoices, and I saw it myself."

"Let me guess, you drove by in the evening when lighting wasn't great." It would be the only way to ensure that small patch of fencing along the drive closest to the pasture would look sturdy enough to hold back charging horses.

He paused, letting out a sigh. "You're saying they misled me?"

"Could be a miscommunication. I can ask them when I see them tomorrow."

"I'm sure it's nothing nefarious."

I wasn't, or at least I wasn't sure it wasn't on purpose. His three friends were likely thinking this was a cushy job with the friend-slash-boss in London working insane hours, so they'd never be held accountable. But I should give them the benefit of the doubt. My own experience over the years working my father's ranch didn't mean the same ratio of lazy to good workers would prove true here.

"I texted your assistant about the farm truck?"

"Aye, it's a beauty, isn't it? The lads picked it up. Sent photos from the dealership."

"It's not here. Do you know if one of them drove it home?"

"You were without transportation today? I'm so sorry. Dunbar must have needed it last night. I hope you had Gresham take you anywhere you needed."

"Gresham was nice enough to offer, yes. Thank you."

"Well, keep me updated. If you can't get me, Marcy has her mobile practically implanted."

I signed off and let out a sigh. This had the potential to blow up in my face. He'd been blithely believing his friends had his back and were working hard to help build out the grounds on his dream country estate. Instead, he might find out his friends have been taking advantage of the rich guy.

To unpack or not? That was the question of the hour. If this thing with his friends and the construction crew blew up in my face, he'd put me right back on a plane out of here. Unpacking seemed like jinxing the outcome of those potential confrontations. Then again, I'd committed to four months at a minimum. With the status of the barn construction, it was looking more like six months. Unpacking would fortify my resolve to get through this bumpy beginning and make this work. I'd left behind the life I'd always worked toward. This was my new reality. Settling in would only help me accept it.

After getting everything into the closet and bathroom, I headed to the kitchen and opened the fridge to decide on dinner. Pasta sounded good. Quick to make and easy to keep for leftovers. Locating the cutting boards, I starting dicing the tomatoes, mushrooms, zucchini, basil, and onions for the sauce and placed a pot of water on a burner.

As the sauce came to a boil, the front door opened and closed. I was on the verge of calling out a greeting, but Damisi's footsteps padded up the stairs. Just when I thought she might ignore the fact she now had a roommate, her footsteps sounded again. Gone was the smart skirt and blouse from this morning, replaced with comfy crop pants and a t-shirt. Also gone was the reticence on her expression, replaced now with reluctant acceptance.

"Hello. How was your day?" I asked.

She gave me a half smile. "Fine, and yours?"

"Surprising. Not much is going as expected, but that makes life more fun, right?"

"One of those, yeah?" She seemed to be teasing about my optimistic response.

As she turned to check the fridge, I offered, "There's plenty if you like pasta."

Her back straightened, and she swiveled to look at me. "Very kind."

"Very kind, as in you'll join me for dinner? Or, very kind, you dimwit, now be gone from me."

A split second of silence passed before her mouth opened and a bark of laughter spilled forth. Not at all delicate or soft or cute. The absolute best kind of laugh. "I can't ask you to be gone; you'd abscond with my tea."

And she was funny. Gorgeous, smart, great body, even better laugh, and she's funny? At least she lived forty-five hundred miles away. That made it fair. She was totally out of my network plan.

"I'm about to add these vegetables to the sauce, unless you have an aversion to any of them?" I indicated the cutting board.

"I don't. Shall I set the table?"

What a breath of fresh air. I cooked dinner for many people, and only my best friend and her mother ever offered to help. Others made efforts like bringing the wine to the table and clearing their own plates, but to take over one of the jobs associated with getting dinner on the table was nice.

"Were you at Edinburgh or Glasgow today?" I asked after setting platters of spaghetti and broccoli on the table. Damisi brought over the garlic bread and salad, then took a seat at one of the place settings. I sat across from her and offered the spaghetti platter to her first while I dished some broccoli and salad onto my plate.

She paused, either waiting for me to finish loading my plate so we could begin eating or she was surprised I remembered where she worked. "Edinburgh." She took a bite of the pasta and contemplated the taste for a moment. Since she didn't spit it out, she must have found it acceptable. "How do the grounds look? When Hearn said he would be adding horses, I was surprised. He's got enough going with his business and charities, and now this estate. He's going to add a horse business, too? It's mental."

"Are you worried about him?"

"He always dives full in. Gets wrapped up, adds more, I've never seen anyone work harder."

I smiled around a mouth full of pasta. She was protective and worried about her friend. "That's why he hires people who know what they're doing. At least, I hope that's what he's done. I'm not sure about the construction crew."

She gave a snort. "When they're here."

"I noticed that today. Do you know the college friends he's hired to work the horse business?"

"Dunbar went to uni with us. The other two are his friends. They leech off Hearn. I've tried to tell him as delicately as possible, but when you're as wealthy as he, you hold onto friends you had before you became wealthy."

"Do they do any work?"

"When they first started, aye. Now they seem to spend all their time riding motorbikes and coming up with things Hearn needs to buy for the grounds."

I've dealt with worse. Some of my brothers' friends would try working the ranch, thinking they'd get to hang out with their friends on a job that couldn't be harder than mowing their parents' lawn. When reality set in, even with my brothers' leniency, they all quit.

"Will you be in charge of them?" Her smile was teasing.

"I'm getting everything up and going. We'll see if they want to join in."

A hint of unease touched me when her smile grew.

CHAPTER 5

THE CONSTRUCTION FOREMAN was more accommodating this morning. Marcy must have called and reminded him I was the project manager for the stables. Or it could be with a full night's rest, I was back to my even-keeled self and found things less irritating today.

"Drains in the floors?" he asked, rubbing his chin again.

"It makes cleaning easier."

"I don't know what you're used to over there in America, but here, a barn is a barn. You muck out the stalls, walk the horses in and out, and close the barn door at night. You don't scrub the floors and spray them down." He turned away as if that ended the subject.

"Actually, we do." Not as often as I clean my bathroom and kitchen floors, but we do wash out the barn aisles and the stalls. The contractor turned back with a look of distaste as if imagining the chore. "When can we expect the concrete floors to go in?"

His eyes widened and flicked away. "That's not in the plans."

"It is, and if you're not up to it, we'll get a subcontractor who is."

"We know what we're doing here, lass."

I resisted the desire to call him "boy" when I addressed him to point out just how condescending he sounded every time he called me "lass." Pointing out facts would be more effective than condescension. "And yet, you're seven weeks behind and cutting corners. You have one week to get the drains placed, concrete poured, and roof framing redone for the apex windows or we'll be looking for another contractor."

"Hey, now, wait a minute."

Now he was getting it. I left him with one parting instruction. "I've been tasked with project management, and I plan to do my job. You can decide if you want to do yours."

The three friend-workers still hadn't shown up to work today. They'd better be here soon. We had a lot of work to do. A skid steer was being delivered later this week for the regrading, trenching, and fence post driving. Grazing grass needed to be at a specific length before horses could be turned out into the pasture. That would take a few weeks to grow.

For now, I'd finish walking the property to look for other problem areas. I followed the secondary road we'd driven yesterday. A crying baby sounded in the distance. As I rounded a bend, the former gatekeeper's cottage came into view. The baby's cry grew louder. A silver haired man walked the edge of the property rocking and cooing at the crying baby.

"Hello," I called out to keep from creeping up on them.

"Hello," the man replied, glancing down at the crying baby and back up at me as I approached.

I took my hat off and stepped up to get a better look. Cute little thing with almost exactly the same champagne blond hair color as mine, even the red highlights matched. If we added some product to her hair, she'd have a matching hairdo as well. "Who've we got here?"

"This wee lass is my first granddaughter, Isla Campbell Baird."

"Great name, Isla. I'm Nora Cleary," I told her. "Who's your granddad?"

"Alastair Campbell, nice to meet you. Don't let her crying convince you she isn't happy to meet you."

"I wouldn't do that. Isla's just trying to tell us something."

"I've been trying to figure it out. Her twin brother and mum are inside taking a much-needed nap, but this one rarely sleeps."

"She likes to be alert. Nothing wrong with that."

I glanced toward the house and something caught my eye. The familiar deep grooves from the ATVs tore through the pasture next to their animal pen, and at one edge, broke through to the pen. Fencing lay prone across in that corner.

"I'm new to the Ogilvie estate next door and assessing the work that needs to be done to get these pastures ready for horses. I see the same people who ripped through our property took out some of yours."

The baby grew quiet when he shifted her in his arms. "Aye. My daughter talked to one of your colleagues to get this fixed. That was before this wee one was born. She hasn't had time to follow it up with his boss."

My suspicions about who caused this damage was confirmed. I'd been hoping it wasn't anyone working for Hearn, but no such luck. "I haven't had a chance to meet the employees yet, but I assure you, this will be fixed." Glancing at the still upright fencing, I asked, "Do you keep sheep or goats here?"

"Sheep, but we've had to move them to my farm because of the damage to the fence."

"I apologize for the inconvenience. My plan is to regrade and reseed the estate's pasture lands, and if your daughter will allow, hers as well. We're going to fence much of the pasture lands. If she's okay with it, we'll take your border fencing down and replace it with ours for a consistent look."

"It's not for me to say, but that sounds like a wonderful offer. I hate to disturb my daughter right now, but she should hear this."

"No, please. Pass along my phone number, and she can call at her convenience. New mothers need all the sleep they can get." I wrote my name and number in my notebook and tore out the page for him. My finger itched to brush along Isla's cheek when she started crying again, but my hands weren't sanitized and this looked like a newborn.

"Are you a mum?"

"I'm not, but I have done a lot of babysitting in my time. How old?"

"Three weeks, and she was early."

"She was ready to face the world."

"Would you like to hold her?"

"I would, but I should get her mama's permission first."

Alastair looked surprised and a little flustered. "Oh-aye, you're right about that. It was nice meeting you, Nora. I hope we see a lot of you."

"Let your daughter know about the pasture and fence. I'll want to coordinate a time when she's away from home so I don't disturb the kids."

"That's grand of you."

"It's the least we can do." I waved and headed northwest to finish my perimeter walk.

About a mile away, I heard engines in the distance. Could the construction foreman be adding more crew now that he had a deadline to keep? A flash of color showed through a copse of trees to the left. The whine of a small engine followed. One of the ATV riders was on the property. I double-timed my steps to catch up or find their towing vehicle.

Four other ATVs cut through the pasture past three SUVs up ahead. Hearn had mentioned three workers. How could five, no, now six, ATVs be tearing around this place if only three guys worked here?

It was a half-hour wait before a rider came close enough and saw me leaning against a new SUV. He skidded to a stop, ripping up more of the terrain. He flipped up his visor, giving me a peek of bright green eyes. "All right?"

"Do you work here?"

"Aye. Need something?"

"You can get your buddies off their ATVs and actually put in some work."

His eyes narrowed. "That's out of order. Who do you think you are?"

"I'm your interim boss, Nora Cleary. Not only are you not working, but you're making more work for us by ripping up the pasture lands with these things."

He dismounted and pulled off his helmet. A full shock of brown hair fell past his shoulders. "We're just having some fun on our break, no need to get your knickers in a twist. We have an agreement with Hearn."

"All agreements now go through me. If you want Hearn to give you a different job, call him. If you want to keep this job, you'll do as I ask."

He spoke into the radio mic in his helmet, asking his friends to come in. "We'll see about that."

Three of the riders surrounded him in a matter of moments. The others took a little longer. After some chatter among them, one pulled out his phone, and the rest stepped closer to me. As if their combined mass would put me off. I'd been directing older and taller male ranch hands my entire life. These joyriding fools wouldn't faze me.

"Fellas," I greeted casually. "Ready to get to work?"

"We've already put in several hours today." A strong accent made the blonde one difficult to understand, but he'd clearly understood me.

"Not here, you haven't. Why don't you load up your ATVs, say goodbye to your friends, and meet me back at the barn in ten minutes. Oh, and these grounds are off limits to ATV pleasure riding from now on."

"You can't do that." The blonde looked indignant, staring at the brunette to do something about it.

"But I just did," I turned and left them gaping after me. No doubt they'd be on the phone complaining to Hearn, but I didn't care. If Hearn wanted me to stay on, he'd set these lazy asses straight about who gave the orders here.

Twenty minutes later, they finally came rolling down the drive, two SUVs with trailers and two ATVs loaded on each. The other two ATVs must have gone off with the three guys who didn't work here. The brunette and a taller redhead stepped out of one SUV and the blonde exited the other.

"Hello again. I'm Nora, and you are?"

"Dunbar." This from the bulky guy with brown hair.

"Ryan." The slight guy with the blond hair next to bulky spoke up.

"Oisin." The redhead had a different accent than the others. Not English. Irish, maybe? I should know being of Irish descent myself, but I'd already made the mistake of misidentifying the accent of the woman sitting next to me on the plane and received the silent treatment for the rest of the trip. Either way, he stood out as the only one not scowling.

"Great. Which one of you drove the work truck home last night?"

"No lorries here."

"Pickup, passenger truck," I clarified. "The vehicle Hearn said you bought for use on the farm?"

They all glanced at each other as if this were a quiz show where they needed to consult on the answer.

"Not ready yet." Dunbar said.

"It died out in the west pasture," Oisin replied at the same time, which scored him two glares from his mates.

"It died?"

"It wasn't the greatest to begin with, but yeah, we think the transmission blew."

How could a brand-new truck blow a transmission so soon? "And you didn't take it back? Don't you have lemon laws here?" They stared blankly at me. "Laws to protect you from buying a car that stops running after you've driven it off the lot?"

"We haven't gotten around to it." Dunbar looked satisfied with his answer.

"Let's get on that. How far away is it?"

"Just down this way," Oisin said helpfully, again getting glares from his buddies.

I followed him as we walked into the pasture farther down the lane past where I'd explored so far. The men stayed quiet as we walked, conspicuously not taking note of the deep trenches we had to step over. Out in the middle of the next field was what looked like a small pickup from the eighties, old body style, low to the ground, tiny bed. It was completely insufficient for a work truck. As I got closer, I noted all the rust spots and dents adorning the body.

"Funny joke, guys, but we really don't have time. Now where's the real pickup?"

"This is it."

I pulled out my phone and clicked through the emails Hearn's assistant sent me yesterday. One of the attachments had a bill of sale. "This is a brand-new Mercedes X-class?" I'd never heard of that pickup model, but one glance at the familiar VW logo on the grill told me this wasn't a match.

"We couldn't actually get that one. They didn't have it in stock."

"And yet, here you two are standing beside one on a lot. A brand spanking new pickup." I showed them the photo Marcy had attached of Dunbar and Ryan leaning against the truck.

"Aye, well, we couldn't take that one."

"Here's the paid invoice for the same color and model, with all the same options listed on this window sticker right by your head, Dunbar."

"Well, we couldn't get it," he came back, sticking a finger in my face.

I chuckled at his intimidation tactic. "I'll give you one chance to tell me what happened so I can try to help."

"Or else what?"

"When Hearn calls for a status chat and asks about the pickup, I'll have to let him know what I think happened to it." They stared at me blankly, so I continued, "It looks to me like you had Hearn pay for the pickup in this picture, then you canceled the order before you took delivery, having them write you the refund check. You took that money, bought this piece of shit, and used the rest for those beautiful little ATVs."

Oisin whipped his head around, not able to help his surprise. So, he wasn't in the loop on the embezzlement scheme. Interesting.

"Hearn knows we bought the ATVs."

"But does he know you bought six of them and used his money earmarked for the pickup?" I flicked a glance at them. "Thought not. So, let's move onto the fencing that you were supposed to have put up by now. Where can we find those supplies?"

They looked down and out again, anywhere but at me. Oisin gave a small shake of his head. He must be the friend of the friend, rather than Hearn's friend, or he would be outraged right now. I'd be outraged if I found out someone ripped off my friend.

"Same thing? Did it give you the down payments for your nice new SUVs?" A blush rose up on Ryan's face. Dunbar continued to look unbothered. "You guys are unbelievable. I suggest you give Hearn a call and let him know everything you've done. If you're lucky, he'll just fire you. If it were me, I'd call the cops."

"Sod off. Let's go, lads," Dunbar said. "We'll see what Hearn has to say about her."

Ryan followed closely, but Oisin just stared at me, panic in his eyes. "I don't want to toss anyone into the creek, but I don't feel right about this. Dunbar never said—," he cut himself off and looked at me with the expression of someone caught between two things. "I need this job."

The sincerity in his voice was enough for me. "If you're ready to work, Oisin, I'm happy to have you."

"Oisin!" Dunbar called. "Let's boogie."

"I'm grand, D. You go on."

Dunbar didn't stick around long enough to be offended by his friend choosing to stay. Oisin ran a hand over his curly hair. He looked devastated, and I couldn't blame him. He probably thought this was a part-time job with land use privileges and liked hanging out with his friends. Instead, he just found out his friends roped him into stealing from their boss.

"Can you find a number for a tow truck and call them out here? We'll have them haul this to the scrap yard. Hearn will have to take a write-off on this." I snapped a picture of the pickup and turned back to Oisin. "Do you have any construction skills?"

"I'm good with my hands."

"Good. We'll start putting the forms up for the foundation of the storage building as we wait for the pickup to be towed. I'm going to put in a call to Hearn."

I didn't look forward to ratting out his friends, but I'd have to explain needing additional funds for the equipment and supplies they neglected to get. We'd see just how enthusiastic Hearn was about my employment after finishing this call. It was one thing to be told your friends were lazy, quite another to find out they'd been ripping you off.

CHAPTER 6

A LOUD WHOOP-WHOOP sound got closer and closer. My gaze automatically went to the sky. A helicopter descended toward the estate. I set the nail gun down, having borrowed it from one of the absent construction crew. With their deadline looming, they should be here in full force, working two shifts a day and weekends. Instead, it was mid-afternoon on Saturday, and no sign of them. Oisin, on the other hand, was working right beside me, trying to make up for the bad his friends had done.

Which was why Hearn was arriving. We'd spoken on the phone after he'd gotten Dunbar's side of the story. My side differed enough to make him want to come up and see it for himself. He was ducking out of the afternoon festivities at a tech conference he was attending in Manchester to fly up here.

"That'll be Hearn," Oisin stated the obvious. He looked a little sick, ready to own up to his part in the Lazy Three. I told him he didn't have to, but since he occasionally hung out with Hearn, he felt like he needed to.

Gresham brought Hearn over in a beautiful classic convertible and stopped in front of the barn. Hearn stepped out and approached. He edged me out by about an inch with a lanky build. His hair was medium brown, a touch too long for his face, and no style at all. He looked like a true geek rather than how television shows portray their geeks.

I took off my work gloves and shook his hand. "Good to see you."

"Hey, Nora. The barn and storage building look good. Last time I was here, they'd barely cleared the location for the storage building. They're working quickly."

"We just finished putting the framing together for the storage building."

His gaze snapped back to mine. "You did this?" He didn't seem shocked I knew how to do all this, rather why I was doing this.

"Oisin and I did. He's a good worker."

He tipped his chin up at Oisin, who'd stayed near the barn. "Tell me what went on here. Dunbar said it was all a misunderstanding."

"And it could have been." How he decided he wanted to deal with his friends was his business. If he wanted the excuse to give them a pass, it was up to him. At dinner last night, Damisi told me she thought he'd end up letting them keep the ATVs and vehicle down payments as severance pay, but he wouldn't be hanging out with them much, if ever again. That seemed incredibly generous to me, but I'd never been ripped off by people I considered good friends. I might be lenient as well. "Marcy sent me copies of paid invoices for a new pickup and the livestock fencing I recommended. What the guys showed me was a broken-down pickup and a sliver of fencing suitable for chicken coops. They'd cancelled the orders and got refund checks from the car dealer and fencing supplier." I paused to give him time to digest that his friends really had taken that money from him. They were probably going to tell Marcy they miscalculated and needed more fencing material to cover the shortage at some point in the future. "When I asked if they were ready to get to work, only Oisin stayed behind."

"I just can't believe it." His wire-rimmed glasses slid down his nose with a head shake. He impatiently pushed them back up. He'd likely had many so-called friends disappoint him since selling his first company for millions. It seemed like these guys, or at least Dunbar, had been a true friend until he became greedy like so many before him.

Oisin came jogging up. "Hey, Hearn. Sorry about, well, everything. I didn't ask enough questions."

"What did Dunbar tell you about the pickup?" Hearn's tone held the remains of hope that this was all just a misunderstanding.

"He said he had to get a used 4x4 for the stables."

"And the fencing?"

"We worked on that one section, but the lads said the shop didn't have enough for the whole property, so we were waiting on the delivery." He reached out to grip Hearn's shoulder. "Listen, I don't want to get them in trouble. I probably just asked the wrong questions. I appreciate you giving me this job but understand if you want to make me redundant."

Hearn flicked his wrist to wave away that concern. As much as he must be reeling from this blow, he wouldn't hear of tossing someone out when they were ready to work. "I don't even know what to say. This isn't how I thought things would go once you got here."

Me neither, but I didn't need to rub it in. "We'll muddle through."

"You shouldn't have to." He gestured for us to walk toward the barn. "Show me what you mean about the pastures."

I gave a thumbs up to Oisin, letting him know he'd done okay and would probably best show Hearn his sincerity by getting back to work. He'd been fun to work beside this past week. So far, his only flaw was his inexperience with horses. He'd need a lot of guidance once they arrived. Construction wise, he was proficient, and he had a great attitude. A few more employees like Oisin and the ranch would be set up nicely.

Hearn walked at my side, his tennis shoes getting dirtier by the stride. The tech conference lanyard flipped up and over his shoulder as a gust of wind swept by. He yanked it over his head and stuffed it in his pocket. "As depressing as this situation is, it's still more enjoyable than that yawn of a tech con I was at this morning."

Amused, I nudged his shoulder. We'd gotten closer over the last couple of years, sharing occasional texts and meeting up at two or three competitions each summer. I looked forward to getting to know him better as we got this ranch in working order. A tech genius like Hearn who thinks tech conferences were boring was worth getting to know.

We were coming up on one of the ripped-up pastures I hadn't yet gone over with the grader. "If they hadn't run the ATVs after it rained many times, the damage might not have been too bad. Horses are used to rough terrain, but these deep ruts are treacherous. I started regrading at the northeast corner. Oisin will continue the rest of the property next week while I follow behind and reseed."

"Whatever you think." His eyes locked onto the first of the grooves in the grassy lands and found a large circular area of bare ground just beyond. He shook his head as he looked over the multiple tire tracks up and down as far as he could see. "Is this everywhere?"

"They've gone over most of the pastures we planned to fence in for the horses. They also knocked down your neighbor's fence."

His head swung around. "Jack's? Are his cattle getting through?"

"No, the neighbor down the end of that road over there." My hand waved in the direction of the former gatehouse. "I met an Alastair with his granddaughter."

"Oh, no, Ainsley? She doesn't need that. She just had her bairns. Early, too."

Early bairns? "Is that a breed of sheep?"

He laughed and slapped my back. "Babies. She had twins, earlier than expected. She doesn't have time to deal with property issues."

"I promised to fix it for her, at your expense, by the way."

"Yes, good, good." He pulled out his phone and tapped in a text faster than a teenage girl. "Just sent her an apology. She helped with the plans on the estate, you know."

I didn't. Hearn seemed to work from a standpoint of everyone being up to speed on everything. That may be the case on a tech project where everyone's work is uploaded to a shared drive. It didn't work in everyday relationships.

"Sorry, I'm in my head. You wouldn't know. She and Damisi are historians. They did the research on the property and what stood here in the past."

"Gresham said it was a replica. Nice that you have historians at your fingertips."

"Damisi's the best. She and I were at uni together." His brow creased as he must be thinking about Dunbar being at college with them. "She's about the only person I knew from back then that didn't turn up looking for something, a job, a loan, a handout. She even pays me rent for the cottage if you can believe it. I offered it up when she needed a place between Glasgow and Edinburgh while she works both unis, but she wouldn't take it unless she could pay rent."

Interesting. She hadn't given up much more about herself or her life during our two other dinners together. We'd kept things light to avoid stepping on any hot button issues. So far, it was pleasant enough. She was getting used to the idea of a housemate, and I was getting used to the idea of her not wanting to kill me in the night.

"What's your plan here?"

I got us started back toward the barn. No reason for him to dwell on the state of the land at present. "Grading first, then reseeding. We'll put in access roads along the property lines and dig some drainage trenches. Flexible fencing is the last step to prep the fields for horses."

"I really thought you could hit the ground running once you got here, but it seems like you're doing more prep work than the crews I hired to do that work."

"It's all part of being a ranch manager. As long as you're not in any hurry to get the horses in, trained, and ready for competition, then we don't need to rush. I know Kenzi's eager, but she'll need a lot of practice before her first competition." It didn't matter how often his niece had been on a horse before, she'd need to learn to ride a cutting horse properly.

He waved his hand again. "I'd like this done correctly. Kenzi's excited, but she's a good lass, she can be patient."

"Good, then we'll get this set up exactly and bring in the horses when it's ready."

"Thank you, Nora. I'm glad you're adaptable."

"Life of a rancher, Hearn. You'll learn not to rush things." I watched a smile crest on his face. He liked the idea of being a rancher.

"Not to rush things?" Damisi's voice called out as she approached. "More has been done in this past week than over the past two months. Speed and efficiency are all this one knows." Her chin tipped in my direction and my stomach flipped at the compliment. She was still in her work clothes, a pair of charcoal colored slacks and a silk blouse in burnt orange. Both were tailored to fit. She had an incredible work wardrobe. Just one more tick in the sexy column for her. As if she needed more things to make her attractive.

"Damisi. Good to see you." Hearn went over and wrapped an arm around her shoulders. They made a beautiful couple, even with his slightly too long hair and lanky frame. She'd make a beautiful couple with anyone.

"You arrived in style. Glad you're here. Have you seen all she's done?"

My head tilted at her tone. She was being overly complimentary, which was out of character for our interactions. Perhaps she was glad Dunbar was gone and wanted to throw some support behind the person who got rid of him.

"Just tallied up. She's been a grand addition, don't ya think?"

"That she has, my friend. You'll have your stables ready in no time." She gave me one of those beautiful fleeting smiles that turned her mouth into an inescapable temptation.

My heart thumped as she looped her arm through Hearn's and tugged him toward the cottage. In the matter of a moment, she'd reassured my boss, shown support for me, and ignited my libido. Talented all around.

Chapter 7

"**Are you going** to do this every night?"

Damisi's question pulled my attention from the chicken browning in the pan. She gave me an expectant look. I tried to interpret it, but she was still a mystery to me after two weeks of interaction. "Do what?"

"Make my tea?"

I chuckled and looked back at the pan. "I'm making dinner for myself. If you want to join me, there will always be enough. If you don't, I have leftovers for lunch the next day."

"I've been eating your lunch?" Concern marked her tone.

"We've been keeping each other company over dinner."

Her eyes narrowed, not trusting my easygoing answer. "What do you do for lunch?"

"I make a sandwich or a salad. What do you do?"

"Pick up something at one of the canteens on campus."

During my college years, dorm and café food were the only options until I'd moved into an apartment. It made me appreciate being able to make my own food again. I'd grown up on homecooked meals every night. When I moved out of the dorms, it became automatic for me. I never really thought of it as unusual.

"You cook every night?" She obviously did think it was unusual.

"I have been to a restaurant, you know. I'm not a complete hick."

"Hick?"

"Country girl, bumpkin."

Her eyebrows rose. She'd probably never heard either of those terms either. "You really don't mind me eating your supper?"

I chuckled at her obvious disbelief. "I would if you were eating my dinner, but like I said, I make enough."

"May I put in for it?"

"Why don't you get all the breakfast groceries, and I'll get all the dinner groceries?"

"Breakfast is less expensive. I wouldn't feel right about that."

I took the pan off the stove and turned to her. "Okay. Toss in salad stuff and we'll take turns getting the coffee, wine, and beer."

"Are you going to make me breakfast, too?" Her tone was teasing this time.

"If you're here when I make breakfast and want whatever I'm making, sure."

"It's really that easy for you?"

It was. One of my chores growing up was to help make the meals. If we wanted to eat, I had to help. It was expected. Either I learned to like it, or I'd be miserable every day. It was easier to learn to like it. I shrugged in response to her question. Anything else might bring out the circumstances for why I had to get used to making dinner every night. We weren't on that kind of personal level yet.

"May I make requests?" The tease was back. She was going to be fun to get to know if she ever dropped her guard.

"Can't guarantee I'll make them well, but you can always make the request."

She gave me the sexiest side-eye I've ever seen. I laughed and finished plating the chicken fajitas. She'd once again set the table without my needing to ask, and she'd do the dishes afterward at her insistence as well. Several meals shared so far, and her help still marveled.

"Tell me your favorite story from Scottish history," I asked as we sat at the table together.

Her eyes narrowed. She had some major suspicions about me, or she had trust issues in general. "Story?"

"That's what history is. Forget facts and figures, tell me the story of the people at the time. You teach medieval and modern, right? Lots of colorful stuff in both. There's gotta be something you love telling."

She smiled and my heart thumped. God, her mouth. Absolutely beautiful. Wide and full-lipped. I couldn't help but imagine kissing it.

She began telling me about the House of Dunkeld and one of its more colorful kings. In between bites, after which she'd occasionally sigh in pleasure, she spelled out the story of its rise to rule. Details came out and seemed to surprise even her. She didn't even get to finish a quarter of the tale before we were done with dinner and she was into the dishes.

"You know, telling you this and hearing questions from someone not familiar with this history has opened my eyes to new details to explore. Ta for that." Her eyes danced as she grabbed the pan I managed to dry before she could and put it back in the cabinet.

"I enjoyed the story. You can pick up where you left off next time."

"I'm going to get started on my next paper." She tapped me on the shoulder as she sauntered by. In seconds, her bare feet were padding up the stairs to her mysterious domain. My curiosity nagged at me to check it out while she was at work, but by unspoken agreement, we kept to our corners of the house.

Despite having a sore shoulder from adding plywood to the framing of the storage building the last couple of days, I headed back outside to clear more debris from what would become our composting area. The construction crew was doing better, but nowhere near finished with the barn. Oisin and I were taking up their slack on the easy projects for the outbuildings and setting up the aerated composting system to ensure the most necessary elements were in place before the horses got here.

Tomorrow, I'd be back at work on the neighboring property. Ainsley and her wife and kids were joining Damisi for a private tour of the castle before it opened for public tours next weekend. As much work as these past two weeks had been, I loved ticking off each accomplished task and enjoyed the sense of belonging on these grounds.

CHAPTER 8

WITH AN AUDIBLE huff, I loaded the last of the French drain pipes into the new pickup Hearn had helped choose. To temper his frustration with his friends' misuse of funds, I made a stereotypical decision that he might like to go car shopping and suggested we take Gresham on the hunt with us. Hearn got very excited when we found a Nissan in a green color matching his family tartan. I was still getting used to the gearshift on the left, but otherwise it was nice to have transportation again.

A black Volkswagen hatchback crawled up the road. It paused several times, obviously letting the passengers study the progress made on the barn. I lifted a hand to wave as they passed by. The passenger window rolled down and a dark-haired woman waved back. Unless the neighbors had a third car hidden away in their garage, it wasn't them. Damisi mentioned inviting two other friends to tour the estate. I was dying to take a look at the castle's interior as well, but repairing the damage to the neighbors' property was more important.

Over the past week and a half, whenever Ainsley was scheduled to be out of the house with the babies, Oisin and I headed over to grade and seed their sheep pen and drive in the fence posts. On my own today, I had to get the trenches dug and add the drain pipes and gravel. I doubted it would get done in one day, but only the trenches required heavy equipment. The remaining gravel could be shoveled in later so as not to disturb the babies.

On my way back to the house, a compact Range Rover came up the road and parked next to the VW. This was one of the cars I'd seen in the neighbors' driveway. I'd spoken to Ainsley on the phone three times already but hadn't met her or her spouse in person yet.

I cut through the side yard and went in through the mudroom, unlacing my boots and leaving them by the door. Then I turned to the sink and washed my hands and arms up to my elbows. My hope was to get my now clean hands on that cute baby. Her brother would be okay to hold, too.

Noises came from the foyer. Everyone must have gone out front to meet the neighbors' car. I stepped through into the living room just as they made their way down the hall.

"Oh, hello. You must be Nora," a beautiful full-figured brunette spoke in a lovely tone of voice, the kind usually belonging to professional singers or stage actors. "I'm Celia. This is my partner, Zoey." She indicated the petite brunette beside her. The woman smiled her hello as Celia's arm snaked around Damisi's shoulders. "Damisi's told us very little about you."

My eyes shot to Damisi, who was biting back a smile. "Other than my being a complete surprise, you mean?" That got a laugh from everyone. I wondered if Damisi told them just how much of a surprise and what state I'd found her in. Heat bloomed in my chest as a sudden memory of her glorious nakedness flashed in my head.

"I don't get it," a pretty redhead spoke up in an American accent. She was holding a baby carrier in her right hand and sliding a tote onto the floor with the other. "Hearn has run several successful businesses, but he seems so forgetful at times. Was he always like that, Damisi?"

"Distracted unless he was coding, yes," Damisi agreed.

"You must be Skye." I said as she shifted the baby carrier to her left hand to shake mine.

"What gave me away?"

"I've spoken to Ainsley on the phone." My hand reached to greet the beautiful blonde holding the other baby carrier. Neither baby was making any noise at the moment. "I apologize for the damage done to your property. It's unacceptable and a great inconvenience."

Skye smiled and waved a hand like it wasn't a big deal. Of course, it could be the exhaustion speaking. She probably thought nothing but trying to get an hour of sleep was a big deal these days. "What you've done so far to make up for it is amazing. I was just telling Ainsley how we no longer have any puddles forming around the back patio."

I'd noticed the slight slope toward their house draining water from the animal pasture into their backyard. It was an easy fix with the grader, tilting the plane back toward the fence line where the French drains would redirect the flow.

Ainsley shifted the carrier in her hand again. She eyed the couch and the sleeping baby and made a decision to keep hold of the carrier instead of risking a shift that might wake the baby.

"Want me to take her, hon?" Skye asked her.

She shook her head, and her eyes dropped back down to the baby. "We don't want to chance she'll wake up. This is only the second hour she's slept in more than twelve."

My feet took an involuntary step toward her. "Would you mind a tip on making those things easier to carry?"

Her blue eyes flipped up to meet mine. "Easier?"

I reached out and slid my hands under the carrier to keep it level and take its weight. "Stick your arm under the handle and through, then curl your hand around the base of the handle closest to you." I waited for her to get a grip on the rounded curve of the handlebar base and let her take back the weight of it. "How does that feel?"

"Grand. Oh, darling," she turned to Skye, "you have to try this. So much easier."

Skye shifted her grip to try it and smiled. "Amazing, the difference. Thanks, Nora. They should really teach this to new parents. We've been killing ourselves when we have to carry both babies at the same time. Do you have kids?"

I shook my head. "A lot of babysitting." More like nannying for my best friend's cousin as she was finishing her medical residency with a newborn. We'd take shifts carrying the baby around in a pouch at work. After a month, we barely noticed having the extra weight and only needed to switch when we had heavy lifting or riding to do. I'd never been sure about wanting kids before my time with little Jared, but it made my desire clear. I only hoped the woman I fell for would also want children in the future.

"You're quite handy, aren't you?" Celia said and drifted over to Ainsley. "I know you say she never sleeps, but I really want her to wake up so I can hold my godbaby."

They chuckled, but I noticed neither of them gave up the sleeping babies. Ainsley's father also mentioned Isla not being much of a sleeper. These poor parents.

"She'll be up soon enough, and you can have her for the rest of the day."

"Hey," Zoey chimed in. "She's my godbaby, too."

"There are enough babies to go around," Damisi joked.

Neither said the boy was their godbaby. Was Damisi his godparent? And did Zoey have an American accent, too?

Remarkable that Damisi knew two lesbian couples of mixed citizenship. Two lesbian couples were amazing enough. I had to go off to college before I met more than one lesbian couple in the same room. Should I assume Damisi was gay? Would that make me a stereotyping jerkface, or just a wishful jerkface? To think all that lovely gorgeousness might play on the same team. I fought the impulse to shiver. Did she want babies? I shook my head of the ridiculous thought.

"I've met Ms. Isla, here," I said to Ainsley and looked at Skye, "But who's the little gentleman?"

"Sorry, we're sleep-deprived and have lost our manners. This is our son, Tavish. Alastair said he'd met you with Isla when Tavs was sleeping."

"Isla Campbell Baird and Tavish What Baird?"

"Baird Campbell."

I blinked, processing. Ah, their last names. "Campbell? Baird?" I asked of Ainsley and Skye respectively.

Skye laughed and shook her head. "You were right," she said to her wife before turning back to me. "Ainsley's a Campbell Baird. She did all the work bringing these two into the world. It's only right they get her family names."

Interesting. Made me like Skye even more than her easy forgiveness of Hearn's employees trashing her animal pen. Two kids would be the easiest way to get both parents' last names into the mix, but apparently, Skye Unknown-Last-Name didn't have the same ego as most parents.

"I should get to work so we don't keep you out of your house for too long. It was nice meeting you all."

"Do you need help?" Zoey offered up after a moment of silence.

If I knew her better, I might take her up on the offer. It was going to be a long hard day, but she didn't work for me and I didn't know her well enough to ask for help. More importantly, she was stick figure thin and short. She might break in half while shoveling gravel.

"Thanks so much for the offer, but it's mostly tractor work today."

"You don't want to miss the estate tour, Zoey." Celia's tone reflected her surprise.

"I'm sure Damisi could get me in another day."

"I know people." Damisi smiled at her.

As she got another round of chuckles, Isla started to wake up. Everyone held their collective breath to see if it was a momentary blip or if she was truly awake. Her next soft cry told us she was awake. Celia's hands reached forward immediately, drawing more laughter.

"She's just the best baby in the world," Celia cooed down at her when she was safely wrapped in her arms.

"She's got a brother, who's also a baby," Damisi joked. She didn't look as baby crazy as Celia seemed to be, but she did seem enchanted enough.

"When I'm holding him, he'll be the best baby in the world."

"I see." Damisi patted her friend's back and glanced down at Isla.

Ainsley must have noticed me tracking the baby's movements. "Would you like to hold her before you leave? If we can prise her out of Celia's arms, that is."

Celia looked up with wide eyes before sheepishly chuckling. "Of course. You must. We get her all day, and you're off to work. You need a treat first."

"I'd love to, thanks." I directed my comments to Isla's mothers before reaching to tuck one hand under her neck and the other under her body. She was light as a piece of paper. Tiny as a newborn, but even more so being early and a twin. Her blue eyes stared up at me before she let out a cry. I repositioned my grip and started a bouncing motion. She immediately stopped.

"Oh my God, how did you do that?" Ainsley asked. "She always cries with new people. They get so upset when she won't let them hold her."

"Some kids like a good bounce instead of rocking."

"You're like a baby whisperer," Skye said, setting the baby seat on the ground and lifting her son out to Zoey. Not one peep out of the still sleeping baby as Zoey cradled him close.

I gave little Isla one last bounce before handing her back to Celia and turned to her mothers. "Thanks for the baby cuddle. Let me know when you're headed back to the homestead, and I can pick up on the work another day."

"We've got three capable sets of hands ready to help us haul these kids around and three history nerds to keep us occupied in the manor," Skye joked.

"Castle," both Ainsley and Damisi corrected.

"Do you think there was a difference to the servants who worked there?"

"Actually," they both said again and laughed.

"Save it for the tour," Celia told them.

"I'll leave you to it," I said and made my exit.

Chapter 9

THREE QUARTERS OF the way through digging the trench along the border fence, I spotted two figures walking over the crest of the road leading down toward Skye and Ainsley's house from the estate. One of them lifted a hand to wave as they moved close enough for me to make out Zoey and Damisi with one of the babies riding in a pouch on Zoey's chest.

I shut down the skid steer and hopped out to meet them on the path. "Is my time up?"

"We made it partway through the tour before Tavish had enough and Skye looked like she was about to pass out," Damisi reported. "They're relaxing in the living room while Celia is getting her baby fix."

"And you've bolted with the other."

"She apparently doesn't like sitting around while her brother sleeps."

"She's a go-getter." I came closer and took my hat off. Isla's eyes tracked the motion, little hands reaching out to grip the brim.

"She might crush it," Zoey told me.

"It's just a hat."

She beamed at me. I loved my hat, most cowgirls did, but when something fascinates a baby, you don't throw up any roadblocks.

"You've made some progress." Damisi spoke to the length of the trench as if not wanting to give me the compliment. She was an odd one to figure out. Not hot and cold, more like warm and cool for the most part, but she never stayed with one opinion of me for too long.

"All part of my master plan."

Zoey chuckled as she rocked up onto her toes then down to her heels to keep the constant motion that Isla liked.

"Where's Oisin today?" Damisi asked.

"He's worked twelve days straight. I forced him to take the weekend off."

"But you're working."

I waited for her to look at me. It wasn't a teasing or mocking tone, really. But there was a slight edge of humorous disbelief. "There's work to be done and a timetable."

"It looks amazing," Zoey commented. "All over the grounds, but especially Skye's backyard. After they added the master bedroom addition, every time it rained, the yard would turn into a pond."

"I'm glad something good has come out of willful property damage."

"That looks fun." Damisi gestured to the skid steer.

"Have at it."

She gave me her full attention now. Those dark brown eyes peered at me with a scrutiny befitting a weapons inspector.

I stepped up to the front of the skid and motioned her forward. She looked at me skeptically. "It's here, it's a rental, you may never get another chance. I doubt they have these sitting around your department at the university. Hop in and give it a go."

Zoey flashed a bright smile and encouraged Damisi with a nod. Isla made a soft cry in agreement.

"I'll muddle what you're trying to achieve."

"Not possible. Step up here and slide in."

I reached to grip her hand. After a long moment, her soft, clean hand gripped my rough, dusty one. She didn't seem to mind the disparity, too eager to get into the machine. With a second more certain step, she twisted and slid her backside onto the seat.

"Left throttle controls vehicle movement. Right throttle controls the arm. Ignition switch, here."

She tentatively reached out and cranked the ignition, bringing the skid to life. Before she could grip the throttles, I jumped down and to the side, calling out more instructions. She pushed slightly on the left throttle and when the skid bounced forward, she ripped her hand back and searched my eyes for further instruction.

"You're doing great. As long as you don't swing left and knock down the fence posts I put in last week, you can't hurt anything. If you want to keep trenching follow the line forward. If you want to have more fun with it, pull back on the right throttle to lift the arm and take it out into the field here anywhere you like."

Her right hand tweaked the throttle and raised the trenching attachment on the arm, clearing the ground by a few inches. I indicated she should go up a bit more in case the skid dipped, then I shooed her off to the right. After a few more startled starts, she slowly turned and headed into the field. It took all of a minute before she increased the speed and was making turns this way and that. When she came back toward the half-finished trench and managed to set the trencher back into the groove, it looked like I might never get back into the machine. Soon enough, she grew bored of trenching a straight-line and turned it off.

"I was right, definitely fun."

"Zoey?" I turned to her. "Want to get in on that action?"

She looked down at the baby in the pouch carrier and seemed about to say no, but I doused my hands with some water from a bottle and dried them on the hem of my shirt. It wasn't ideal, but the mothers didn't seem too fussy about sanitizing hands before handling their babies. Zoey was already lifting Isla out of the pouch and handing her over. She squeaked a little before settling into my arms.

Damisi gave Zoey a quick guide and stepped close to me when Zoey was off like a shot into the field, not tentative at all. I chuckled at her enthusiasm.

"She doesn't say a whole lot, but she's absolutely fearless."

I tilted Isla toward Damisi, assuming she'd want to take her friends' baby from me. She glanced down and up to my eyes, a smile playing on her lips.

"You like babies."

"Who doesn't?"

She gave me an incredulous look. "Are you serious? You've never met someone who doesn't like babies?"

I jiggled Isla and gave her my finger to grip. "I've met people who say they don't like babies, but they really mean they don't want to have a baby of their own. Or they don't like hearing a baby cry on a plane. I've never actually met anyone who can look down at a baby in someone's arms and say, 'Nope, can't stand babies.' It just doesn't happen. Have you?"

She flicked her eyes up and to the left. "That could be. They certainly protest loudly. You, though, seem especially enamored. Are you planning a large family?"

Well, well, the first real personal question from Ms. Damisi. "I'll take as many as my partner wants to have or adopt with me."

Damisi's eyes skimmed down my front and back up to my face, a long, invasive perusal. My body heated in its wake. "Not going to be having those babies yourself?"

I laughed. "Not that brave, no."

"What if she doesn't want them?"

"I have to hope I fall for someone who wants kids."

"Optimistic."

I shrugged. "My general outlook on life."

She smiled and nodded. "I've noticed."

"What about you? Are kids in your future?" I shouldn't be asking. She could misinterpret my question, which might make her revert to her cool behavior. Still, I had to know.

Her examining gaze came back and swept over me again. "I've thought about being a mum."

Not exactly a definitive answer. Should I try to get a rise out of her and ask if she wants to have babies with me? That would immediately dowse any warm feelings she might have at the moment. Better to play it safe. I tilted Isla toward her. "Do you want her?"

Her hands came up. "I had both kids during part of the tour. You enjoy your baby time."

Zoey brought the skid back to the starting point and jumped down with a huge smile on her face. "Awesome."

"Better than the tour?" Damisi asked her.

Zoey looked conflicted. "I learned a lot on the tour. This was a bit of fun."

"I've got it for another week. You're welcome to come for a ride any time."

She grinned and nodded with enthusiasm. Her hands came out to scoop Isla from me and deposit her back into the pouch. "Thanks."

"You're welcome."

Damisi gave me a brief smile as they started back toward the cottage. After a few steps, she looked back and flashed the smile again. It touched off a swarm of butterflies in my stomach. Looked like I might have done at least one thing right today.

CHAPTER 10

OUR NEW THREE-PERSON team was exponentially more efficient than Oisin and I had been alone. Paisley, the newest addition to our ranch crew, came from the infrastructure engineering unit of the British Army where she helped plan, design, and build many structures during her service, including a tour in Iraq and assisting the UN in several countries. Out for all of five months, she confessed she'd had a hard time holding down a job due to her ongoing treatment of PTSD.

Paisley outshined all nine other interviewees even without any ranching experience. It wasn't just her skillset, which would come in handy as we built out this ranch, but her attitude. I expected a slight difference between the usually overenthusiastic hires on my dad's ranch and what I might find here, but there was British reserve, which Paisley possessed, and indifference, which many of the other candidates showed during their interviews.

When I offered her the job on the spot, she fought against tears. Apparently, she'd had three other employers who lost their understanding of her need for a semi-flexible schedule on therapy days. My assurance that she could come and go as needed for those sessions probably did as much to advance her recovery as her therapist was doing. One week in, she'd had one unscheduled appointment, for which she'd given a couple hours' notice, and she'd returned to finish out her shift. Working a ranch gave me an appreciation for employees willing to go the extra mile and put in an hour or three more from time to time. The least I could do was understand when they needed flexibility in their own schedules.

"Paisley, you're putting me to shame," Oisin called out from his fence post three back. Paisley had leapfrogged past his post and completed two others. The expertise with which she used a drill would have her catching up to me marking the location of the brackets on the corner post.

"You'll be the one lugging those rolls of fence rail to lay out next week."

"My muscular physique will rise to the challenge." He started laughing before he finished his statement. He had a quirky sense of humor, much appreciated with all the hard work we'd been putting in. He accepted Paisley at nearly a foot shorter than his six-three frame onto the team as easily as he'd accepted me as his boss in this traditionally male field.

"Get to the corner here, and we'll pack it in for the day." I marked the top bracket spot.

Oisin chuckled as he realized he wouldn't beat Paisley to the corner post. "We've still got forty minutes on the clock, boss."

"You've kicked ass this week, and we're ahead of schedule. Get an early start to your weekend." I packed up my tools. "You going by the train station, O?"

"I can run you all the way into the city tonight, Paisley. My mates and I are hitting a pub. You're both welcome to join." He knocked a fist against Paisley's shoulder. Once we found out Paisley didn't have a car, we coordinated rides to and from the train station to spare her a three-mile trek. Oisin timed it perfectly most days. On others, I made the trip, including dropping her at her therapy session under the guise of getting my hair cut in the city. Paisley didn't like us making a fuss, but after the kind of work we'd been doing, she was grateful for the rides. I didn't want to ask about her financial situation, but with an apartment in Edinburgh and only part-time work since leaving the army, she probably wanted to avoid starting a car payment until she was solid with this job.

"Ta," Paisley told him.

It sounded fun, but if one of his mates was Dunbar, I probably wouldn't be a welcome addition to a night out. Plus, it wasn't always good to hang out with your employees before a true employer-employee relationship was set. "I'm bushed, Oisin, but thanks for the invite. Maybe next time."

We walked back to the storage building to drop off our tools. They jumped into Oisin's car wearing big smiles about getting out early. I wondered if Paisley would join Oisin's crew tonight. She never mentioned doing anything outside of work, but this was her first week. She could be training tigers every weekend and not ready to tell her new workmates about it for all I knew.

As I rounded the bend in the road separating the barnyard from the cottage, I noticed a red sedan parked in the semi-circular drive. The driver's door opened and a middle-aged black woman exited the car. She had heart stopping good looks with medium-length curls pushed back from her forehead by a colorful fabric wrap and a sleeveless duster dress with black leggings showing off shapely calves and a slim frame.

"Hello there," she called in what sounded like a West African accent.

"Hi." Close enough now to study her features, I could see she was very attractive with light brown flawless skin and dark brown friendly eyes and a beautiful mouth that could only be rivaled by—ah, sure, that made sense. "Are you Damisi's mom?" She was just as gorgeous and their face shapes were identical, and those mouths—heaven have mercy. I'd had to stop myself from staring at Damisi's mouth whenever she spoke; it was that irresistible.

The woman's eyes grew wide, and that gorgeous mouth spread into a smile. "I am. You must be Nora, the flatmate."

It didn't come out as an accusation, so Damisi must have shared at least one good thing about me. Or perhaps it was only a neutral relay of the facts. Her name's Nora, she's American, she works and cooks. Yeah, that would be more like Damisi.

"Is she not home yet?"

"No, and I did not want to let myself in now that she has a flatmate."

So, the mom had the lock code. Good to know. "That's kind of you, but please, let's go inside where it's more comfortable."

"Thank you." She ducked back into the car to grab a cloth bag and followed me up the three steps to the door.

"I'm Eni Dalziel."

I turned, shutting the door after her. "Nora Cleary."

Her eyes moved over the interior as I unlaced my boots. "Should I take off my sandals?"

"Your choice. I change out my boots for sneakers. Your daughter seems to prefer bare feet."

She smiled at the mention of her daughter. "Me, too." She kicked off her sandals and followed me into the living room. "Are you sure you do not mind me invading your space while I wait for Damisi?"

"Not at all. It's nice to have company. I was about to start making dinner. There's plenty if you'd like to join."

"That is very kind of you to offer. Damisi tells me you cook. I do not want to presume, but I hoped to use your kitchen to make her favorite tonight."

"Please do. I'll grab something quick and let you have the space."

Her hand reached out to grip my arm, keeping me from moving to the refrigerator. "You must join us. Damisi tells me of your meals together."

Normally, I wouldn't hesitate, but Damisi still kept her personal shields at eighty percent around me. She might resent my horning in on a dinner with her mother.

"Damisi will insist."

I smiled at her telepathy. "Only if you let me help."

"Delighted." She started pulling food items from her cloth bag as I gave my hands and arms a wash.

"What are we making?"

"Jollof rice and fried plantains."

"A Nigerian dish, right?"

She turned with a curious gaze. "Are you a worldly chef?"

"I've been lucky enough to share apartments with several international students. The one who liked Jollof rice was from Lagos." He'd been nice enough but wasn't around much for that summer session. He also wasn't much of a cook, unlike my favorite international roommate who loved cooking the Thai dishes she missed from home.

"Ah, yes. I am from Abuja."

"The capitol. Do you go back often?"

"I am just returned today."

"And you decided to bring something from your trip to your daughter."

"I missed her and thought she needed spoiling."

I had to stop myself from clapping a hand to my heart. What a great mother. So eager to see her daughter, she rushed over after a long travel day to spoil her daughter with a favorite meal. That was the kind of mother I hoped to be one day.

"Mama?" Damisi's voice called out from the foyer. "You're back early!" There was an unfamiliar excitement to her normally unaffected tone.

When she appeared in the living room, her gait stuttered. She hadn't expected me to be in the kitchen with her mother. It didn't look like she was upset, but she wasn't the easiest person to read. In the next moment, she was hugging her mother and chattering happily.

"Nora and I were just about to make your favorite," Eni told her.

"I'm sure Nora has other things to do."

"I enjoy learning how to make new things. If you don't mind me joining you."

Both sets of beautiful eyes locked onto me, one curious, the other wary. Standing next to each other, their resemblance was unmistakable. Damisi's father must have a sharper nose, straight or wavy hair, and was possibly Caucasian or mixed race given Damisi's lighter skin tone, but otherwise, her features were a carbon copy of her mother's. Based on how gorgeous Damisi was, her father would no doubt be as good looking as this twosome.

"Of course not," Damisi assured, losing most of the excited tone, but not all.

"Nora shared a flat with someone from Lagos, did she tell you?" Eni slipped her arm around Damisi's waist.

"Just for a summer. He didn't cook, so I never learned to make any of the Nigerian dishes he raved about." I nodded my head at Eni. "Your mom offered a culinary class."

"What are you making?" she asked her mom, something she never asked me before our dinners together. Perhaps she felt it was a presumptive question, not wanting to put pressure on me to provide dinner for her.

"You can guess, my daughter."

Damisi's eyes lit up and she smiled, spotting the ingredients we'd laid out. "How was the conference, Mama?"

Eni passed me the tomatoes to dice while she got the rice cooking. "Not well organized, but I made connections."

"Helpful?"

"Yes. Someone to call on when documents are needed."

Damisi caught my curious glance. "Mama is an immigration lawyer."

"Hard work and not often rewarding, or at least that's true in the US."

"Unfortunately, it is becoming that way here, too."

"You help so many people. Don't get discouraged."

Eni cupped her daughter's face. "Never. It is too important."

Damisi's eyes glowed with pride. They clearly had a close relationship. My stomach tightened at the sight. I'd once shared a close relationship with my mother, but as I got older and could see how my gender dictated so much about my standing in the family, I kept more and more to myself, withdrawing from both parents and my brothers.

"You work with horses? In what capacity? Damisi has not said." Eni turned her attention back to me as we finished the prep work and the rice dish was cooking.

"Training and competing."

"What kind of competition?" She placed the plantains carefully in the hot fryer.

"It's called cutting. Riders separate a cow from the herd and keep it from rejoining." My description was met with baffled stares. To the uninitiated, the competition could appear pointless. "Imagine trying to stop me from leaving this kitchen without touching me. Now apply that side to side dance to a horse and cow."

Their eyes widened. The skill of cutting was a lot more complex than I described, especially when it came to scoring, but basically it hinged on the athleticism of the horse and guidance of the rider.

"How long have you been competing?" Eni asked.

"Started training when I was seven, competing at ten."

"Is there a ranking system?" Damisi asked with a spark of challenge in her eyes.

I grinned and shot her my own challenging look. "Yes."

Her brow lifted in obvious question. Eni pushed at her shoulder and made a grumbling noise to let her know she didn't approve of the challenge. It didn't deter Damisi from demanding an answer.

"Bounced between first and second in my region every year. I have one particularly fierce competitor, and lots of good competition from others." If I'd kept a game face on at all times and not been friendly with my competitors, especially my main competitor, I probably could have come in first always. Instead, we all became friends and could be happy for whoever won. Yes, there was a difference between first and second prize money, but for me, it wasn't about the prize money. That was only part of my annual income once I started competing for my own ranch. The more important benefit was the prestige to our training program. First for my father, then in more recent years, my ranch.

"The best, of course. Like my Damisi."

Damisi gave a slight grimace before beaming at her mother. "Second best, Mama."

"Pssh," she waved off.

I studied Damisi as we brought the full platters over to the table and took our seats. The quick correction of her mother's assessment was interesting, and not because she was being modest. She truly believed she was second to someone else.

"You will compete here for Hearn?" Eni asked as she dished out portions for all of us.

My mouth started watering as she passed me a plate. "His niece, Kenzi, wants to learn. There's a competitive circuit in Europe, or she can go to America. Hearn wants to get a breeding and training program in place here."

She sent a questioning glance at her daughter. "A whim?"

Damisi shook her head and finished the bite she'd taken. "He seems quite serious about it. You know he loves horses. I'm not sure how seriously Kenzi will take it, but keeping horses here works for the estate."

"Will you stay to run the stables?" Eni asked me.

"I'm getting everything set up. Kenzi will need a coach and the stables will need a trainer. I'll help hire and train both."

Damisi's eyes narrowed briefly as if she didn't believe me. Or maybe she was calculating the amount of time until she'd have this place back to herself. She planned another year teaching at both Glasgow and Edinburgh. The cottage's location was ideal for traveling between the two. I'd tried to get more information about why she'd taken the placement at Glasgow when she had a full load at Edinburgh, but she'd been close-lipped about it. Perhaps, her perceived status as second best had something to do with it. Teaching at two universities would up her profile, not that it needed it. Based on our dinner talks, she had to be more knowledgeable than any other Scottish history professor at either school.

"Will these be spoilt horses?" Eni drew my attention back.

"All my horses are treated well, but they're for riding and competing, not just show." I studied her. "Are you a rider, Eni? Damisi?"

"I love to ride." Hope shined brightly in Eni's eyes. "Damisi is not used to horses."

"You'll have to come back for a ride once the horses are settled in." My eyes shifted to Damisi. "We can start you out slowly if you like."

The barest hint of a blush touched her cheeks. My pulse shifted at the sight. "I'm happy to watch."

That blush made me determined to push her out of her comfort zone. I had faith in my horses to draw her out. She'd be up on a horse before the end of my time here. For now, I could let her off the hook.

I took my first bite of the rice and followed it with a fried plantain, barely suppressing the moan at the burst of flavors. "This is excellent, Eni. Thank you for showing me how to make it."

"You are quite welcome."

"Thank you both," Damisi said. "It's as delicious as ever, Mama."

"Only the best for my girl."

I could tell she wasn't just saying that. She meant to give and wish only the best for her daughter. What a wonderful feeling that must be.

CHAPTER 11

GRESHAM PULLED THE Rolls around the curve and smoothly slid to a stop next to me. The back doors opened and out popped my best friend and her mom. Despite a five-hour train trip up from London, they looked refreshed and excited to see me.

"Nora!" Sayen reached for a hug that her mother, Melanie, joined by wrapping her arms around both of us.

I pulled back and studied the twosome. Both had long, straight black hair surrounding oval faces with narrow noses and sculpted cheekbones. Equally beautiful on the inside and out, they made a fearsome duo when confronted. Their relationship was as beautiful as they were. Melanie was only nineteen when she had Sayen and raised her on her own. It made for a dynamic that most others in similar situations would have botched. Melanie's ingrained calm helped bring a maturity to her impending motherhood lacking from many others her age.

Sayen and I met when she transferred from her school on the Fort Hall Reservation to play for our high school's state winning soccer team. It was a difficult choice for her, leaving her friends on the Reservation for a high school with a predominately white student body. Her soccer skills were exceptional, though, and her high school didn't have a team.

If she wanted a chance at a college scholarship, she had to make the switch.

Transferring a few weeks into the year, she was assigned the last available locker in the freshman section, which happened to be next to mine. The door didn't close properly, and after a few of her things went missing, I offered to share mine. We didn't know each other well, but when I found out who'd stolen her stuff, I offered. She was hesitant at first because she guessed correctly that her stuff had been taken by a few racist asswipes who felt their white privilege was being threatened by everyone, not just the Shoshone people. As a white privileged person, I couldn't blame her for not trusting me right off. But over the next few weeks until maintenance fixed her locker, we'd struck up a friendship that was now in its eighteenth year.

"Thanks for coming all this way."

"We get to visit with you and your boss is paying for the trip? No brainer," Melanie assured.

I grinned and hugged her again. She had been a calming influence in my life, so different from how my parents treated my brothers and me. Our parents were more traditional, focusing more on providing and teaching and setting expectations. Melanie was all support and love and encouragement. She could pretend the free trip was one of the reasons she was visiting, but I knew she would have come on her own dime if I'd called for help. Thankfully, Hearn understood the importance of having trained handlers here to get the horses settled when they arrived and offered to fly them over.

"Not much to do back at the ranch, anyway," Sayen added with a wink. Because of the delay in getting the horses here, a few of the chosen horses were sold to other customers when we couldn't confirm a delivery date. That left us three short.

Sayen and Melanie agreed to bring over a long yearling and a three-year-old in addition to the champion mare I'd sold to Hearn to make up two of the three. They'd be a lot of work to train, but for the long-term, better than several of the horses I'd bid on at auction. I knew their bloodlines, coming directly from my champion stud and their champion mares.

Left at my ranch now would be their two mares and my stallion, easily taken care of by Sayen's cousin while she was here helping me. When I started my ranch, Sayen and Melanie took me up on my offer to stable, train, compete, and breed horses for each of them. For Sayen, who worked with me on the ranch, it was a labor of love. For Melanie it was both an investment and a way to show her support for us. At first, I only intended to keep horses for the ability to compete occasionally, but when I found myself with access to a champion stud and three champion mares, it made sense to start a breeding program. It was nowhere near the scale of my father's ranch, nor would it match what Hearn was planning. Still, it brought in enough income for me to pay Sayen a good wage and add a little extra to my competition earnings and full-time job. Sayen and her mom also made extra money with each sale of a foal from their mares.

"How do you possibly look better than when you left?" Melanie asked, gripping my face and tilting it for inspection. "With all the work you've had to do here? How is that possible?"

I didn't know about looking better, but I certainly felt better. Breaking away from the pressures of the family and the family business, even with the responsibility of getting this ranch up and going, my stress level was almost non-existent. I hadn't realized how bad it had gotten, but having complete autonomy and someone with faith in my abilities to do what needed to be done made work and life so much easier.

"Helps not to be criticized every minute of your workday, doesn't it?" Sayen muttered as she squeezed my shoulder. She knew firsthand how much I had to deal with on the family ranch, having worked there with me for a few years before I got my own ranch and she jumped at working there instead.

"Let me show you around, then we'll get you settled at the B&B."

"We're ready to get to work," Sayen offered and I wanted to hug her again. We'd been keeping in touch by email mostly, a few Skype calls, but she knew how much work still needed to be done here.

"You get one evening off, then I'll need you on the hiring committee starting tomorrow."

"Wherever you need us."

When we rounded the curve in the back driveway and the barn came into view, my companions stopped. Small sounds came from their mouths. The stables were grander in scale than they'd ever seen. Even the best stable yards in Kentucky and Florida couldn't match the luxury this building and the pastures exuded.

"This is nicer than some of those celebrity homes in Sun Valley, and it's for horses," Melanie breathed as we stepped into the wide corridor of the stables.

We giggled at her description. Not quite as splendid as the homes in the opulent ski resort town of our home state, but these horses would want for nothing here.

"You could rent out these stalls on Airbnb. I'm serious." Melanie's hand ran over the top of the low-profile U-shaped stall fronts. She unlatched the first stall and stepped inside, bouncing up onto her toes to check the padding on the stall floor.

"This is really amazing, Nora." Sayen's eyes bounced from feature to feature. My own barn was decent. It had a lot of the same basic features, but where I'd gone for efficient but economical, Hearn had gone for efficient and magnificent.

"The horses should be happy here," I said, glancing up at the windows lining the apex of the ceiling. Two on each side could prop open for extra ventilation in the hotter months of summer. Large sliding doors stood at the end of each aisle in the barn and on the crossway, and every stall had Dutch doors to allow for constant fresh air for the horses. Every door, window, skylight, light, and temperature gauge could be operated via an electronic system from the stable office. Cameras in every stall and along the aisles allowed for constant monitoring. It had all the elements of a smart home and was more sophisticated than my own home.

"From the pictures you sent on your first day to now, it's really amazing." Sayen led the way out the rear door of the barn.

Her eyes landed on the storage building to the left and the hay barn just beyond. Set apart from the stables was the building where the ranch hands would have lockers, bathrooms, a kitchen, lunch tables, and on the upper floor, three dorm style rooms for the nights during foaling season. It was still about two weeks from being finished, but it was progressing far more quickly than the barn had. Apparently, the contractor had more residential contracting experience than stable experience.

"It's amazing you stayed," Melanie said. "You walked into a completely different situation than you were led to believe was here."

"Yeah, but I'm glad they weren't done before I got here because the stables wouldn't have turned out right. And we all know how bad the fields would have been, not to mention the fencing."

"It was meant to be," Melanie said.

"Come on, let's head back to the cottage. I've got dinner planned before we get you over to the B&B in town."

"Does your housemate know we'll be staying for dinner?"

I glanced at Sayen and smiled. She knew about Damisi and was eager to see which version we'd get tonight: warm or cool. "She's aware." I'd warned her last week, asking permission in a show of politeness.

"This is nice," Melanie commented as we entered the foyer.

"This is a guesthouse? It's almost as big as your place." Sayen said as we moved down the hall toward the living room.

"Bigger, I think. There's at least two bedrooms upstairs."

"At least? You don't know?" Melanie's dark brown eyes grew wide.

I shook my head. "No, ma'am. That's Damisi's area. I'm not about to go traipsing through."

Sayen's brow rose. "Is she here?"

"She usually gets back on Wednesdays about now. I asked her to join us for dinner, but it'll depend on how her classes went today."

"A professor, huh?" Sayen teased, knowing just how much I liked smart women.

"Of Scottish history. Quite well known, or so Hearn tells me. Same with the neighbor down the road. The one with the twins I told you about."

"Ooh, babies." Melanie's eyes danced. "We should invite them over and grill out."

"We should." I'd run into both Ainsley and Skye a few times over the past few weeks and they were always funny and nice. Both had the summer off and were probably going stir crazy with the babies at home. "One for the new employees, too." Although, I'd definitely need to clear that with Damisi.

The front door opened before they could respond. Both whirled to catch a glimpse of Damisi, but as usual, she went straight up the stairs first. Over the past several weeks, I wondered if it had more to do with her need to decompress once she got home than her need to ready herself for dealing with a roommate.

"Something to drink?" I offered, moving to the refrigerator and pulling out a chilled bottle of wine and the fresh-squeezed lemonade I'd made this morning. Sayen reached for the lemonade and Melanie pointed at the wine.

I grabbed two wine goblets and two glasses, figuring Damisi would want wine. If she joined us. "Several options for dinner tonight. Do you feel like a chicken, pork, or a veggie dish?"

"Do you have the stuff for artichoke chicken or arroz con pollo?" Sayen opened the refrigerator to answer her own question. "Both, excellent. Ma?"

"Mexican sounds good, if Damisi likes Mexican."

"I do," Damisi said as she entered the living room with a bright smile on her face.

I gave a sweeping gesture and introduced them. "Melanie and Sayen Honovi, meet Damisi Dalziel."

She shook Melanie's hand and turned to catch Sayen winking at me before greeting her. Damisi shot me a questioning look, but I brushed it off. Leave it to Sayen to try to embarrass me in front of a gorgeous woman. For someone not sexually inclined, Sayen sure did like to play matchmaker with me and her other friends. One shared trait that bonded us so tightly when we first met was the fact that neither of us liked boys. It turned out she didn't like girls, either, but we commiserated over having to listen to our friends be exhaustingly boy-crazy while we couldn't have cared less.

"Nora's been looking forward to your visit. Was your trip all right?"

"Very nice."

"They stopped off in London for a few days," I said as Sayen helped me arrange the ingredients.

"Have you never been?" Damisi asked them, giving me an approving nod as I tipped the wine bottle toward the empty goblet.

"I've only ever been to Canada," Melanie responded. "Sayen's been to Mexico, Belize, and Argentina."

"And Canada," Sayen added.

Damisi gave me another questioning look. "A few cities in Canada and Mexico for me. But I've been to 41 of the 50 states."

She shook her head in dismay. For a Brit with dozens of countries within a few hours flight, it was hard to believe anyone else couldn't have been to more than three countries. "I've been telling this one she needs to explore more."

"Not till this place is up and running, I bet," Sayen kidded and bumped against my shoulder as we started the rice cooking.

"You must know her well," Damisi said with a playful grin. Was she trying to flirt with Sayen? Of course, she'd find Sayen attractive. Who wouldn't? But really, the gorgeous woman I've been living with finally decides to show some interest and it's for my best friend? So not fair.

"We'll get her out and around, won't we?" Melanie made it seem like it was a question, but I knew better.

"Yes, ma'am," I replied.

Damisi shot me an amused look. "Ma'am?" she copied my accent well.

"Melanie's a queen where we come from." She basically was, and not just to Sayen and me. Her coworkers and friends thought just as highly of her.

Both Sayen and Melanie cut us confused looks. "The Brits pronounce 'ma'am' differently, unless addressing the queen."

"Right." Sayen snapped her fingers. "From that movie we saw that time with what's his name as the king and that woman with the hair as the queen."

Damisi and Melanie laughed at our communication shortcuts. "She uses that term a lot," Damisi told Melanie.

"Her parents insisted on respect for her elders and authority figures. Unlike this one," Melanie poked her daughter's arm, "who is nothing but sass."

"All for you, Mom," Sayen deadpanned.

"You're a fun lot," Damisi said.

Her expression gave me hope that having this "fun lot" around for the next week and a half might help crash through the last of Damisi's defensive walls and we'd get to see more of the intriguing woman I'd only seen glimpses of so far.

CHAPTER 12

AFTER THREE LACKLUSTER interviews, this one was a breath of fresh air. It helped that he was a referral from Paisley. Melanie walked out of the last interview, not wanting to waste more time on someone she knew we wouldn't hire. I needed to tick all the hiring practices boxes so the interviewee wouldn't sue us for not giving her the same chance as all the other applicants.

This candidate was also a veteran, deployed with Paisley's unit to Iraq. He'd left the army a few years before Paisley, moving into municipal government work until his wife was killed in a car accident and he became solely responsible for their two young children.

"I've been taking two or three part-time jobs to work around the kids' school schedule." His eyes went from mine, to Sayen's, to Melanie's, not spending more time on anyone over the other. "Unless I want to work overnight, I can't get a full-time job, but Paisley said you'd be okay with a flexible part-time schedule."

I was glad Paisley felt comfortable recommending a few applicants. Having tried working with friends in the past at my dad's ranch, it wasn't always a comfortable experience. Our first interview today had been with one of her friends, but it became clear within a half hour, the job wouldn't hold the woman's interest long. Besides not being an animal person, she wasn't much of an outdoor person.

My eyes flicked to Melanie. She'd asked a few questions, but mostly she sat and watched. Sayen and I were always amazed by her mother's ability to assess someone's potential without much exposure. She glanced over at me and gave a single nod.

"We can offer full-time flexible hours as well," I told him. "We've got work from early morning till late night seven days a week."

His brown eyes widened. "You'd be open to that? Work school hours and come back to put in a couple more after dinner when my mum can take over with the kids?"

"We're adding more staff, so you can choose your hours, and if unplanned kid things come up, we're covered. Paisley recommended you and we all like you, so I say we give it a try. Are you up for it?"

"Absolutely. I don't even need to know how much you'll pay. One full-time flexible job at minimum is worth more than several part-time jobs paying well."

I smiled, happy to hear that. My only requirement for sustained employment was their contentment with the job. No amount of money could make someone happy to go to work. It could make them go to work, but not be happy doing it.

"You'll be happy to hear we pay better than minimum, Roderick." I stood to shake his hand. "Let us know when you can start and we'll get your schedule ironed out."

"Thank you, Ms. Cleary."

"Nora," Sayen and I said together. She knew how much I didn't like standing on ceremony. Too many of my dad's employees still called him Mr. Cleary, and my brother Niall made all new employees call him the same.

"Looking forward to starting, Nora."

"One down," Sayen said after walking him out. "We get a couple more like him and you're set."

It took three more interviews before we found another suitable candidate, and he had horse experience. Better yet, he was okay working Thursday through Monday. I thought I'd have to fill weekend spots with part-time workers, but having Andrew would eliminate the need for three part-timers. As a ranch owner, I was used to working weekends, but it was a lot to ask of ranch hands not getting room and board as part of their wages.

"Have we run through everyone?" Melanie asked.

"Everyone who applied, yes. I'll see if Paisley has any other recommendations and get on the phone to the vet org later. For now, let's head to the feed store."

We piled into the pickup and got onto the motorway toward Edinburgh. I'd been warned the feed stores here didn't have everything we'd need to outfit and feed the horses. The vet I knew who taught at University of Edinburgh had given me a brief rundown on how all things horses went over here. Lots of specializations rather than an all-in-one shop like we could find in most farming communities in the States. I'd placed a preliminary order for feed and supplements at the store we were visiting. They could become our regular supplier if all went well today. I tried out my suppliers as carefully as my employees.

"May I help you?" a young woman greeted as we walked in. On closer look, she appeared younger than eighteen with a wary look in her hazel eyes, despite the professional greeting.

"We're picking up an order for Ogilvie."

"I'll take care of this, Rhona." Another woman brushed her aside with a dismissive tone. "You can load their order as soon as you deal with that spill I asked you to clean earlier.

Rhona's gaze flicked to hers. The woman wasn't much older than she. It was hard to believe she could be her boss. Rhona gave a polite nod as she moved around us.

"You're with the Ogilvie Estate?" The woman's eyes sparked to life with a gleam that made me slightly uncomfortable. "We want to do whatever we need to for your business."

Not whatever they could do, but whatever they need to do. She didn't look like she'd stop short of anything criminal to win our business. Typical overzealous salesperson.

"We've placed an order," I repeated.

"You're American." She tried to modulate her voice, but whatever distaste she had for Americans came through. "Right, let me see about that order."

Sayen knocked her shoulder against me, tipping her head in the woman's direction. She didn't need to say anything. The surprise at our nationality wasn't anything new, but the woman either expected Hearn himself or she really disliked Americans.

"Have you been helped?" an older gentleman with similar facial features as the woman asked.

"We have, thank you," Melanie supplied.

"Did I hear you're with the Ogilvie Estate?" He barely waited for my nod. "We're very excited to be your feed supplier. Mr. Ogilvie's plans for the stables are grand, and we're thrilled to be part of it." This guy was even more slick than his daughter when it came to sales. Always assume a close, or so my marketing classes in school taught me. "We can set up an automated weekly order today to make things easier for you."

I could feel Sayen dying to laugh at his boldness. She knew how I did business, and this guy's pushiness was grating on everyone's nerves. Melanie had already turned away to find the young woman who would be loading our order, knowing she'd never keep her opinion to herself.

"We're not yet sure of our needs. Most of the horses are coming from different farms and we'll have to assess their preferences first. Thank you, though." The finality in my tone was clear to me, but probably not to overconfident sales guy. I hoped the other feed store recommendations would work out better than this one.

"Of course, keep us apprised. Let's ring up the order. Or would you like to start an account and be billed?"

"All set to pay now, thanks." I pulled the company card from my wallet and handed it over as the woman instructed the younger woman to bring our order to the loading bay before she came toward us again.

"I've already started the account setup, Dad. Hit F5 and you'll see the saved account screen."

"She's going to pay now," he told her.

"It'll be much easier to bill you. Your operation is going to need weekly deliveries."

Like this woman would know best what "my" operation will need. "We'll pay now, thank you." I thrust the card forward, my action now matching my tone. Next week, we'd try the other feed store closer to the vet school. And if that one didn't work out, there were two more outside of Glasgow.

The man reluctantly took the card, swiping to complete the sale. I let the guy mutter on about what he'd be able to do for the ranch, their excitement at the prospect of serving such a prestigious estate, and on and on. Finally, when he let himself breathe, I shook his hand and went to join both Melanie and Sayen out at the truck where they were helping the younger woman load the feed. She and Sayen were joking about something, both stopping to laugh before picking up the final bags of feed.

The know-it-all woman stepped out of the store and grasped the girl's arm. "You've been warned about this, Rhona. Your flirting is unwelcome and unprofessional. Not to mention, unnatural." Her gaze shifted to Sayen, and a clear appreciation of her beauty flashed despite her stated disgust. Sayen's beauty was hard to ignore. "I'm terribly sorry if she offended you. She'll be dealt with, I assure you."

"Excuse me?" Melanie's tone was pure protective mother. "Why would she be offended? And what do you mean by unnatural?"

The woman was too surprised to mask her honest reaction. "Rhona shouldn't be coming onto our female customers. It makes them uncomfortable. She's been warned several times. If she weren't my stepbrother's friend, she'd have been fired months ago."

"I wasn't flirting." Rhona jerked away from her grasp, pink cresting her cheeks. She ran a hand over her dark blond ponytail, flicking the end as her eyes furtively glanced at Sayen. Even if she'd been flirting with Sayen, it would have been harmless. Most people flirted with Sayen; she had that kind of draw.

"We'll see what Dad has to say about this." The woman marched off into the store.

My gaze caught Melanie's. Her intent was clear. Even if we hadn't been interrupted, I had a feeling Melanie would have nudged me anyway based on how hard they'd been working together. "Hi, Rhona. I'm Nora and I'm hiring if you're interested."

Her eyes widened, skipping from me to Sayen and Melanie and back to me. She didn't even bother looking toward the shop door. She had a million questions she wanted to ask, that she should ask, but was interrupted before she could.

"Please excuse my employee." The man rushed out of the shop.

"For what?" I asked. "She's doing her job expertly and quickly."

"We don't condone—"

"Just stop," Melanie told him. "You're digging a hole you'll never get out of with us."

"We're simply trying to apologize for any offense our—"

"You're going to need a ladder to get out of that hole, guy. You best be quiet." Sayen looked at Rhona, who was trying to hold back her smile. "Think about Nora's offer. You know where the ranch is?"

"Stables," I added the word the locals kept using to describe the ranch.

She nodded and flicked her gaze between all of us again. Mine went to the owner and his daughter. He probably guessed I'd tried to poach his employee, but he didn't look like he cared if he lost her, just that he'd lose face over losing her to someone else. He glanced back at us and I could see he was dying to give us one last sales pitch, but our demeanor had changed. He'd lost Melanie and Sayen for sure, he probably didn't want to push his luck with the woman who had the credit card. He swept back into the shop, his daughter following.

"I hope we didn't just force your hand, Rhona," I told her, realizing too late that by standing up to that guy he'd likely take it out on her. And if she wasn't interested in working on the ranch, she might be out of the job she liked here.

"They've been holding the 'we might make you redundant' threat over me for weeks. My mate begged a favor to have me hired on, but it's been strained the whole way. I appreciate the offer if you were serious."

"Definitely serious." I studied her more closely. "I'm probably not supposed to ask this of a potential employee, but aren't you young to be done with school already?"

She glanced away, swallowing roughly. "I had to leave school."

Melanie gripped her arm and gave her a sympathetic look as if she knew exactly why Rhona had to leave school without her needing to say. Melanie could sometimes do that. It made me curious to learn her story, but this wasn't the right place.

"If you decide to join our team, we can go over your options and come up with a schedule that will work for all of us including if you want to go back to school. You do like horses, don't you?"

"Love them." A wide smile confirmed the feeling I had about her. Very few teenage hires worked out on our family ranch, but my instincts told me she'd be different.

CHAPTER 13

FOR THE FIRST time in two months, the barn smelled equal parts new construction and horse. Not that "horse" was a labeled aroma, but to equine ranchers, it was. Eleven noses jutted over the wide u-shaped stable enclosures. Three were very familiar, coming from my ranch. The other eight were from auctions in Montana and Wyoming. Originally, Hearn wanted me to fill the stables, but I talked him into starting smaller. If he was really serious about this breeding and training program, I'd find a few others for him when I went back to the States.

My mare bobbed her head in greeting, instantly recognizing me even after our time apart. Moisture pricked my eyes, happy to see her but sad to be leaving her here. She was the first horse I'd bought on my own. First horse I'd competed with under my own ranch's name. But each year, the blazing heat of Idaho's summers seemed to affect her more and more. Scotland's more mild summers would suit her better. If Hearn's offer hadn't come along, I was considering selling her to a friend on the cutting circuit whose ranch near Portland would have provided a similar mild climate.

My hand stroked her velvety nose as I spoke quietly to her. She didn't appear worse for wear, but the quarantine protocols, long flight, and long drive was hard on humans, let alone a horse used to being turned out with freedom to roam and graze as she wished most days.

Down the line, I greeted each horse, spending a little extra time with the long yearling. Sayen hadn't planned to sell him until he was fully trained and possibly not even then, but Hearn offered an amount equal to what she'd get if he'd been fully trained and she couldn't pass it up. Her mare was due to be inseminated in the fall, so she'd have another foal next year.

"I'm not going to ask if you slept in here last night; I don't want to know."

I grinned and turned to find Damisi entering the barn. "I only sleep in the barn if necessary."

"What could possibly necessitate someone sleeping in a barn?" She came closer, sticking to the center of the wide aisle.

"When a large part of your income depends on a mare having an uncomplicated birth, you tend to stick close when she's ready to drop."

Her brow spiked. She'd been joking, but not being a rancher, she wouldn't have known just how many people do spend nights in barns or in fields keeping tabs on their livestock. "I'd like to see a live birth."

"Stick around long enough and you will. For now," I cut her a sly glance, noticing she still hadn't stepped closer to the stalls on either side. "Come meet the youngest in the group. This is Inky Lander, or Inky, for short. He'll turn two next month."

She inched forward. The minute she saw his beautiful black body, her eyes went wide. Yeah, he had that effect on people. "He's beautiful."

"He knows it, too."

"Is his name a combination of the mother and father's?"

"Dam and sire, and yes. Sayen's mare is Inkswept. She's all black like Inky. My stallion, Salander, is chestnut colored."

She tore her gaze away from Inky. "Interesting names."

"Sayen and Melanie like to use descriptive names. I go for kickass literary women when I name mine." I reached over and scratched my mare's face. "This is Angelou. Her first born was Lou Landy." My hand stroked Melanie's buckskin filly in the next stall. "This is Sunbeam Sala, or Subi, for short. She comes from Melanie's mare, Sunbringer."

She breathed out a laugh as her eyes flipped between the three horses, always coming back to rest on Inky. Her head swiveled and looked at the others, a hand gesturing to ask.

"The other eight are new to us. I picked them up at auctions for Hearn. They haven't competed yet, so I had Hearn and Kenzi help me name them before getting them passports."

I crossed back to Inky's stall and gestured Damisi closer, but she stood rooted to the ground. "He likes his nose rubbed."

"That's all right."

My lips curled into a smile as I recognized her hesitancy for what it was. "You aren't afraid of horses, are you?"

"No," she denied automatically, but her eyes kept straying to the colt.

"Once you touch his nose, you'll never be able to stop."

She snorted and rolled her eyes at me. "I'm sure he's lovely. I just wanted to see if you'd truly stopped the night out here."

My brow furrowed before taking her words in context. I'd been slowly picking up more of the Scots language as well as Oisin's Irish idioms. I'd probably have to learn some English sayings as soon as Andrew started on Thursday. "Your hand, please, ma'am."

Her grin flared, as it always seemed to whenever I referred to anyone as ma'am or sir. She brought it up to wave off my offer, but I caught it and tugged her forward. I didn't let my thoughts drift to how soft her hand was. How my callouses could imprint divots in her glorious skin. Or how her citrus scent made me want to bury my nose into her neck. I had a mission and it was to make sure this woman never feared these animals when she lived so close. Over the past few weeks, our dinner conversations touched on the future of the ranch and the original intended use of the cottage. I got the impression she wasn't certain she'd be able to stay on once the new ranch manager took over. Hearn would need to assure her as my own assurances didn't seem to be setting in.

I placed my left hand on Inky's face, and raised Damisi's hand to touch his muzzle. If I hadn't already given him two carrots, he might have taken a playful nip at Damisi's hand, but for once, he was behaving himself.

A breath pushed out as her hand automatically began stoking the velvety muzzle. She giggled as his whiskers brushed against her palm. I moved her hand to his neck, showing her how he liked to be stroked. My motive was only partially impure as my body brushed up against hers to complete the stretch to Inky's neck. He really did like his neck scratched.

"You don't want to stop touching him, do you?"

She took her hand off him and twisted to face me, enticingly close. For a second, her breath mingled with mine, then she shoved me with that soft hand. I stumbled back a step and laughed. "We'll have a bit of hush from you."

A truck engine sounded outside. I glanced down the aisle and felt regret at losing the excuse to keep touching Damisi but excited for the visitor.

"Dr. Luskin," I called out, moving toward the woman who stepped out of the passenger side of the specialized truck. "So glad you could make it."

"Nora, good to see you again. I was eager to see what you're building here and wanted to introduce you to my former pupil."

A tall brunette stepped up next to her. Probably late twenties, which meant she wasn't long out of Dr. Luskin's veterinary program. "Ms. Cleary," she greeted in a gorgeous low voice. "I'm Finola Pullar."

I took her hand. "Nice to meet you, Dr. Pullar. Call me, Nora."

"Finola," she insisted. "Fin, actually."

"Dr. Fin," I insisted right back with a smile.

"Damisi?" Dr. Luskin peered farther into the barn where Damisi was still petting Inky.

"Agatha." Damisi came forward with a smile for Dr. Luskin. When it looked like she'd be swallowed up in a massive hug, she managed to shift it to a brief one-armed squeeze. This wasn't the first time I'd seen her avoid close contact with someone. Not with her mom or Celia, but everyone else was limited to a brief touch. Finding out why became a new goal for me since getting a hug was likely out of the question.

"I'm doing house calls with my favorite former student. Got to keep my skills up to date." Her hand came down to grip my shoulder. "Nora called for a referee, and I was all too happy to oblige."

Damisi's eyes flicked between us. "Have you met?"

"At one of her lectures in the States." I'd been one of the few Agriculture Business students at UC Davis sitting in on her guest lecture series. The material was impressive enough, but she'd blown me away by taking as much time with my fellow AgriBiz students as she had with the veterinary students. We shared the belief that ranch owners needed to understand the basics of veterinary medicine in order to keep their flocks whole and hearty. So many of my classmates didn't get that. "We've kept in touch. I knew she'd know someone we could rely on for the horses here."

"That I do. Fin's just getting her mobile operation going."

I gestured to her truck. "Let's take a look at your rig."

Fin took me over and started opening various hatches, showing me the equipment. She filled me in on her experience while we checked everything out. She'd worked for four years in a city vet hospital, seeing almost exclusively small animals and volunteering for any farm work they'd get. She saved up and bought the truck and equipment and struck out on her own three months ago. We'd be her largest client operation to date, which should make me nervous, but something about this calm, sure woman dispelled any concern.

When we joined Dr. Luskin and Damisi in the barn again, it looked like Damisi had forgotten she was in a barn half full of animals she'd denied being afraid of. Dr. Luskin was stroking my mare's neck and Damisi's hand was rubbing her nose.

"Quick check over or something more?" Fin asked me.

"They had cursory checks before and after the flight, but I want them looked over completely before we start training and insemination. The works, please."

Her eyes lit up, and not because of the invoice she'd be sending. She liked working with animals, and if she'd only been in business for three months, it was likely she'd barely had a chance to work on horses.

"I'll leave you all to it," Damisi said, shaking Dr. Luskin's hand. "Mama will be here this evening. I wouldn't be surprised if others drop by as well. Hearn's in tomorrow."

"We'll be ready," I assured her, my gaze lingering on her retreating form.

Two hours and a thorough exam confirmed my first impression of the new vet. Fin knew what she was doing. We came to an agreement on which of the unfamiliar mares would be best suited for insemination this year and made a tentative schedule.

"Let me call round to the neighbors' farms to put in a good word for you." I waved at Oisin and Paisley as their car pulled into the parking area. "Oisin knows them pretty well. We'll have a visit to see if we can't get you a few more clients around here."

"I appreciate that, Nora."

"I'll let you know when we're ready for insemination." I shook both their hands, and walked them out of the barn.

Their truck met Gresham's car on the way in to drop off Sayen and Melanie. Both back doors popped open and Rhona exited with Sayen. We'd spoken on the phone twice already. I thought she was starting on Monday, but I was thrilled she showed up today for the first handling session with the horses.

With Sayen and Melanie's help, we'd get everyone comfortable harnessing, tacking, and riding the horses before their visit ended. Finally, two months after arriving, I was jazzed to start the work I'd been hired to do. Surprisingly, I didn't feel frustrated about the delay in getting started. Keeping busy and the intriguing company of a somewhat prickly housemate made my time here anything but frustrating.

CHAPTER 14

HEARN'S SMILE SPLIT his face as he glanced up from the box to me and back to the box. Almost as if he'd never received a gift before. Perhaps once someone reaches a certain level of wealth, people stop giving gifts? Completely unfair, especially since he most likely gave gifts to people he cared about for every occasion.

"For me?" he asked with a hitch in his voice, causing Damisi to reach over and squeeze his shoulder in support.

He'd come up from London for the weekend to see the horses finally installed on his ranch. He caught us heading back to the cottage for lunch when he arrived at the estate. At first, he seemed shocked by the invitation to join us for lunch, and now, he couldn't comprehend the box I placed in his hands. Did no one at his company headquarters in London treat him like a normal human? No wonder he'd held onto friends like Dunbar if he was getting choked up by the invitation to share panini sandwiches and a simple gift.

"Shake it," Damisi prompted him out of his stupor. She'd become more comfortable hanging out with us since Melanie and Sayen had arrived. She'd even gone with us into Glasgow last evening for a brief tour and a museum visit, making the trip far more interesting by dropping historical facts throughout. She glanced at me, "Or is it fragile?"

"He can shake all he wants."

Hearn gave it a small jerk back and forth. When no sound came out, he started to peel off the wrapping paper carefully. His eyes widened as he took the lid off the hat box. Inside was a dark brown cowboy hat with a low crown, shallow pinch, and three-and-a-half-inch brim. Custom ordered and handmade, it wasn't a typical first cowboy hat. Most men went for the cattleman's high crown and deep pinch and crease. That style wouldn't suit Hearn's narrow face, but he needed a serious hat now that he was a serious rancher. He took it out and fingered the brim and the thin leather band.

"Try it on, Cowboy," I said.

He looked up with a grin and clapped the hat onto his head. A perfect fit, thanks to his admin's help. A couple of styles would have fit him, but since he'd never worn one, I thought the standard cattleman's tall brow and folds might be a bit much. I ordered something less stereotypical with a lower pinch front style. He might change it out in a couple of years, but this should suit him for his first.

"Thank you, Nora. This is so unexpected."

"You need a good hat now that you're a rancher." It wasn't as nice as mine, which was a custom design that blended the gambler and pinch front styles and done in a natural dyed felt landing somewhere between bone and sand on the color scale. Sayen had made a hat band from colorful beads, making my hat different from any other on the cutting circuit. I received compliments all the time.

He walked down the hall to the half bath to check out his new look. Damisi came close and brushed a hand down my arm. Goosebumps broke out, even as heat bloomed inside me.

"You know what you've done there." Her chin tipped toward Hearn.

"Every man wants to be a cowboy at some point in his life."

She glanced over at him again and shook her head in disbelief. Perhaps she thought she knew him really well and never guessed he'd be so fascinated by a cowboy hat, but one thing was clear, she was happy for him.

"Let's go try it out," I suggested when he came back.

Sayen and Melanie encouraged Damisi to join us as we headed for the barn. She'd been out a few times, stroking the noses of every horse while she pretended to check with me on dinner options. I hadn't gotten her to muck out a stall yet, but I was slowly making her into a horse lover.

"It's just grand," Hearn said. "Can I say that about my own place or does that make me a fandan?"

"Not sure what a fandan is, but I think you're allowed to admire your own stables," I said.

Damisi laughed and knocked a hand against his shoulder. "He has to curb his Scots jargon at work with those Londoners. It all comes tumbling out whenever he comes back home."

"As it should," Melanie agreed. Sayen and I grinned at each other. Melanie was heavily involved in the language revitalization efforts on the Reservation. She and Sayen were among a dwindling number of people fluent in Shoshoni.

"I should come back home more often."

"You should move back home," Damisi encouraged. We'd talked about Hearn's decision to start his tech company in London rather than his home city of Edinburgh. It was an understandable decision, but now that he'd made it big, he had the clout to relocate. She'd been slowly planting the idea in his mind over time. With the estate now up and running, he seemed closer and closer to making that move. After seeing what he was like around here among his friends Damisi, Gresham, Oisin, and Ainsley, I wholeheartedly agreed.

"One step at a time." His eyes flicked back toward the castle as if cementing the idea of a move. His sister and niece would be arriving next weekend and would stay for most of the summer. They, too, had been living in London since his sister's divorce. After the summer, though, they planned to move back to Edinburgh for Kenzi to attend a new school. That move might be the thing to tip the scales in favor of Hearn relocating as well. They were a close family.

When we arrived at the barn, our new employees, Andrew and Rhona, were just finishing saddling up the horses for our ride. Both had been able to start right away and their skills with horses were much appreciated. With Melanie and Sayen leaving next week, I'd need their help getting Oisin, Paisley, and Roderick up to their level of comfort with the horses. Their riding skills were getting better by the day, but it would take a while longer for them to handle anything other than a well-trained horse.

Damisi stopped before entering the barn. I reached back and grasped her elbow, pulling her inside with us. She'd agreed to get up on my mare and walk the corral when her mother had been with us, but she still wasn't a horsewoman.

"Short ride, you'll love it," I encouraged.

She studied me, trying to decide if she could trust my word. Over the past week, she'd stopped showing any reticence where I was concerned. She joked around more and almost seemed glad to have me as a housemate.

She hadn't shown any signs of attraction toward me, but I was hopeful. It might be stupid to harbor the beginnings of a crush on her, but she was so damn alluring. It was impossible to fight the attraction. Thanks to her friend Celia, I knew Damisi was a lesbian and single. Celia tried to be subtle about adding that tidbit to the conversation. Zoey's snort-laugh at the lack of subtlety made us all laugh. On the inside, I was jumping for joy. The more I got to know Damisi, the more I wanted to know about her.

CHAPTER 15

A SMILE BLOOMED on my lips when I heard Damisi's footsteps come up behind me outside Inky's stall. She usually reserved her visits for after work or dinner, but Mondays were her toughest scheduled day. A quick visit with Inky always put her in a good mood.

"How's my favorite boy this morn?"

"Feisty and ready for some treats." I turned to face her. She was dressed in cream-colored trousers and a patterned blouse. The only concession for her trip out to the barn before work were the stylish sneakers.

Her hand reached out, palm up, waiting. I grinned and plucked two carrots from the bag in the wheelbarrow beside me and placed them in her palm. She turned to Inky who had rushed to the stall door as soon as he heard her voice. They had the start of a love affair going. I felt a little stupid for being jealous of a horse, but I couldn't deny it.

She spent ten minutes loving on him and feeding him an extra carrot. Finally, she turned her attention to me. "He's so sweet."

"I can already tell he's going to be the toughest horse to train. It should make him quite the competitor." I smiled fondly at him and jerked the wheelbarrow into motion to walk her out.

One of Hearn's beautiful cars appeared on the road leading up to the barn, gliding with a deep rumble up to us. Paisley was in the passenger seat, chatting away with Gresham, who always seemed to have an official need to be driving past the train station at the exact moment Paisley would be coming to work. Melanie and Sayen were in the back seat. He'd insisted on bringing them here from the B&B each day, for which I was grateful.

Melanie emerged from the backseat, and an unfamiliar woman slid out to stand beside her. She was short and plump and probably in her sixties with a cap of white hair and a tentative smile on her face. "Elizabeth Helm, meet Nora Cleary. Nora, we ran into Elizabeth applying for work at the B&B this morning. She's your newest hire."

Elizabeth jolted in place. The surprise she was too shocked to express verbally ended up coming from Damisi, Paisley, and Gresham. "Gracious, I was only hoping to apply," Elizabeth looked panicked at Melanie's assertiveness. She obviously didn't want to insult me or the hiring process.

Melanie placed a hand on her forearm. "Elizabeth ran a seven-child household. She's going to be a scheduling genius. She was applying to cook at the B&B, but they don't have any openings. You do."

Poor Elizabeth had grown even more pale as Melanie continued to declare her hired. Her eyes pinged around the stables, obviously wondering how being a cook at a B&B would translate here.

I smiled, understanding what Melanie had in mind. Providing a meal for the employees would keep the team on time with their tasks in addition to being a nice fringe benefit. Help with their scheduling, requests for time off, and keeping track of everyone's whereabouts on the property throughout their workdays would also leave me and the future ranch manager time to focus on horse training rather than HR duties.

"Our kitchen isn't put together yet, but you can help get that squared away," I told her. "We'll have a few full and part-time employees with varying schedules to cover a twelve to fifteen-hour workday. Scheduling will be a headache and not something I'll have time for, and lunch needs to be provided. If you're up for it, we can talk about any other duties that might interest you."

"The job is mine?" Elizabeth asked, incredulity dripping from her tone.

It wasn't just how quickly we'd made the hiring decision. Something else was making her skeptical of the offer. Perhaps she'd been looking for work for a while. Given her age, she'd probably been rejected before even getting to some interviews, so yes, this might be hard to believe. But I knew Melanie would have assessed her in her own way, probably while the woman was trying to fill out her application at the B&B and on the drive here. We needed someone and my opinion wouldn't be better than Melanie's when it came to evaluating someone for a personnel-oriented position.

"Melanie is an excellent recruiter. The job's yours if you want it." I glanced over at Paisley. "Would you show Elizabeth what she'll be working with in the unfinished kitchen. Maybe she'll have some suggestions we haven't thought of."

Paisley tipped her head at me and gestured for Elizabeth to follow her. Slightly dazed, the older woman followed. Gresham, out of politeness for Elizabeth's return trip and what I was beginning to think was a crush on Paisley, made a comment about wanting to see how the building was coming along and rushed to join them.

"Didn't mean to put you on the spot there, Nora," Melanie said. "She's an unconventional hire, but I have a feeling about her."

"That was something to behold. I think you just made her year." Damisi's eyes twinkled.

"I did tell you Melanie is a queen where I come from."

"That she seems."

"And my subjects still have a load of work to do before my daughter and I leave you with a ranch full of novices."

"Yes, ma'am," I responded immediately and grinned when Damisi snorted. "Hope your day is as awesome as ours will be."

She chuckled and shook her head. "Cowgirl."

"Professor," I retorted because she seemed to like to point out this difference between us.

Her eyes twinkled again as she waved at Melanie and Sayen before sauntering off. Melanie shot me a meaningful glance as Sayen kept swinging her head back and forth between Damisi's retreating form and me.

"Stop it," I told them.

"She seems to have your number."

"She thinks I'm a simple country girl whose only interest and therefore knowledge surrounds horses."

"I don't think that's true, and you could correct that impression," Melanie said.

"Yeah, blow her mind with your dual career. Just because you've taken a break from lecturing at the U doesn't mean you're not still an academic," Sayen pointed out.

"It's been fun this way." For the first time I didn't mind someone underestimating me. If she ever found out I spent more time teaching college students than I did ranching she'd probably shudder to paralysis. Which would be fun as well, but I would wait. There will be a perfect time to tilt her Nora View in the future.

We made our way around the barn and into the still unfinished bunkhouse structure. The construction crew was with Oisin at the storage building putting in the finish work. Our locker room/kitchen/breakroom/occasional bunkhouse was last on their list to complete. Paisley, Oisin, and I were the ones to get it from stick framing to the drywall stage. Paisley's friend, Roderick would be starting in about an hour and had as much experience as Paisley with construction, having been in the same engineering unit with her. The three of them could project manage the bunkhouse and other nonessential structures after Sayen, Melanie, and I got everyone up to speed on caring for and working with the horses.

"What do you think?" Melanie called out to Elizabeth as we entered.

Since it was a completely unfinished blank room, I rushed to assure her, "It will have a nice kitchen and a long table for meals and lockers lined up over here. Did you show her the bathrooms?" I asked Paisley.

"Aye, and assured her they'd be done soon, too."

"We've had to put the human amenities on hold to get ready for the horses," I told Elizabeth. "They should finish the last ag building today or tomorrow, and then they'll get started on outfitting this place next week."

"It's grand," Elizabeth's eyes pinged around the building, noting the skylights and the view out the windows.

"Grand enough to keep your interest? We're not a restaurant, but you'll have people to feed each day and schedules and supplies to coordinate to keep the day from getting boring."

"It sounds a treat," Elizabeth said.

"When can you start?"

"Now, if you need me to."

We all chuckled. "You can get started on the paperwork, but we can wait till tomorrow for your official start."

It felt wonderful to have most of the pieces in place before my friends left. Things were starting to feel more like home every day here.

CHAPTER 16

KENZI'S EXCITEMENT WAS catching. Hearn and her mother looked on as she greeted each of the horses. She wanted to know everything about each one. Melanie's filly would make a nice mount for her once Subi was fully trained. I'd start her out on Angelou for her rider training, but she could ride any of the others for trail rides. Her summer plans were fairly open. Unlike most wealthy mothers, Kayla didn't have Kenzi overscheduled with activities.

I was already missing Melanie and Sayen. They'd left on Wednesday for a quick trip to Spain and Italy before heading back home. It was hard not to take advantage of how close some of these other countries were. If I could convince them to come back before my contract ended, I'd join them on some of those explorations.

Inky poked his head over the stall door. He stayed like that for a second before turning away. I bit back a grin, knowing he was looking for Damisi. She would make an appearance today, even if she was busy all day going into the city to meet up with some work colleagues. She always made time for him.

"Which one can I ride first?" Kenzi's dark blue eyes blinked up at me. She barely came up to my shoulder, but her energy was boundless.

"First, you meet the employees."

Her expression fell and a groan sounded. Her mother wrapped an arm around her shoulders and patted her cheek.

"This is a large property. You're going to have the run of it on horseback. You'll need to be aware of any strangers who come onto the property." I glanced up at Hearn and her mother. We'd had a long discussion about how to handle her safety while she was at the stables. They wanted to give her some freedom, but being the only niece of a billionaire made her a target. Thankfully, Hearn was the type of tech billionaire whose name was recognized, but not his face. He could walk freely through most of Britain without anyone recognizing him. That would keep Kenzi relatively safe. Making sure one of the employees was with her at all times while she was on the stable grounds would be the other.

Outside, I introduced her to Rhona. They immediately hit it off, which wasn't surprising as Rhona was just as personable and hard working as when we'd met her at the feed store. At barely sixteen, Rhona's age made me nervous, but her ease with the horses and following directions made her the ideal employee. She hadn't yet opened up about why she wasn't in school anymore. Before the end of the summer, I hoped to reignite her interest in going back if it was possible for her. I wouldn't be much of a college lecturer if I didn't encourage her to at least try for college.

"Now, can we ride?" Kenzi asked after she met Andrew and our newest employee, Lewa.

"Now, we learn all the rules. First one being, you are never to be up on a horse without an adult present."

"Aww, come on, Nora."

"My rule, enforced by your mother."

"Mum," she whined to her mom.

"Listen to Nora. She's in charge while you're here." For which I was grateful. Kayla was happy to turn the horse thing, as she called it, over to her brother and me.

"Helmets any time you're around the horses."

"I know. Mum already said."

"Good. One last thing, then we're up on horses." I guided her to Subi's stall. "This one is your responsibility. Wheelbarrow and fork are in the equipment room. Shavings are in the supply building. Manure gets dumped out back onto the UTV trailer. If it's full, you find someone and go with them to dump it at the compost pile."

"I have to clean?"

"You want to be a horsewoman? You take care of your horses and your farm. Clear?" I didn't mean to sound lecturey but whining always set me off. Any time my students tried to pull a pout I'd double up on whatever they were whining about.

"I want to be a cowgirl, so yeah."

"Good answer, Kenzi. Let's find your ride." I walked over and laid a hand on Angelou's neck as she watched us from her stall. "Angelou will be a good trainer for you. Once Subi is suitably trained, we'll work on her together. All right?"

"They're both beautiful." Kenzi had gone into a horse trance as she stroked her.

We tacked Angelou together. Rhona got one of the new horses ready for me, and Andrew made a subtle correction to Hearn's tack. Kenzi's mom was content to watch.

Swinging up onto Wollstonecraft, my favorite of the new horses, I led our procession out and along the east pasture. As a daily occurrence, riding a horse shouldn't still thrill me, but there was no feeling like it. Riding a bike or a motorcycle wasn't the same. Horses had power and grace and didn't tear up the land. I could absorb that on horseback.

Hearn was especially giddy this morning, finally able to share his ranch with his niece. Over the past two months, I'd gotten to know him much better. He spent too much time working or attending software focused functions. As Damisi pointed out, he had few true friends, and spent most of his free time with his sister and niece. Since I'd been here, he'd made trips up from London every weekend. With anyone else, I might think he was checking up on my progress, but he was just happy to have a new pastime. No one bothered him for any decisions here. He could just be Hearn and hang out with the horses and his friends. We saw more of the neighbors when he was here, and Damisi joined us on the ranch or hanging out in the cottage. It was laidback and stress-free for him. Plus, he was becoming a real cowboy, and he looked the part in that stellar hat.

"How's Jacobus feel today?" I rode up beside him.

"No hitch in his gait anymore. Did you do that?" He leaned down to pat Jac's neck.

"A bit of training. He'll need more to be competition ready, but I think he's going to make a nice competitor."

"What did you decide about the cattle you'll need for training?"

Keeping fresh cattle for training was an expensive part of cutting. Once cows became complacent about being separated from their herd, their training worth was minimal. A constant supply of fresh cows was the best way to get horses competition-ready. Back home, I took my horses to a cattle ranch in Blackfoot. For a small fee, I could round up as many cattle as needed for training before each competition season. Thanks to Oisin, that wouldn't be necessary here.

"Oisin hooked us up with your neighbor Jack. His cattle will use some of our acreage for grazing, and we'll have access for training."

"That's a great idea." He glanced around. "What else are you planning?"

I chuckled because he truly was leaving the running of this ranch to me. "First up, we're planting an acre of pine trees around the composting system to camouflage the area and mask any odors. We'll reach out to nearby farms to sell the resulting fertilizer for a discount if they'll come pick it up." I had a similar arrangement with a neighboring farm at home. "Then, I'd like to test how well carrots and apple trees will grow in this climate before planting a full orchard. After that, we'll plant a hundred acres of pine tree seedlings, which will become a sustainable source of stall shavings for us after a few years. We should have a chat about wind turbines as well." I tested the waters on the touchy subject. Some people found them offensive to the sightline of any landscape, let alone their own.

"Sounds grand," he replied easily. "Are you sure you don't want to stay on? Seems like you might like it here."

"I love it here, Hearn. Thanks for that."

"Is that a yes?"

"That's an 'I appreciate the offer, but' response. You know I've got obligations at home. If not, I'd stay on here as long as you'd have me. It's a wonderful place to work, and the cottage feels like home."

"Glad you and Damisi are getting along so well. I'm hoping she'll stay at the cottage."

So was I. She seemed content there. She'd been living in a flat in Edinburgh when she and another professor volunteered to take over a friend's class load at Glasgow while their friend went through chemo and radiation treatments. Having a place halfway between the two cities cut down on her commute considerably. The cottage was safe and comfortable and she'd never have landlord issues. Her last two apartments were temporary, but she was settling into the cottage. The new ranch manager could stay in the guest quarters of the castle or rent a house in town until another cottage could be constructed for his or her use when the rest of the estate was built out.

"Maybe you should tell her again the cottage is hers for as long as she wants."

He looked chagrinned. "Fair enough."

"How's your seat feel, Kenzi?" I twisted to look at her, slowing Crafty to slide in beside her.

"My bum hurts, but I love Angelou."

We chuckled at her enthusiasm. "Your bum will get used to it. You've got all summer to toughen it up."

"Do I want a tough bum?" she joked.

I thought back to dealing with my younger brothers when they were her age. She'd probably be just as much of a handful, but unlike with my brothers, she wasn't purposefully annoying.

"If you want to be a cowgirl, you do. Let's head back and give your bum a break."

When we got back to the barn, we found Damisi chatting with Lewa in front of Inky's stall. He was grabbing up all the scratches he could get from them both.

"Damisi!" Kenzi greeted in her perpetual cheerful mood.

"Hello, Kenzi. How did your first ride go?"

"Amazing. Nora's going to teach me to be a champion." She wrapped her arms around Damisi in a quick hug and greeted Lewa again.

"Nora's going to teach you to untack before you do anything else," I reminded her.

"Oh, right." She trudged back and got started on the saddle.

Lewa smiled and excused herself. Damisi's hand never left Inky as she turned to me. "Nice ride?"

"Kenzi's a pro already."

She gave a worried glance at Inky and leaned toward me. "She's not going to be competing on Inky, is she?"

I grinned. She thought she was so clever hiding her affection for this animal. "Inky hasn't even been saddled yet. We'll start with that first, then it's six months to a year of training before he can compete. Subi will likely be her mount, but she'll train on Angelou. You can continue your secret affair with Inky, and no one will be the wiser."

She shot me a glare and quick as a snake strike, shoved me. I felt giddy when she joined my laughter. "This horse is exceptional."

"He's going to be a champion."

"You're cocky."

"About my horses, yes."

"Nothing else?"

That sounded dangerously like flirting. "You'll just have to find out."

"Hey, you two," Hearn interrupted. "We're going to finish getting Kayla and Kenzi settled in the house. Come out for tea with us later?"

I checked with Damisi automatically. Even though we'd been getting friendlier, I wasn't always sure where we stood. She flicked a quick glance at me. "Sounds good, unless you want to come to the cottage? Nora makes a wicked tea." Her eyes found mine. "If that's all right with you."

"Of course." And preferable, actually. I'd eaten out a few times since getting here and most of the entrée offerings were tasty but not exactly healthy. I'd play it safe and order a salad, which Damisi had apparently noticed.

"We don't want to be a bother," Kayla said.

"It's no trouble. I like cooking and Damisi makes a great sous chef."

"Only if we can return the favor next week."

Damisi had given me a tour of the public portion of the castle a couple weeks ago. Very impressive, but I was curious to see how their modernized west wing compared to the historically accurate east wing of the home.

"We'll be in each other's pockets all summer, I imagine."

They waved and headed off to the estate. Damisi's hand landed on my arm. "Sorry to nominate you. I noticed you prefer tea at home to dining out."

My chest warmed at her observation. "I'm not a picky eater. I can go out."

"I know." She looked surprised when I gestured us back toward the cottage. "Are you done for the day?"

"I've got dinner to worry about now." I smirked.

"You hired one of my mum's clients." She glanced back and caught sight of Lewa wheeling a bale of hay into the barn. "How did that happen?"

"Eni mentioned she had a client with horse experience at dinner the other night."

"Did she tell you Lewa was on the verge of losing her visa status because her employer went out of business?"

Eni had shared a bit about some of her clients' struggles while Damisi made a phone call. Lewa had been working as a cleaner for a now defunct agency. Her professional background was in banking, but office cleaning was the only work she could get after leaving Nigeria. She'd grown up around horses, which was all I needed to know for an interview. We clicked right away, and even knowing I might lose her if a banking position was ever offered to her, I snapped her up. "Didn't matter. I had an opening; she knew someone with experience."

Damisi watched me as I unlocked the side door and waved her through first. She kept watching me as I pulled off my boots, hung up my hat, and washed my hands.

"Something else up?" Not that I minded her eyes on me.

"How did you know she was my mum when you first met? Had you seen one of my photos?"

I studied her furrowed brow. "I haven't gone through your things, Damisi. I wouldn't do that."

She nodded, holding up a placating hand. "I wasn't saying that. I thought maybe I'd shown you a picture and didn't remember."

"You haven't. She looks like you. Or I should say you look like her."

She scoffed and glanced away. Something that looked like remorse flitted into her expression.

"That can't be the first time you've heard that."

"Growing up, most people thought she was my nanny."

A stone dropped in my stomach as an involuntary sound left my lips. "That's terrible. I'm sorry you had to deal with such ignorance."

"When Dad was with us, it was easier. People could do the maths." She tried for some levity, but there was nothing light about this subject. My family issues were nothing compared to having to deal with a lifetime of racial bigotry. "Once it was just Mama and me, people saw a black woman and a fair-skinned child."

I shook my head. "People can be idiots. It's easy to see how alike you are. Not just your mannerisms, but you have the same eye shape and color, same cheekbones and jaw line. You even stand the same way. And don't get me started on..." My face flamed even as I managed to stop myself from admitting how appealing her mouth was.

"Started on...?" She goaded with a sinister stretch of her gorgeous mouth.

"Nothing, not important, never mind," I fumbled through my embarrassment. "Do you have a picture of your dad handy?"

Her eyes brightened and then dimmed. She'd mentioned him over dinner a few times. It was clear how much she'd loved and idolized him. Following his chosen profession was just one of the hints. A brain aneurism took him when she was fifteen, and the loss was still so raw for her.

She reached for her phone on the island counter. Scrolling through her photo album, she brought up a photo she wanted and thrust the phone at me. A man with dark blond hair and hazel eyes smiled at the camera. He looked to be in his thirties but had the youthful glow of someone very happy. I'd been right. Damisi had his nose, the same loose curls, and her skin tone more closely matched his than her mom's.

"He's very handsome. Not surprising since he snagged your beautiful mom." I glanced up and met her smile. "I'm sorry you lost him."

She nodded and swallowed roughly. "He was the best. Mama still hasn't gotten over him."

"She doesn't date?"

"She has, but she says no one can compare."

I wanted a love like that. My past relationships haven't come close to that level of trust and need and love. As sad as it was to think of Eni not having someone else in her life, it was beautiful to know she'd loved and been loved so deeply.

"It's sad but romantic, and my dad was worth that level of devotion." Her lips pressed together in a determined line. Perhaps she, too, was looking for that kind of love despite her standoffish ways.

CHAPTER 17

THE CLUB WAS a nice size, not as big as the ones in San Francisco or L.A., but a decent space for a city this size. It had been a while since I'd been out to a gay club, not since the last time I competed in a town outside of Dallas. The lesbians on the competition circuit wanted to go out on the last night and dragged me along with them. I'd missed winning by two points and was feeling bruised about it, but Maddie, the winner and good friend, wouldn't let me wallow by leaving that night instead of in the morning as planned.

The pack of women with me tonight had pretty much done the same thing. Not that I'd been wallowing, but Damisi's friends had decided we were all going out, me included, and to a gay club, because all but two of these friends were lesbians. All were beautiful in their own way, but four were particularly good-looking. Zoey and Celia, whom I'd gotten to know well over the past two and a half months, and Yashika and Regan, who were introduced tonight. One was a former actress in India, now an acting professor at Celia's university, and the other was a museum director originally from Ireland. The other seven women were very nice and kind to include me in their fun. Celia was the one to press Damisi into inviting me. It was nice to be included. I'd be here for another three months and now that the horses were settled, I needed to get out and enjoy life a bit more. As per usual, Damisi was neither excited nor unhappy I'd been included. Two and a half months of knowing her and she was still somewhat neutral where I was concerned, except for dinners and Inky. She wasn't cavalier about either.

She was also a great dancer, lively conversationalist, and seemingly doing everything she could to avoid dancing with me. After introducing me to everyone, Damisi had been whisked to the dancefloor by one of the singles in the group. The former actress had grasped my hand and pulled me onto the dancefloor as well. Hours later, I'd danced with everyone in the group, several times, everyone except Damisi. And damn, the way she moved, it felt like a compulsion to want to dance with her.

But she was determined not to dance with me. I could read it in her expression, in the way she'd turn away any time I made a move toward her. Maybe it was the looks her friends were giving her. My friends gave me the same looks whenever an eligible woman showed any interest. She might not want to encourage their imaginings about what we were to each other. Or maybe she was hung up on someone here at the club. Then again, it could be she really didn't like me and our interactions at the cottage were nothing but ingrained politeness on her behalf.

She did like me, though. She did. I was certain of it. She came out to the barn after work every day now, seeking me out, not just the horses. She had dinner with me every night. She'd even gotten a bunch of Celia's DVD collection to introduce me to some British television shows. Celia taught television studies, which turned her personal DVD collection into her own version of a still operating Blockbuster store. Yes, Damisi definitely liked me, but she didn't want to dance with me. At least, not in front of her friends.

Returning from the bar with two bottles of water and three martinis, I spotted a newcomer to our table. Almost my height, the woman's long brown-black hair and flawless tan skin made for a beautiful sight. Seems all of Damisi's friends were beautiful.

Celia had a tight expression on her face as she stood close to Damisi, who had risen from the table. We'd all taken a break from dancing, and Zoey and I had gone to the bar to get another round of drinks for the group.

"Get over yourself, Gina," Celia was saying as I set the martinis on the table before sliding them to the women who'd ordered them.

"Always so protective, Celia. Better watch out. Your wife might get jealous about your obsession with Damisi. Oh, but wait, she's not really your wife, is she?"

"Stop it," Damisi's voice was soft but clear. "Just go, Gina. You won't accomplish anything here."

Gina's eyes twinkled and flicked over to me as I set the other bottle of water in front of Damisi on the table. "What do we have here? A newbie? Is that a buckle and are those cowboy boots? A cowboy, Damisi? Haven't learned your lesson from slumming, have you?"

Celia grabbed Gina's arm and turned her away. "Leave now."

Zoey was suddenly at Celia's side. A menacing stare accompanied her protective hand sliding around Celia's middle.

"What? She always made me feel like I wasn't good enough and now she's with a—"

"You're not winning here." Normally quiet Zoey rounded on her. "That's all that matters to you, isn't it? Winning? Look around," she ordered, waving a hand at the group. "Everyone here is on Damisi's side."

"What do you know about it, Celia's-Not-Wife?"

This woman needed to be taught some manners. She had to be an ex of Damisi's, and by her actions, she wasn't anywhere near over her. Lashing out at Zoey was uncalled for.

Damisi placed a hand on Zoey's arm. "Just leave, Gina. We have nothing left to say to each other."

Gina looked like she had plenty left to say, but a glance around the table proved Zoey was right. Her look lingered on me for a second with a smile playing at her lips. "Giddyup," she gave a parting shot to Damisi before leaving.

"What a bitch," the sweetest one in the group said.

Damisi flinched and turned away from the table, scooting through the crowd to the restroom. Celia followed and caught up to her before they disappeared into the back hall. My curiosity had me glancing at Zoey first, then moved on to everyone else in our group. There was a lot more to the story, obviously. Yet, no one was speaking up.

I'd had plenty of people judge me based on my boots, belt buckle, and hat in the past, but I didn't think my boots and understated buckle screamed cowgirl tonight. I'd purposely worn a sleeveless solid shirt rather than anything overtly western. Not that I wasn't proud of being a cowgirl, but I didn't always dress like one.

"You look great," Zoey whispered to me as she sat down. Her reassurance was calming. She exuded quiet confidence, something the horses appreciated when she came around for a ride or just to walk through the stable grounds. She was assuring me when I should be doing the same to her. I hadn't pushed for the story behind why she and Celia weren't legally married because they were more married than most couples I knew. Who cared if there was a legal document behind it? Gina had no right to judge them.

"She sure does. Love the cowboy look," Regan said.

"Cowgirl," another corrected.

"Hot," someone practically slurred.

"All right," one of the cute brunettes gathered up the tipsy one. "Time to get home." She stood and pulled the woman with her, waving at all of us as they made their way to the exit.

Celia and Damisi returned from the bathroom, neither mentioning their need for a breather. Zoey glanced at me, a slight flare in her eyes. I knew better than to ask in front of everyone.

One of the more talkative ones of the group started in on a running commentary of everyone nearby. Apparently, she was at the club a lot. Damisi's professor friend leaned in to ask how I was liking Scotland and working for Hearn. We had a conversation while everyone took a break from the dance floor and had the latest round of drinks. Damisi and Celia went to the dancefloor for one of Celia's favorite hip-hop songs. The Irish woman joined them. Yashika continued to chat me up. It could be polite interest, but something said it was more. She was very pretty and so far, extremely engaging, but a hookup wasn't on my mind.

Damisi called an end to the evening soon enough. I was happy for it, but glad I'd been invited. We drove back to the cottage mostly silent. The incident with her ex was still bothering her. Didn't take a genius to figure that out. I was curious, but I'd hold onto my questions until she seemed more receptive. Based on how she reacted, that might never come around.

Chapter 18

A SIGH SOUNDED from her as we walked into the kitchen, both going for the kettle. "I should apologize for what Gina said to you. It was uncalled for."

I leaned against the counter and let her fill the kettle. "No biggie."

Damisi turned and shot me a disbelieving look. "She insulted you for how you look."

She did more than that. She insulted me for who I am based on how I looked. Plenty of people in cities did that; well, they didn't go so far as to insult me personally, but I could tell they felt superior when they saw a cowgirl walking around a city.

"I'm okay with how I look and who I am. She clearly isn't."

Damisi snorted and reached for two cups and saucers. "She's always had an inferiority complex. I didn't realize it until the end."

"That's how it goes with ex-girlfriends sometimes."

"Ex-wife."

My head shook into a double-take. You married that? I wanted to say, but thankfully, my tongue wasn't too loosened by the beers I'd had at the bar. You married that judgmental, selfish bitch? was more like what I wanted to ask, but again, my mind was still in control of my mouth.

"How long were you married?" my mouth finally asked.

"Not long." She turned back and busied herself with the tea prep. After my continued silence, she turned back. "We were together four years, married for one." She let out a long breath. "Technically."

"Technically?"

"We got married when it was first legal here. We'd been together for a while. I already felt like we were married, but when the law changed, Gina wanted to make it official."

"Something happened?" Something must have or they wouldn't have gotten divorced.

"I should have seen it for what it was." She waited for me to ask, most people probably would, but she needed to tell me this on her own. "She got caught up in the cause. That was more important to her than our relationship. The buildup, the ceremony, the honeymoon, she loved the attention and thrived on it all. But when we settled back into our flat and life went back to normal for us, I guess she decided we'd been at the end rather than the beginning of our time together. I was fighting for a permanent contract at work, building up my classes, and getting my second textbook through publication. I didn't put enough time into the relationship. Three months after the wedding, she tells me she wants a divorce. We went through therapy for a while, but it was clear she'd made up her mind. It took the rest of the year for the paperwork. Biggest mistake of my life."

I let that sink in for a bit. "It wasn't a mistake, Damisi. She misled you. She was trying to prove something and using you to do it. Instead of being honest with you, she pushed through without examining her feelings or yours." Which probably accounted for the majority of Damisi's trust issues. Who wouldn't have issues when your partner of three years shows equal excitement about the prospect of marriage only to want to back out a few months later?

"I still should have seen something." She shook her head and turned away, defeat slumping her shoulders.

"Stop beating yourself up. You deserve better, and from what I saw tonight, you're far better off without her."

"But as a divorcee."

"It just means you'll be more prepared next time." For someone who deserves you and will treat you right, I silently told her.

"You have an answer for everything, don't you, Cowgirl?"

"Not everything, Professor." I smiled and took a swig of the tea she'd made.

"Did you have fun tonight?"

"I did. Your friends are really great."

"Seems like you had a nice time." Some of her usual sparkle came back to her dark eyes.

"Could have been nicer." I let that hang in the air, hoping she'd pick up on it. For weeks now, we'd been on the verge of flirtation. Not really flirting, just comments that could be construed as flirting if she wasn't so hard to read.

Apparently, she couldn't resist the bait. "Oh?"

I turned to face her fully. She was leaning back against the countertop closest to the fridge. "You wouldn't dance with me."

Her chin lifted. "You didn't ask."

My chin matched her height. "You wouldn't let me. You did everything to avoid it." Her eyes narrowed, and I went in for the kill. "But you wanted to dance with me. That was clear."

"Hardly," she said in an unconvincing dismissive tone.

"Oh, but it was. You wanted to dance with me but didn't want your friends to know how much you wanted to dance with me."

"What do you know about what I want?"

"A lot." I moved closer to her. Heat came off her in waves, drawing me in.

"I doubt it." Her tone wasn't as dismissive this time.

My hands reached out to grip the counter on each side of her, blocking her in. Her eyes widened and breaths increased, but she didn't try to move. She was being defiant, which was sexy as hell, and I was being confident and trying for seductive. It might be the wrong play with her, but all night, she'd been denying me the dance I wanted. And now, I wanted more than just a dance.

"You don't—"

"I do. You wanted to dance with me."

"You're getting quite cocky all of a sudden." She raked her gaze over me from head to toe.

"You can handle it."

Her hand pressed against my chest, very little force behind it. She could shove me out of her way at any moment, but she didn't. My heart pounded under her palm. She was so beautiful I couldn't take my eyes from her. "I can handle anything."

Before I could toss out another challenge, her fist bunched into my shirt and pulled me close. In the next moment, her glorious mouth was on mine. It felt even better than I imagined. Firm and oh so supple. Her kiss felt both familiar and foreign, like we'd been kissing for years but every movement of her lips and brush of her tongue was unexpected. Pure bliss in kissing form.

I grasped her hips and pressed her back against the counter. Her hands let go of my shirt and came around to grip my ass. A bolt of heat shot through me as her fingers flexed and pulled me closer.

My lips savored every slide and pull of her mouth. For months I'd been staring at her mouth, wondering what it would taste like, what it would feel like, and nothing could have prepared me for this. I didn't have time to consider why this was happening when her hands drifted upward and palmed my breasts. A groan incited my own hands to shove under her shirt and stroke her stomach. Her skin was on fire, so smooth and warm and soft. Up, up, up they went until lace covered breasts filled my hands.

I shoved her shirt up and flicked her bra open. Forcing myself to abandon her kiss, I let my gaze wander over her chest. Firm breasts with dark nipples had me salivating. I leaned down and kissed my way toward one nipple, sucking her in.

"God," she moaned.

My hands dipped under her legs and lifted her to sit on the counter. I pressed into the vee of her thighs and moved my mouth from one breast to the other. Her breathing hitched as my tongue lashed against the puckered nipple. Her hands stalled for a moment before frantically starting to unbutton my shirt. She didn't bother to unhook my bra, just shoved it up to my sternum and had my naked breasts in her hands in the next instant. I rose up and took her mouth again while her fingers squeezed and plucked at my nipples.

I popped the button on her jeans and unzipped them. With a little encouragement, she lifted up so I could shimmy her jeans down and off. My mouth started dragging down her throat past the bunched-up shirt and back to a breast. She tilted back against the cabinet, her pelvis thrusting up against my bare stomach. Her underwear was soaked.

I kissed my way over her ribs to her flat stomach and skimmed my tongue under the band of lacy underwear. My fingers hooked under the material and pulled, taking away the barrier to my ultimate goal. For a moment, I stopped and just looked, getting my fill of her beauty. She had a neatly trimmed tuft of hair and slick naked lips. Saliva gathered in my mouth as I slowly went down to a knee. My mouth skimmed, slid, and smooched along her inner thigh, closing in on her center. Her thighs were straining as I lapped against her clit. Her hips jerked off the counter and her thighs closed against my head as I attached my mouth to her clit and sucked hard.

"Oh, yes, so good," she moaned as her butt lifted up, pushing herself fully into my mouth.

My tongue swirled around her clit and slid along her folds, dipping once into her hot center before snaking back up to sweep against her clit. Her taste was exquisite and uniquely Damisi. I glided a hand up her body and grasped a breast, squeezing once and pulling at her nipple while my other hand stroked her inner thigh.

"Inside, inside," she breathed out.

My fingers followed her command, sliding along her creases, teasing her opening before plunging inside. I sucked her clit back into my mouth as I began a firm thrust all the way in and back out to the tips of my fingers. Her hips rocked with the motion as her breathing grew ragged. She barely lasted a dozen strokes before crying out and shuddering hard. I softened my assault, drawing out her orgasm. When she slumped, she fell forward and I had to stand to keep her steady. I reluctantly pulled free of her tight sheath as I kissed her neck up to her jaw and onto her mouth.

I barely got a chance to finish the kiss before she was shoving me back and sliding off the counter. Her fists bunched in my shirt again and she swung me around to press against the counter. Her mouth was back on mine as her fingers tugged at my nipples. My clit throbbed against the seam of my jeans. I was so turned on from her taste and touch and kisses, she could probably make me come just by leaning back and staring at me. A breath of air would make me explode at this point.

Her hands skated down my torso and worked to loosen my jeans. She shoved them over my hips, taking the underwear with them. A hand was suddenly there, pushing against me, rubbing and teasing. Her fingers tunneled through and down to my opening. She circled and circled and forced me to tilt toward her before two fingers pushed inside.

A sound escaped my throat, part word, part groan and made absolutely no sense. As much sense as how quickly this evening had turned sexy. She took her lips off mine and swooped down to pull my nipple into her mouth. She held her fingers steady, waiting for a sign from me. I stood frozen, memorizing every sensation she was giving before rocking toward her. She notched her thumb against my clit and pumped her fingers in and out. I didn't want this to end but she felt so good, so right and she'd made me so hot with her mouth and her climax.

"Do it." Her mouth was back at my ear, hot breath spilling over the shell with words that compelled me to follow her direction.

I lurched into climax, shivering and moaning as the contractions rolled through every part of me. My mouth brushed against her neck as her hands came around my back while I recovered. I stood in her embrace, soaking in her heat and aroma and feeling totally blissed out. My mouth brushed soft kisses along her throat. Her pulse beat against my lips, fast then slower and finally steady.

When she pulled back, she smiled and pressed a kiss to my lips. "Mmm, that was pleasant."

Pleasant? Is she kidding me? Pleasant? Like I'd just given her a quick neck rub instead of the fucking of her life. Sure, it was frenzied and mostly upright while partially clothed, but the unexpected coupling was better than any I'd experienced or even fantasized. No way she didn't feel the same, or at least think it was damn good sex. Pleasant? Pleasant made me want to throw her down on the floor and give her pleasant again. Over and over until she screamed another word. Exciting. Electrifying. Inspiring. Galvanizing. Sensational. Earth Shattering. Hell, I'd take "fun" in a pinch, but pleasant? Pleasant was a picnic in the park. Pleasant was an evening at the symphony or a quick peck on the lips. Pleasant wasn't a fiery, frantic, fantastic fuck.

"Pleasant?" I heard myself echo.

Her softly blinking eyes landed on mine, a smile curving her lips. "It wasn't unpleasant."

"It wasn't torture either, but you can do better than pleasant, can't you?"

"Fishing for compliments, Cowgirl?" She paused after stepping into her pants.

I could respond in any number of ways. Instead, I stared dumbly at her as she slid her pants up over her hips and started buttoning her shirt.

Almost completely put together, she ran a finger down my cheek. "I'm pleasantly knackered."

Pleasant, again. This time it seemed less of a praise and more of an explanation for what led to our encounter. Like she would never have gotten to sleep without a good orgasm. Since I was there and handy, she might as well take advantage of the situation and get what she needed.

With a tap to my cheek, she winked and made her way around me. I turned, not caring that my shirt was still open, bra bunched up, and pants still slouched low on my hips while she was completely put back together. I watched as she made her way back down the hallway, bare feet slapping softly on the floor and then the risers to her domain upstairs. Our encounter barely acknowledged and definitely over.

CHAPTER 19

SEVEN DAYS. SEVEN days and no mention of our tryst in the kitchen. She'd disappeared for the entire following day, and since then, she'd been almost as scarce. When we did dine together, the topics were casual about our days or questions about whatever subject she was currently researching for her next paper. Her evening trips to the barn to say hello to Inky were shorter than normal as well. She wasn't avoiding me, but she wasn't looking to spend as much time together as usual.

"Showering in the middle of the day?" Damisi's voice surprised me as I walked from my bedroom to the laundry room, toweling my hair dry.

I halted and stared at her. She was in shorts and a tank top, lounging on the couch and reading a book. So much of her velvety skin was on display. I swallowed hard. She hadn't been there ten minutes ago when I came in from the stables. She was supposed to be at Celia's today. Not that I minded she was here, it was just a surprise, and because I was expecting company, slightly awkward.

"Weren't you going to Celia's today?"

"Skye had to go to London for a work thing, so Celia's over at Ainsley's helping with the kids."

"No babysitting for you?" I'd seen both parents and their kids many times over the past three months. The kids would sit quietly mesmerized by our activities with the horses, giving their parents time to zone out or take a power nap. They were quite a handful for one parent. Their friends and Ainsley's parents kicked in to help whenever they could.

"Didn't feel like it today." She shrugged and glanced back down at her book. I knew her well enough to know she was disappointed not to be hanging out with Celia as planned. She was a creature of habit. Changing plans got under her skin a bit. "Did you fall into some manure or something? Normally you don't shower until you're done with work."

"I'm technically done for the day."

Her brow lifted sharply as she glanced at the clock in the kitchen. I knew what she was thinking. Even when we'd gone for a night out, I'd put in a full day of work.

"I'm expecting a visitor." I paused, gauging her reaction. "Yashika."

This time her back straightened and lifted off the sofa. Interest sparked in her eyes.

Yashika had asked for my number last weekend, hoping to get to know me better. Code for a casual hookup, if I wanted to read it that way. She was a beauty for certain. Back home, I would have jumped at the chance to get to know her better in any fashion, with or without a potential hookup. Too bad my head could think of nothing other than Damisi since last weekend. I wasn't about to toss out a chance at friendship with Yashika, though.

"To take you out or look over the stables?"

My head tilted as I tried to read her tone. A slight edge kept it from being mere curiosity, but not enough to determine if she didn't like me hijacking her friend or if she might be a touch jealous her beautiful friend was showing interest in me.

"We're hanging out. Is that a problem?"

Her eyes slit fractionally before returning to normal. "No. I'm just surprised. I didn't notice you chatting to her last weekend."

"You were on the dance floor most of the night." I paused and added, "Dancing with everyone but me."

Her head shook and she sucked in a deep breath. It looked like she might actually bring up our time together after the club, but the doorbell rang. I glanced at the door and back to my room. I wasn't finished getting ready. Even if this wasn't a date, I still wanted to look nice. It didn't hurt that my making an effort might irk Damisi more. Maybe jolt her out of her stasis and make another move with me.

I dashed back to my bathroom to rub product into my hair and added a smidge of eyeliner. After washing my hands, I made my way back toward the front door, only to stop at the sight of Damisi and Yashika chatting in the living room.

"Hi, Nora." Yashika's bright smile barely eclipsed the bright colors of her sundress.

"Hey there. Glad you could make it."

"I was just telling Damisi I hoped we could go to dinner after you show me around."

Damisi looked over to see how I'd respond. "Let's see how much energy you have after you bond with the horses."

She gave a jaunty nod. Damisi smirked at me but smiled encouragingly at her. I grabbed my competition boots, dressier than my work boots, and gestured toward the door. Over my shoulder I glanced at Damisi and raised my eyebrows in question. She ran a hand through the air, telling us to go without her.

So, it wasn't jealousy. Even if it felt like it was a little bit.

"I've been looking forward to this all week," Yashika was saying as she looped her arm through mine on our way to the barn.

"Do you ride?"

"On movie sets only."

That was the fourth or fifth time she mentioned being a former actress. Of course, I probably mentioned horses in some fashion or another whenever I talked to new acquaintances. Couldn't really hold it against her, but it did feel a touch boastful.

"We can get you up on a horse today if you like." I already knew her answer before posing the offer. Her dress and shoes were designer. I was surprised she was willing to go into the barn, but riding would be a step too far.

"Not today. Maybe next visit."

"Sure." I led her up to the corral where Rhona was working with Kenzi on stops and starts. Lewa was looking on from the other side of the corral. As good as Rhona was with horses, I still wanted an adult around when Kenzi was riding. The responsibility for Kenzi's health and safety couldn't be left to a sixteen-year-old. "Helmet, Rhona."

Her head whipped around and a sheepish smile came over her face. "I'm not on the horse."

"You're working with a horse. Helmet, please." I didn't want to sound like a parent, but she and Kenzi were still kids. No one else liked wearing the helmets either, but until they were experts, I was making everyone but Andrew and Lewa, two expert riders, wear helmets. Once the rest of the adults got comfortable enough riding, I'd let them decide if they wanted to keep wearing helmets. Rhona still had two years until I'd let her make that decision for herself. She rolled her eyes but grinned as she trotted over to a post, pulled the helmet free, and placed it on her head.

"Are they both Hearn's nieces?" Yashika asked from beside me.

"Kenzi is. Rhona works here."

She made a humming sound before commenting, "Young."

I wasn't about to share Rhona's circumstances without her permission, but yes, she was even younger than I thought when we first met. Elizabeth had coaxed most of her story from her, and it was concerning. A new stepmother with small children combined with how the woman felt about Rhona's sexuality made living at home unbearable. She'd stuck it out for six months until she'd been left in charge of babysitting the stepbrothers and invited her girlfriend over to help watch the kids. The stepmother freaked out, accused her of being a dangerous influence on the kids, and demanded her father send her back to her mother's. Her mother had an addiction problem, which made living with her difficult. Soon, Rhona found herself couch surfing with friends and needing to drop out of school to work full-time to save up for an apartment share. Elizabeth encouraged her to talk to me, and after hearing her circumstances, I offered one of the rooms in the bunkhouse. It was unconventional. Basically, we were taking over the care of a teenager, but she'd been through a lot, and she was mature beyond her years. She signed up for summer school to make up for her lost semester. With a free place to stay, she could go back to school in the fall and work part-time at the ranch. Most of the time, she was my star employee, but she was still a kid at times. Like when I had to remind her to wear a riding helmet if she was working around the horses.

"She knows more about horses than most of the others. Used to live on a farm when she was younger, and she's great with Kenzi." That was the biggest bonus to having her as an employee. Kenzi's enthusiasm never got under Rhona's skin.

"Am I keeping you from working?" Yashika drew her hand down my arm. Her soft fingers stroked my forearm and would have given me goosebumps if not for the lasting impression left by Damisi's hands on me.

"I've got Rhona, Andrew, and Lewa covering things, but I do have a call in to the vet. We'll have a look around the barn and grounds while we wait for her if you don't mind."

"Not at all."

I took her through the barn, introducing her to all the horses. She spoke to each one, stroking their foreheads and noses. She seemed to enjoy horses, so perhaps she would come back for a ride sometime.

Outside, I heard Fin's truck pulling up to the barn. She was making a special trip out for me when I noticed something wrong with my mare's bite. Calling the vet could have waited till tomorrow, but I'd automatically set up an out to this get-together without conscious thought.

"Dr. Fin," I called out. She'd taken to stopping by unannounced over the past month, using the stables as sort of a home base in between appointments. It was a great perk for us and a way for her to keep from needlessly driving around to kill time before her next appointment. She was becoming a good friend, and I knew she didn't mind a quick trip over on her day off. "Thanks for coming out so quickly."

"No problem." She smiled and tipped her head. Her eyes flared when she caught sight of Yashika. Yeah, Yashika was eye-flare worthy.

I introduced them, watching as Yashika checked out Fin. In jeans, work boots, and a short sleeve button up shirt, Fin looked ready to work, even if this would be her only house call for the day. She also looked damn fine, for anyone who went for the butch type. Yashika looked like she might lap her up. I grinned. Perhaps Yashika might get to know someone today after all.

"Angelou's bite is off today. Could be a cracked tooth," I told Fin after I'd given them time to exchange pleasantries and lingering handshakes.

"I'll take a look."

I glanced back outside and made a decision. "I've got to step into the corral with Kenzi for a minute. Do you mind?" I asked Yashika. "I'm sure Dr. Fin would be happy to have you as an assistant for a few minutes."

"Call me Fin," she said to Yashika. "I'd love the help if you're up for it."

Yashika glanced between us and smiled. "Certainly."

I watched them head to my mare's stall before joining Kenzi and Rhona in the corral. I'd give them some time alone before going in to see what Fin had to say about the horse.

An hour later, Fin had cleared Angelou of anything serious and checked on the other horses to be thorough. Or to spend more time with Yashika. Their mutual attraction sparkled in the air around them. When it came time for Fin to leave, I made the excuse of needing to stick around and keeping an eye on Angelou. She took a long moment to study me. We weren't quite at the silent communication stage of friendship yet, but I hoped she was reading my acceptance of the situation and could see Yashika's disappointment of having her plans for dinner set aside.

"I'm off for the rest of the day if you'd like to join me." Fin said to her, clearly understanding I was fine with her stealing my companion for evening. "We could drop my truck back home and head for a bite to eat?"

Yashika glanced at me and back to Fin. She wasn't as sure about ditching me, but Fin was too enticing to pass up, especially since I'd called a halt to the evening. "That sounds lovely. Nora, perhaps we can try again another night?"

"Maybe when you come back for a ride. Thanks for understanding. You two have fun."

I watched them get into Fin's truck and drive up to the cottage where Yashika could collect her car. She followed Fin off the property.

Damisi was halfway through her novel when I got back to the cottage. She looked up, feigning indifference. "Is Yashika still in the barn?"

"She's off to dinner with Fin."

Her eyes widened, scrapping the attempt at indifference. She set the book down, giving me her full attention. "She left with Fin? Is that all right with you?"

"They looked like they would hit it off."

"You set them up?" She couldn't mask the shock in her tone.

"Not on purpose, but I probably would have introduced them eventually."

She tilted her head, brow furrowed. "Yashika's not your type?"

"Yashika seems like she needs someone who is...enraptured by her. She's an actress, even if she teaches now, she's still an actress. I don't know if they'll progress to anything or last if they do, but Fin can fill that role for her. I'd fall short."

A small smile played on her beautiful mouth as she considered my analysis. "I doubt you've ever fallen short on anything, Cowgirl."

"I hope not, Professor. But, no reason to start now."

CHAPTER 20

IT HAD BEEN raining hard all day, ruining Kenzi's plans for training. Rhona and Roderick convinced her to join them for a trail ride, rather than training with the mechanical flag. Two of the horses really didn't like the rain, which was upsetting since rain was part of every season here. They'd be the first two horses we'd sell once they were trained up.

Tomorrow, if it stopped raining, the crew and I would spend the morning hosing down and scrubbing the center aisle of the barn to wash off the muddy tracks. Hearn had taken to showing up unexpectedly, sometimes with business associates to show off the ranch. A muddy barn reflected poorly on the operation.

Down the line, I patted each of the horses, checking they had their hay nets in place and water for the night. They'd be snoozing soon. Time to head in for the night.

"...stay here tonight." Damisi's voice floated out to me from inside as I stepped through the side door. "What if it gets worse? You're right, probably for the best. We'll get it sorted tomorrow. I can ask around the department for recommendations. Someone ought to know the right company to hire. Are you sure you're all right?"

I stopped in the doorway and watched Damisi as she paced and talked. She was so goddamn beautiful. Didn't matter if she was happy or irritated, she always came across as beautiful.

When she ended the call, she caught me staring. I glanced away and said as casually as possible, "Everything all right?"

"Mama's roof is leaking. She came home to a wet carpet, constant drip, and a spreading stain on the ceiling."

I grimaced, thinking about having to deal with that all night. "Give me five minutes to load up the extension ladder and some tarps and meet me out front."

She looked at me strangely. "What?"

"I'm guessing your mom isn't a handyperson?"

"No, that was my dad's thing." Her expression clouded for a moment. She'd lost him when she was still in the hero-worshipping stage of childhood before fathers sometimes become overbearing with their teenage daughters. Although, to hear Eni talk about him, he might never have gotten to that point with Damisi. He might have managed to get through her teenage years unscathed. Not something I could have fathomed with my dad, but everything I'd heard about Damisi's dad made it seem possible.

"Eni said she moved to a newly built home shortly after he died. This is probably the first major thing to go wrong. She's got to be overwhelmed. I can't guarantee a temporary fix, but the least we can do is go assure her it can be fixed by professionals easily enough."

Her hand grasped my arm, the first time she'd touched me since our night together. "Why would you want to do this?"

I stared at her and wondered again what it was that gave her these trust issues. Sure, that ex of hers was a colossal bitch, but Damisi always seemed to be looking for angles in every situation. "Your mom's great. If we can do something to ease her worry after a long day in court, then an hour or two tonight is worth it."

She looked like she might protest but nodded instead and headed up the staircase to grab her shoes. I slipped my boots back on and slid into my raincoat. Repairs came with the life of being a rancher, even in pouring rain.

Two hours later, we were walking back into the cottage. Tarping part of the bungalow's roof stopped the leaking for the night. Tomorrow, I'd bring Roderick and Paisley over to assess the necessary work. They might be able to complete it themselves and save Eni a bundle of money; otherwise, they could find the right professionals and supervise their work. I figured Hearn wouldn't mind us using his employee resources to help out his friend's mom, but I'd check with him tomorrow.

Still in wet clothes, I took a seat on the bench in the foyer to take off my boots. I was tired enough to collapse into bed an hour earlier than normal, but the smiles on mother and daughter's faces was worth the fatigue.

Damisi leaned against the door as she kicked off her shoes and shed her jacket. She pushed out a relieved breath. Her mom was set for the night and a plan in place to tackle the repairs. She turned and smiled at me. "Thank you."

"We've gone over this." I told her, having accepted both her and her mother's thanks several times already.

She placed a hand on my shoulder and squeezed. Her eyes searched mine, relief, gratitude, and desire making them sparkle. She shifted and slid a knee onto the bench beside me. In the next moment, she was straddling me as her other knee followed. My hands automatically went to her hips. Her fingers brushed the strands of hair plastered to my forehead up into their more natural state. Her eyes roamed my face for what seemed like forever. I sat rooted in place, breathless with wonder at this turn to the evening. If she was doing this out of a sense of obligation, I would be devastated.

Before I could form a question, her lips found mine. The kiss was soft and sure, not obligatory. She pulled back and looked at me. "I like how you are."

My fingers flexed against her hips, pulling her closer. My jeans were wet and chilled, but my body felt like it was slowly cooking from the inside. With one sentence, she erased any uncertainty I had about her regard for me. She might act nonchalant, but she could have complimented me on some feature she liked or thanked me again or said she found me sexy to kick this off. Instead, she said she liked how I am. That was deeper than a compliment. Deeper than a seduction. She was saying she liked me for me.

I leaned up to kiss her again, reveling in the suppleness of her lips. Her hands moved down my shirtfront, flicking button after button open. She was as eager to get me out of these wet clothes as I was. My hands reached for the hem of her shirt and pulled it up and off. Tonight, she wore a black satin bra, the outline of her nipples pushing against the delicate material. I licked my lips in anticipation.

She'd gotten my shirt off without me noticing and now she was lifting up to drag my jeans down my thighs. I seized the opportunity to do the same to hers and felt my heart leap when she hastily kicked them off and immediately straddled my lap again. Her mouth came back to lock onto mine, fingers now roaming freely.

The front clasp of her sexy bra was no match for my fingers. Her luscious breasts popped free. I wrenched my mouth from hers and bent to capture one of her nipples. She hissed and threw her head back, rocking against my lap. My hands gripped her ass and pulled her harder against me. I was so turned on she probably wouldn't even need to touch me to get me to come.

"That feels so good," she murmured as my lips found her other nipple and sucked her inside.

The rhythm of her hips sped up as her hands shoved my bra aside and cupped my breasts. Fingers plucked at my nipples, pinching and twisting. My chest pushed into her hands, demanding more contact, more pressure, more pleasure. Her lips grazed my temple down to my ear and pressed kisses to my neck as our thrusts got more fevered.

I pushed a hand between us, cupping her center as she ground against my lap. My fingers slid into her underwear, skating over her slick, swollen lips. Her rocking motion hitched as my thumb found her clit and two fingers slipped inside.

"Tight, silky," I barely managed coherent words as my hand pumped slowly.

She started a sensual grind again. The movement pushed the back of my hand against my throbbing sex. I pulled my mouth from her breast and gasped for air as every swing of her hips electrified me. Her lips came back to mine, devouring my mouth as our thrusts pushed us closer and closer to the edge.

Her head tipped back and a hoarse shout left her lips as she shuddered in my arms, coming apart in a glorious climax. Her hips kept rocking, sliding up and down my fingers, wringing every ounce of pleasure from her orgasm. I was so transfixed by the sight I wasn't aware her hand had dropped to my lap and plunged into my underwear. She swiped her fingers over my clit, circling softly at first. My hips tilted, straining for more. She added more pressure with each pass until I heaved into orgasm.

As we recovered, her hands stroked my back and mine flexed against her sides. When she tilted back to look at me, her eyes roamed over my breasts and down my torso. She blinked drowsily and looked thoroughly fucked. I knew I looked the same, except with less perfect hair.

"Thanks for that," she said in a breathy voice. Her feet found the floor beside my legs, and she lifted off me slowly as if testing the strength of her legs.

"Yeah," was all I could manage as she closed the front of her shirt, bent to pick up her jeans and headed upstairs.

Once again, she'd rocked my world with combustible sex only to brush it aside like it was a mere handshake.

CHAPTER 21

GETTING USED TO frequent kid shrieks wasn't something I'd considered as on-the-job training in the past. Kenzi's prominent joy at the quick side to side movements on horseback made the learning curve practically vertical. Earplugs might be a good investment at this point, but I hoped she'd get used to the movement soon and stop with the shrieking. Shrieking wouldn't work on the cutting competition circuit.

"All right, kiddo, take her around the corral to cool down."

"Aww, are we done already?"

"You and your mom have plans tonight, remember?"

"Oh, aye. Tea at Nan's with Mum." She exaggerated the pronunciation with a grin. "Wish I could stay and keep riding."

"You're riding every day now as it is. Give your behind a rest."

"My bum," she giggled as she swung down off my mare, sliding slowly until her feet touched the ground. She kept giggling all the way through untacking and brushing down her horse.

Kenzi's mom was waiting for us in front of the cottage. I gave a quick rundown of the training session and bid them goodnight. Roderick would be in later to help Rhona bring in the horses and set them up for the night. I didn't need to go back to the barn, but I felt compelled to.

A cab crawling up the drive halted my forward momentum. The back door swung open and my youngest brother popped out with a bright smile and wide arms.

"Sis!" he called and came toward me to swing me into a bear hug.

"Nolan, you're here?" Why? Before I could think of any more questions, our mother stepped out of the other side of the cab. "Mom? What's going on? Is Dad okay? Niall?"

She smiled and came toward me. "Everything's fine, Nora. We wanted to surprise you."

My shock didn't wear off quickly, but I accepted her hug as easily as I'd been swept up by Nolan. "It's definitely a surprise." A massive surprise. Like me, neither my brother nor my mother had been out of North America. In fact, neither of them had even been to Canada or Mexico. My mother didn't take vacations longer than four days. What the hell would possess them to get on a plane to Scotland?

I stepped back and studied her, wondering if something was truly wrong. We looked so alike, her blond hair was a shade darker and her highlights were light brown not red like mine. But her light blue eyes were the same shape and color and our cheekbones carved the same paths on our triangular faces.

"This hair," my mother said, taking my hat off and running her hand over the chopped strands on top. "I'll never get used to it." Which was her way of saying she hated it. As shocking as the news of my taking a job in Scotland had been, she'd been more shocked and upset by the short haircut. She expected me to keep my hair shoulder length or longer. I represented the family ranch in my competitions; it wouldn't do to have a daughter who didn't look like a girl. Girls had long hair, or so my family believed.

"Are you sure everything is okay at home? Is Dad following doctor's orders and taking it easy?"

The precipitating event to me taking this job in Scotland: my dad's heart attack. Took us all by surprise, although, it shouldn't have. His red meat consumption, his salt intake, his temper, and his stress level, all pointed to an impending heart attack. I really shouldn't have been surprised since he passed on his high blood pressure to me. But where I took care with my meals and how rarely I'd eat out or indulged in prepackaged food, my father never did. Neither did my brothers, but their stress level was negligible. It was easy to be stress-free when everything was done for you.

While he recovered from his heart attack, I stepped up to run the family ranch. I'd had to put my full-time lecturing job at the university on hold and have Sayen take over most of the duties on my small ranch, but I was happy to do it. The family ranch would be mine to run one day. That it came five to ten years earlier than expected was a shock, but I was happy to step up. For six months I ran the ranch as I always planned to. Secured sales contracts, hired and trained ranch hands, oversaw the finances, and worked with the horses.

When Dad started to ease back into light duties and his blood pressure eased up in kind, he agreed that he'd need a permanent co-manager until he decided to retire and turn over the business. It wasn't an easy decision on his part. He was a cowboy, born and bred. He'd worked hard every day of his life. That his body was preventing him from doing what he loved made him irritable and insecure. It took a while, but he seemed to settle into the idea that he'd need to turn over the business sooner rather than later for the sake of his health. We gathered at a family dinner, typically loud, typically warm, and Dad announced his retirement. Then, he named his successor.

And it wasn't me.

Thirty-two years of living among horses. Twenty-five years of on-the-job training. Twenty-one years of marketing efforts. Fifteen years of bookkeeping and staff management and horse training and being the go-to fixer. Eight years of everyone knowing, absolutely without-a-doubt knowing, I was the successor. Yet, he didn't choose me, so I decided to find something else.

"Dad's doing about the same. He's working more. The boys are helping." Mom squeezed Nolan's shoulder.

He beamed at the praise and tugged on my arm. "Let's drop these bags in our rooms, and you can show us the operation here."

"What?" I didn't follow. "There's no—you—I don't have any guest rooms, and I share the house with someone."

"Nolan doesn't mind the couch, sweetie." Mom was already up the front steps and reaching for the doorknob.

"No, sorry, Mom. You can't just turn up out of the blue and expect my housemate to deal with guests she doesn't know." I held up my hands in apology for the sharpness of my surprised tone. I'd been taught to always be respectful of my parents. Negating a request or command from them was not done, but I had to respect my living arrangement as well. "There's a nice bed and breakfast not too far from here. I'll drive you over there once I've shown you around. How long were you planning to stay?"

She didn't look happy about being carted off to a B&B. We didn't do that to family, but I wouldn't impose on Damisi. I also wasn't sure what was really going on here. Surprise visits weren't a thing in our family.

"A couple days," Nolan answered for her, barreling through the door as soon as it creaked opened.

I halted, shocked once again. Who flies to another continent to stay for two days? Brushing off the thought, I gestured for them to take a seat in the living room and went to grab a beer for my brother and a glass of wine for my mother.

"Tell us how it's going here." She glanced about the cottage with a critical eye.

"Very well. The horses are settling in. The ranch hands are superb. Kenzi is eager to learn. She'll be ready to start training with cattle soon. Her mom and uncle are really nice people. I'm enjoying it."

She nodded and looked away. "But it's not home."

I didn't know what she was hoping I'd say. It certainly wouldn't be, "It's better than home," which was how it was starting to feel. "I like it here. A lot."

"I'm happy for you, honey. I'd be happier if you were back home, though."

Something must have gone wrong at the ranch. "I'm needed here."

"This isn't your family."

"My family decided they could do just fine without me a few months ago."

"Drama, Nor," Nolan muttered but a glare from me shut him up. He was four years younger and used to me bossing him around.

The front door opened and everyone held their breath as Damisi's footsteps drummed up the stairs. Her evening routine had not changed once since I'd been here. My mom and brother stared the question at me. I shrugged and looked back at them. She'd come down when she'd changed clothes, sometimes after a shower, sometimes immediately if she was starving.

Tonight was an immediate appearance. She was still in a summer dress for work, feet bare, hair piled up on her head. Her mouth pulled wide when she saw me, a certain sparkle in her eye. Damn, she wanted one of those kinds of nights. We'd had several over the past month. No telling when they would happen. Sometimes all it took was a flirty comment or seductive look before we were going at it on the couch or on a bar stool or the kitchen counter. Never a bed, though, and never together longer than the ebbing afterglow of our orgasms. Still, I wasn't complaining. Damisi was the most gorgeous woman I'd ever seen, much less dated. She was fascinating and funny and brilliant. Her love for her mom and her devotion to her late father combined for a vulnerability she rarely showed anyone. I couldn't get enough of it or her. But tonight, my family would put a stop to it. She slid to a halt when she noticed them.

"Surprise visitors." I told her. "My mom, Rebecca Cleary, and my brother Nolan. My housemate, Damisi Dalziel."

Nolan was up immediately and reaching to shake her hand, sliding his other up to cup her elbow. "Wow, so nice to meet you." His exaggerated tone was so obvious it was embarrassing. He had no idea how much he projected his attraction. The added wink he threw at me was over the top.

"We've crashed your home, Damisi." My mom stood to shake her hand. "I hope our surprise doesn't put you out."

"Not at all," she said graciously. "I'm sure Nora is thrilled to see you."

"We're just as thrilled. Even more so if we can convince her to come back with us."

Damisi swung toward me, surprise and the barest hint of disappointment in her eyes. "I didn't realize you were leaving so soon."

"I'm not." My firm tone was for everyone in the room.

Damisi caught onto the tone faster than my family and helped to move the conversation forward. "What do you think of Scotland so far?"

"We've just arrived. Haven't seen much of it yet."

"Perhaps Nora can show you around if you can pull her away from the stables." She flicked a knowing look at me. She kept a running list of all the historical sites I should visit, and so far, only three had been crossed off.

"She's a hard worker," Nolan bragged. "Used to be the first one out to the ranch before anyone, even Dad."

"That's why we need her back home."

"The ranch is fully staffed, Mom. I made sure of that before I left."

"Graciela, Janice, Emily, and Bianca quit," Nolan reported in a sad tone, probably because he had a massive crush on Emily.

"Four of the women I hired and trained." I directed a look at my mom. We'd discussed how Niall, Nolan, and Dad treated female employees differently than the men. Nothing sexual or flirtatious, but a lot of mansplaining and being overly solicitous when it came to some of the more labor-intensive tasks. "Something Niall said?" I directed the question at Nolan.

He puffed up ready to defend his older brother, but Mom interrupted. "Of course not. They just weren't good fits."

"Funny how they fit perfectly during the six months I was running the show," I pointed out.

Damisi's eyebrows rose at my comment. Mom shot me a glare and pointedly looked at her, telling me not to bring up family business in front of strangers.

Nolan caught the look and jumped up from the couch. "Why don't I take you to dinner, Damisi. Leave Mom and Nor to catch up. I promise I'm more charming than my sister."

Damisi glanced between us. "Thank you, but I've got some work to do." She went to the fridge and grabbed a bottle of orange juice. "It was a pleasure to meet you." She stepped back through the living room and headed upstairs.

"Would you like to take a look around or tell me why you're really here?" I shifted my gaze to Nolan since Mom was intent on sugarcoating their reason for being here.

He shrugged and said casually, "A few sales orders have fallen through."

"The ones I set up with the women on the circuit?" I guessed, seeing a theme to these problems. "Did Niall wonder aloud how a little lady could run a ranch big enough to need ten new horses annually?" The men in my family believed women were meant to help, not lead. For a woman to run a major ranching operation, well, frankly, that could never happen without a man truly being the one to make all the decisions. And that was the real reason Dad hadn't chosen me to take over.

"That's unfair. Niall is still learning the sales end of things." Mom was preconditioned to jump to the defense of her sons.

"He's an amazing ranch hand," I said. "Great with horses, not great with people." Women especially.

"You can help him with that. It comes naturally to you." She was always great with compliments when she wanted things. "That's why we need you back to straighten out these lost orders and give Niall some pointers."

I let out a breathy laugh. The annoyance that had built to irritation and moved to anger about the unfairness of the gender dynamics in my family as I grew up was what forced me into stepping away and accepting Hearn's offer. "Why?"

She leaned forward, confusion marking her expression. "Why what?"

"Why should I straighten out the orders Niall lost and train him for a job he's not qualified for?"

"Wow," Nolan muttered, surprise kicking his eyebrows up to his floppy bangs. "Bitter much?"

I turned serious eyes on him. "Bitter a lot, Nolan. You would be too if you had twenty-five years of training, six years of higher education, and six months performing the job only to be passed over for a less educated, less qualified, and less experienced person."

"That's not accurate." Mom looked affronted by my assessment. "Nolan, why don't you go out and take a look at the barn? Give us some time to chat." She waited for him to grudgingly follow her instructions before turning back to me. "You know we chose Niall because he has nothing else. The ranch is all he knows. You have so much more. Your competitions. Your university job. Your volunteering at 4-H. You don't need the ranch. Niall does."

My head spun. "Unbelievable. You give a guy a job because he's incapable of anything else? Whose fault is that? He's a thirty-year-old man whose Mommy still does his laundry and cooks his meals. You give him a wage, pay all his expenses, and built him a house on your land. He's never stood on his own. It's not for me to bail him out of this."

She leaned back; eyebrows spiked high. "Where is all this anger coming from, Nora? You get on a plane sweet as can be, then four months in a foreign land, and you're so angry."

I blew out a breath to remain calm despite my now roiling stomach. We should have had this talk a long time ago. When I started high school, or went off to college, or any time before it festered to the point where I needed to leave the country for a break. "I've always been angry, Mom. There was just no point showing it. Nothing would change. You and Dad set a double standard for me from birth, and it had nothing to do with me being the oldest. As a girl, I was given hours of domestic chores at home every week. The boys got to trade off their one and only chore of mowing the lawn. At work, I had far more responsibilities than they did and was paid less for it. Now, Niall has been handed a career without being ready for it, and you expect me to step in and do everything for the men in my family again. Well, no longer." My heart was pounding as I ticked through many of the grievances I'd held since first being handed a scrub brush and told to clean the boys' bathroom while my brothers got to keep watching cartoons on a Saturday morning.

"Why would you have wanted to run the ranch then if we're so unfair to you?" Her self-satisfied look told me she thought she won the argument and I'd accede to her wishes, as usual. She was in for a surprise.

"Because other than my pay, there was no unfairness at the ranch. Dad expected me to know how to do everything, to train and lead the workers, to attract potential customers. He let me do my job, and he gave me and everyone the impression the ranch was mine to have."

"But you have a job at the university!" she protested.

"I do love lecturing, but ranching is in my blood. I was willing to take a sabbatical from my job when Dad got sick. Even at the risk of losing that position, I dove in at the ranch because I assumed it would become mine one day."

She threw up her hands. "This is getting us nowhere. Our farm needs help. Your family needs you."

I could tell her about my blood pressure being consistently thirty points lower, how I didn't have to fear needing BP medication on my next doctor visit, or that my hair no longer seemed to be falling out every time I washed it. If she glanced at my hands, she could see my fingernails were short but smooth, not bitten, and not one ripped cuticle in sight. Things she usually concerned herself with, but there was no point. She'd attribute my lack of stress here to what she would think was an easier job.

"I'm committed here, Mom. You knew that. It was a wasted trip for you." I spoke calmly, no accusation or haughtiness. She wasn't going to suddenly understand my point of view when she's always supported Dad in whatever he wanted or believed.

"It shouldn't be wasted," she sighed.

An idea formed in my head, something I hoped would soothe her surely frayed nerves, no matter how out there the idea was. "The good news is you're only a short, cheap flight away from your fantasy destination of Paris. You should take advantage."

Her eyebrows shot up again. "We came to visit you."

"To convince me to come home early. You've got your answer." I grasped her hands, trying to soften the shock. "I'm happy to show you around, but I think you'll enjoy Paris more." I wasn't shoving her out the door, but it would be awkward for her to stay after this highly charged and eye-opening conversation.

"I wish things were different. We've only ever wanted the best for you."

Her idea of what was best for me and my idea clashed significantly, but she didn't seem to understand that. I would have to accept that she may never truly comprehend where I stood on certain things. "I know." I tilted against her for a brief connection. "Now let's see if we can find you a flight to Paris. It will be more glamorous than following me around the ranch for a couple of days."

She nodded and heaved a sigh. "If you're sure."

I met her direct gaze, and for the first time in our relationship, my expression held nothing back. "I am."

CHAPTER 22

IT WAS LATE when I got back to the cottage after taking Mom and Nolan out to dinner and driving them to a hotel near the Glasgow airport. We'd found inexpensive tickets to Paris and pushed their return trip a couple of days. They'd skip the first part of their return flight and catch the connecting flight through Amsterdam back home. I wished she would have added several days so she could explore more of France and take a train to Amsterdam, but she didn't want to leave Dad alone that long. He would have had his fill of eating out and the house would be a mess when she got back, but she'd see a country she'd always wanted to see.

The TV was on at a low volume and Damisi was lounging on the couch. I checked my watch, surprised she was still up on a school night. My eyes flicked to the screen and warmth pulsed through me as I realized she wasn't watching the next episode of the borrowed crime drama we'd been watching together. It wasn't like we had an agreement not to watch the series without each other, but I'd been holding off whenever she had papers to grade or she was out for the evening. Our current series featured a female police partnership and had well thought out mysteries and character subplots. Apparently, it was already off the air, something I was learning happened more quickly in Britain. A few of the shows she'd shown me only had two seasons to them and not because they'd been cancelled. This one had five seasons and was far more dynamic than the ironically titled Happy Valley we'd watched before this one.

She hit mute and asked, "Did you have a nice dinner out with your family?"

"We did, thanks. Sorry to have run you off earlier."

"Quite all right. Nice to have family visit." There was an unspoken question in her eyes.

"A complete surprise," I answered the question.

"Seemed like. Is everything all right at your home?"

I let out a soft laugh. Everything wasn't all right and yet entirely the same. It was difficult not to care, not to jump in and try to fix everything. An ingrained impulse I had to fight. The distance helped. By the time I got back home, I hoped to have the impulse smothered. "The family ranch has had a few setbacks."

Her eyebrows shot up. "Were they hoping you'd fix it?"

"They were."

She waited, question in her eyes, a mysterious smile forming on her face. "And?"

"I no longer have anything to do with the family business." It was still difficult to say. Even more difficult to convince myself it was true.

"I see." But it was clear she didn't. "I couldn't help overhearing some of what your mother said as I made my way upstairs. You were running the family business at some point?"

"My father had a heart attack and needed to recuperate, so I took over for a few months."

"I'm sorry to hear about his health. Is he well now?" She couldn't hide her worry. She'd lost her father to a sudden medical event. The thought of someone else losing a father the same way troubled her.

"Recovering well, yes. I left when he'd started back to work close to full-time. He couldn't keep his usual pace, so he asked my brother Niall to step up and fill those roles."

Her brow wrinkled. "Because you needed to go back to your own ranch?"

I hesitated. We hadn't delved too deeply on many subjects, keeping our interactions mostly casual, both conversationally and sexually, but something in her expression told me she wouldn't be satisfied with a breezy reply. "Because he believes a woman's duty is to care for and support her man, not stand on her own." I held up my hand to stop her interjection. "It's his old-fashioned point of view. He'll freely admit that I'm smarter than he is, that I'm a better rider than he is, but he and my mom and brothers feel that a woman cannot take care of a large business on her own." Again, I held up my hand because I'd had to say some version of this to a few people over my lifetime and knew all the objections. "I've learned to live with it because I'll never change their minds. From the moment I showed an aptitude for ranch work, he treated me as the person he could rely on. When I took over for him while he recuperated, I thought I'd proven my worth. Apparently, he's had his mind set from our births who would take over the ranch."

"Your brother, even though you're obviously capable?"

"His son, not his daughter, yes."

Her hand landed on my thigh as she let out a breath. She didn't often touch without purpose. She wasn't an affectionate person, but it didn't mean she didn't care. She just didn't feel the need to touch or hug without a reason. With me there was zero physical contact except for when that certain feeling struck and we'd end up tangled together in hot, frantic, fulfilling sex. Our trysts were like a ferocious gust of wind on a blazing hot day. Quick, strong, explosive relief, enough to take the edge off, then back to calm and steady as if nothing happened. Would I change our dynamic if I could? You bet, but would I want her to change for that to happen? Absolutely not. She was a beautiful person who showed how much she cared with words and actions, not casual touches.

I tried not to shift my leg under her hand for fear she'd pull it back. "It's why I finally took Hearn up on his offer. Good to get away and have a new challenge."

"Being busy keeps your mind off the injustice."

Injustice. Yes, exactly that. I kinda loved how she got it after one short conversation. If I were being honest, I kinda loved a lot about her.

"What will you tell your mum and brother?"

"I've already told them I'm committed here and Niall is going to have to start doing the job he was chosen for."

She pulled back her hand. Her lips twitched as she watched my thigh rise to follow the movement of her hand. "How did that go over?"

"About as expected." By the end, better than expected. My mom seemed to accept my reasoning for leaving. She didn't approve, but she accepted it.

"On behalf of Hearn, I'm happy to hear you won't be leaving right away." She nodded once, and with those words, said more than any comforting touch could have. "Will your mum try to persuade you for the rest of her visit?"

"I've convinced her to use the rest of her vacation time to visit Paris. She's always wanted to go."

A full grin this time. "Well done, you."

"It'll be more enjoyable for everyone." Especially me.

CHAPTER 23

THE MISTY AIR cooled us as we rode past the paddocks. Zoey was my riding companion this morning. We were going to scope out the area I was thinking of using to plant thousands of pine trees to be used for stable bedding in a few years. This was a wish of mine for my own land, but I didn't have enough space to make a significant dent in my stall bedding costs.

This morning, Zoey texted to ask if she could stop by for a ride. I'd told her many times she was welcome whenever, but she still insisted on checking first. Her Sunday mornings were usually free unless she was on a work trip somewhere. She had an interesting job doing consulting and marketing for universities. It took her all over the world, but in recent years, she'd stayed mostly in Europe and could do much of her work from home. On Sunday mornings, her partner went to church. Zoey was an atheist. A difference like that usually separated most couples, but Celia and Zoey didn't seem at all affected by it.

On many Sunday mornings, Zoey would often be up for a ride or an excursion somewhere. It took me away from working, even if riding together was technically part of my work. Still, I appreciated hanging out with her. Ranching could be a solitary life. It helped to have friends outside that life.

"Celia mentioned your family visiting?" Zoey pulled at the chinstrap on her riding helmet to adjust the fit.

Damisi must have told Celia, who then told Zoey. Hearn found out the same way and called to see if I needed to take some time off to make a quick trip home. "My mom and brother, yeah. A complete surprise. Neither have been out of the States before."

"Wow."

"Yeah, but it was nice to see them."

She glanced over at me through a new pair of glasses. A long moment passed before she asked, "Did they miss you so much they hopped a plane?"

I chuckled. "They were hoping to persuade me to come home early."

"Ah."

My eyes cut to her. I waited for more, but as was typical for her, she stayed quiet. "My brother's trying his hand at running the ranch to ease my father into retirement. Apparently, it's not going so smoothly."

"I see."

"Did your dad ever want you to take over for his business?"

She let out a snort. "No, not possible."

"Speech therapy isn't your thing?"

A flush hit her cheeks as she shook her head. "My other dad might like it, but I'm not cut out for the Hollywood lifestyle."

She'd mentioned having two dads before. One was a speech therapist, but I couldn't remember what she said the other dad did for a living. Perhaps he was an actor?

"Cinematography," she said, reading my mind.

Oh, right, yes, making movies probably wouldn't suit her quiet personality. Celia would take to it most definitely, but

Zoey would drown in that kind of energy. I marveled at their partnership. Celia was vivacious and talkative; Zoey was serene and quiet. Most would call them opposites, but they were complementary rather than conflicting. Kind of like how Damisi's pseudo surliness could be smothered by my steadfast gusto. The thought made me smile.

"Did I see Agatha's truck parked near the barn when I came in? Is she your vet?"

The question stumped me for a second as I clicked through the many degrees of separation before linking up how they'd know each other. Damisi's department chair was married to a colleague in the school of veterinary studies and enjoyed dinner parties, which was how Damisi got to know Agatha. Celia and Damisi were close friends and must have expanded their friends in common over the years, which was how Zoey must know her.

After playing connect the dots, I answered, "She introduced me to one of her former students, who is our vet."

"Is she checking up on the student?" Her eyebrows popped over the tops of her frames. She didn't normally judge people, but her expression showed a hint of disapproval.

I couldn't hold back a sly grin. "Nope, she's using it as an excuse to be here. Damisi and I introduced her to Hearn a few weeks ago. They hit it off, but he's too focused on work to notice a good thing when she's right in front of him, and she's too locked into the busy, full life she leads to see she's missing an important piece."

"You're hooking them up?" Now her raised eyebrows were directed at me, but in amazement this time.

"Sayen gave us the idea. She's got a flair for matchmaking. Damisi and I invited them both to the barn one weekend, and they clicked immediately. They've been getting to know each other, but I think Hearn's going to ask her out soon. Possibly today. We'll see."

"I wouldn't have picked her for him based on some of the dates he's brought out with us before, but she's kind of perfect." She gave a nod in agreement.

"That's what we thought. He needs someone who is secure and happy with her life as it is. The kind of person who wouldn't even consider quitting her job and buying a mansion if she won the lottery." Essentially, being in a relationship with Hearn would be like winning the lottery. "Agatha needs someone who understands her commitment to her job and students. If she has to change plans at the last minute because something comes up at the vet school, her partner needs to be okay with that." Plus, they had chemistry. She was smart and sophisticated, and he was visionary and dedicated.

"Hope it works out. Hearn's a great guy and people have taken advantage. Agatha's pushed her personal life off for the sake of her classes for too long."

"I think a lot of people in academics fall into that trap." I shot her a careful look. "Are you starting a new university project soon?"

"In the fall. We wanted to be around to help Skye and Ainsley with the babies this summer."

Many of their friends had made the same offer, but it turned out only Celia, Zoey, and Ainsley's parents stepped up more than twice. Yet another quality I admired about them. "Would you normally go somewhere else?"

"We try to get over to Washington for a visit with my dad. Sometimes I take a job in the Northwest and we stay longer."

"Lots of colleges in the area."

She nodded. "Are you still teaching in Twin Falls?"

My head snapped around to look at her. Had Sayen or Melanie told her about my other job? After our discussion about not telling Damisi, I doubted they'd tell Zoey instead. "How did you know I used to teach in Twin Falls?" I'd started my teaching career at a small college in Twin Falls and stayed for two years until getting a lecturing post closer to home.

"I had a branding consultation at your college a few years ago and highlighted the Ag department. My next project may focus on the same, so I pulled up the notes and noticed your name on the faculty roster. Figured there wasn't another Nora Cleary in Idaho."

"That's a lot of research you do to prep, huh?"

"It cuts down on the time I need to spend bothering staff members."

"I'm at the Idaho Falls branch of the U of I now. Had to take a sabbatical this year, and I miss it."

"Plus, your own ranch?"

"Sayen takes care of the daily routine. I'm there in the off hours and compete in the summers. I help out on my family's ranch the rest of the time." Or I did until my trip here. I hadn't given much thought to all the extra time I'd have once I went back without needing to put in a couple hours a day and most weekends at the family ranch.

"Nice." She glanced over at me and seemed to be sizing me up. "You'll be going back, then?"

"That was always the plan." Even if I'd been reconsidering recently. Well, not really reconsidering, just imagining a "what if" scenario. "Why do you ask?"

A blush hit her cheeks again. "I-I...Celia mentioned you and Damisi might be..." She searched and searched for the right words and didn't seem to be able to settle on any.

Damisi must have told her best friend about us, not that I minded. It meant she gave us more than a cursory consideration. "We're having a nice time together."

"I see." She paused to consider her next words. "It's not serious?"

It was getting that way for me, but I didn't think Damisi was in the same place. "I'm her bit of fun, I think."

She huffed a loud breath beside me. "Gina really did a number on her. You could probably tell from the run-in at the club."

I didn't want to violate Damisi's privacy, but it was pretty obvious Gina wasn't in the "friend-ex" category. "Did you know them when they were together?"

"Celia did. She and Damisi shared an apartment after they split."

"What did Gina mean by Damisi not learning about slumming it?" Since Gina had been referring to me, I didn't think it was being too nosy to ask.

It took a while for her to answer. She was probably considering what she could say without crossing a line into something Damisi might object to. "Gina didn't finish college and bounced from job to job trying to find something she might like. She thought she knew something about everything and would snap at anyone who corrected her. Celia said she'd show up at Damisi's faculty parties and try to make everyone feel like they didn't have a clue about the real world outside of academia. It put Damisi on the defensive at work and at home. Not an easy place to be."

No wonder Damisi was so reluctant to get serious with anyone. She'd been completely fooled by this Gina character.

Zoey pulled to a stop beside me at the edge of the planned forestry section. She cleared her throat, hesitated, then asked, "Is Damisi your bit of fun as well?"

We hadn't spent that much time together and certainly not talking about anything too deep, but she somehow had me pegged here. I could be truthful and admit to my deeper feelings for Damisi, which might open an entirely different conversation with this woman who would likely tell her partner who was Damisi's best friend. Or, I could hold back and keep my budding feelings to myself.

I decided on truthful. "She's whatever she wants to be with me."

She studied me for a long moment before gesturing toward the area around us. "How many trees are you thinking of planting?"

I let out a breath, half relieved she let me off the hook and half disappointed she wasn't pushing for more information. It would force me to examine where I really stood with my feelings for Damisi, and if it was possible to make something more out of our casual relationship. Without the push, I could continue to go with the flow where she was concerned. I wasn't really avoiding my feelings, but I wasn't getting out a microscope to analyze every last speck. Probably not the healthiest way to go about continuing a relationship, but anything more might backfire.

CHAPTER 24

MUTING THE NOISE of the crowd, I directed my horse back toward the herd for my third cut of the session. The first two went well with only one-point deduction for needing to use the reins to adjust the first cutback on the cow. Since then, it had only been additions. As the last competitor, I knew I needed two more points to push me into first place.

Wollstonecraft and I zeroed in on our last cow, making sure not to scatter the herd. She'd performed well to this point, nothing like how well Angelou would have performed, but Angelou was already a champion. I wanted to add one or two more to Hearn's stables before I left. Crafty took to the training better than any of the newer horses.

Crafty went into her first switchback without my prompting. I pushed against the saddle horn, keeping upright as she switched back and forth, preventing the cow from returning to the herd. We pranced left, then right, then left and a quick stutter step before going left again. This would be excellent for the scoring. Any cow that tries to fake out the horse always stands out.

When the buzzer sounded, applause rang out. I leaned down and stroked Crafty's neck, giving her praise as we made our way out of the arena. I looked up once we cleared the gate and saw Kenzi jumping up and down in the stands above us. Swinging us around, I waited for the final score to come up.

My heart jumped when the score flashed and we were on top. I heaved a heavy sigh. It was hard not to put pressure on myself to win this event, but it would be a great start for Hearn's stables. I glanced up and saw everyone joining Kenzi's excitement. My heart jumped again at the huge smile on Damisi's face. She made the trip to Sweden with us. Not that it was a hardship for her since they'd flown over on Hearn's private jet. Still, she'd given up her weekend to come to a horse competition. Part of her motivation might have been to spend more time with Hearn and his family, but I was pretty sure she wanted to see me compete.

Kenzi managed to contain her excitement as she approached us in the stables. She leapt into my arms once I stepped away from Crafty. I spun her around, letting her excitement run through me. Hearn's arm came around my shoulders as I set Kenzi down.

"Congratulations, Nora. Wonderful show."

"Congratulations, yourself, Hearn. First win for you." I gripped Kenzi's arm. "First of many, I think."

"Next year, maybe?" Kenzi looked at me for confirmation.

I didn't want to stomp on her hopes of competing, but she had a lot of training to do before she could place in a competition. "With the right coach, you'll be competing in no time."

"Congrats, Nora," Kayla joined us with Damisi at her side.

"Well done, you," Damisi confirmed.

"Thanks. Crafty did most of the work with only one hiccup."

Hearn and Kenzi grilled me about which maneuvers got us the points while we brushed Crafty down. We'd load her into the transport company's trailer after she got some feed and rest in the stall.

Hearn and his family wandered off to check out the other horses and get seats for the reining competition. Damisi stayed behind and grabbed a second brush. She'd gotten into the habit of brushing Inky every night and giving him snacks. I was happy for the company, especially hers.

"That was pretty impressive there, Cowgirl."

My stomach fluttered at her flirtatious tone. "Thank you, Professor. Glad you liked the show."

"Had to make sure you weren't exaggerating about your skills."

My eyebrows wiggled. "I never exaggerate about any of my skills."

Pink crested her cheeks, and my flutters turned to a 6.0 quake. She almost never referred to our encounters unless we were leading up to them. Flirting in a neutral setting was new territory for us. It proved she thought of us together when she wasn't just sexually charged. Perhaps we were becoming more than just roommates with benefits.

"Nora?" a voice called out from behind me. I turned to find someone familiar coming down the center aisle of the stables.

"Josie. What are you doing here?"

"I could ask the same. I thought my eyes were deceiving me when you trotted into the arena. Nice win. Are you on the European tour this year?"

"I'm getting a training facility up and running in Scotland. Tried out one of the new horses here." I felt Damisi's shoulder brush mine as she gave a final brushstroke on Crafty's side. "Damisi, meet Josie, one of the best cutting coaches around."

They shook hands, their eyes lingering. Not in a mutual admiration way; they were sizing each other up. In her late-thirties, Josie's ingrained maternal instincts usually had her looking out for the younger women on the competition circuit. Damisi seemed to be trying to put a label on our relationship.

"Are you coaching someone here?"

"After the mess with the Michems, I wanted to try a new tour."

The "mess with the Michems" put it mildly. Mr. Michem had made an aggressive pass at Josie while she was coaching his son. She put in her notice, and because he was paranoid, she'd tell his wife, he circumvented any attempt by turning the tables on her. The wife was a prominent socialite and blacklisted her with everyone in her horse-riding community. I'd reached out as soon as I heard, thinking she could use the family ranch as a coaching base, but she was already onto a new lead by then.

"Do you have any students here?"

"I'm working out of a training facility in Spain, helping with clients who come in to try it out. No assigned students, so it's not ideal, but Spain is nice."

My smile broadened. "If you're up for a change, I've been looking for a coach for my boss's niece. She's just getting started. During the school year, it would be weekends only, but you'd have the freedom to take on other clients. You'd also have plenty of time to continue designing websites if that's still your side gig."

"Seriously?" Her brown eyes blinked in amazement. Her smile seemed to take some time to catch up to her surprise.

"Seriously. They're here if you have time to meet with them. We can bring you out for a week to give it a try and see if it suits."

"That would be amazing, Nora. I miss coaching." She glanced back over her shoulder and waved at someone down the aisle. "Let me help get some of our horses loaded, and I'll find you again to see what your boss has to say."

I waved as she scurried down the aisle. Damisi tipped a chin at her and turned back to me with an unreadable expression. "Have you known her long?"

My lips rolled inward to prevent a smile. Her expression may have been unreadable, but her tone was pure interest. She couldn't hide how important my response was. "Years. She's coached a few competitors and been on the circuit longer than I have."

"Just acquaintances?"

"What exactly are you asking?" I let my grin flare. She was crossing all sorts of relationship boundaries today.

She shoved at my shoulder and turned away for a split second, then coming back with a furtive glance. "You two were never close?"

"We're friends." I swallowed my nerves and reached out, letting my hand drift slowly toward her, giving her a chance to step away if she wanted. She stayed within reach as my fingers landed on her cheek to trace the contour of her jaw. "Only friends."

Her brown eyes blinked in slow motion as she reached up and captured my fingers for a squeeze. "Good to know."

Then she turned and walked away with an extra swing to her hips.

CHAPTER 25

LIGHT RAIN SPRITZED against my hands and neck as I placed the saddle on Inky. He twitched his head to stare at me, still not used to having a saddle on his back. This was our second week of saddle training and my first day attempting to mount. Given his personality, he probably wouldn't like it. Most horses didn't the first time you tried to ride them, but he'd been exposed to riders getting on and off horses nearby as he got used to the weight of the saddle.

In Inky's line of sight, Rhona was sitting on Jacobus. He and Crafty collected a win each in their categories at competitions in Italy and Germany over the past two weekends. Oisin had traveled and stayed with them rather than flying them back to Scotland between competitions. I'd flown with Hearn, Kenzi, and her mom to compete in each show. Jacobus came in second in Italy but won in Germany. Crafty won at both competitions in her five-year-old group. The training and breeding programs were in good standing now, and I'd made a couple of contacts for potential sales next year after all the horses were trained up.

"Bring him closer, Rhona." I gestured for her to stop five feet away and dismount. I went over and patted Jac and set my palms to give Rhona a leg up onto her saddle again. It was good for Inky to see the process a few times. Then, I mounted

Jac for him to see no harm would come from me, either. My brothers always thought I was ridiculous for taking these extra steps, but my horses never feared their riders.

"Never seen anyone do this before," Rhona commented as I swung up onto Jac one more time.

"It's worked for me in the past. We'll see how Inky takes it."

"He's a feisty one, he is." Rhona grinned and tipped her head at him.

"Let's give it a try." I boosted Rhona up again and waved her back. Jacobus would be a calming influence.

After some whispered words and several pats, I notched my boot into the stirrup and lifted up. Inky walked forward, his head jerking back toward me. I stepped back down and calmed him, then tried again. Only one step this time. On the third attempt, I swung up into the saddle. He jumped forward a few steps, his head coming back over to try to spot me. With some soothing words, he eventually settled into place. We stood like that for five minutes before I lifted the reins and encouraged him into walking. Rhona made an approving noise and walked Jac away from our direction. Ten minutes for this first time. We'd build up our riding time until he was ready to start training in a month. Josie would work with him to make him the champion I expected him to be.

"Awesome, Nora," Rhona exclaimed when I dismounted and untacked.

"I think he's going to be even better than my stallion." My throat grew tight with the knowledge I wouldn't be the one to train and ride him. I could always ask Hearn to fly him to the States for competition season, but this was always the hardest part of ranching: letting go of stellar horses. I had to watch the first colt from my ranch, Lou Landy, take first prize in several competitions last year. Had I held onto him, he might have paid off a chunk of my mortgage with his winnings and sale after his first competition season.

"When does the new guy start?" Rhona walked with me back to the tack room to store our saddles.

Her hesitant tone told me how nervous she was about the new ranch manager I'd selected. Over the summer, we'd grown close. I could feel how much she looked up to me. She would be sorry to see me go and not just because she was reliant on this job to hold onto the remainder of a normal childhood. She would be starting her final year of school in a couple of weeks, something she'd given up on when her mother stopped being able to care for her and her stepmother wouldn't let her move back into her father's house. She could even continue onto college if all went well, but only if she continued working here. Magnus, the new ranch manager, assured me he was happy with keeping everyone on. He'd been managing ranches his whole life and understood the value of good ranch hands. After meeting with him a few times, walking him over the property, and introducing him to Hearn, he was by far the best applicant. With some direction on how things operated here, he'd be able to take over seamlessly.

"Next week. He has the right experience and knows everyone's role here. It should be a smooth transition."

"You have to go?" Rhona glanced away with hunched shoulders. She'd grown into herself over the summer, becoming more and more secure in her duties and surroundings. I was going to miss seeing her every day.

"I've got responsibilities back home." The words were harder to say than I thought.

She nodded and collected the saddle blankets from the horses to take back to the tack room while I started brushing Inky. Without looking, I knew she'd stay behind to collect herself. Leaving was going to be hard on everyone. Kenzi was in denial about it. Paisley needed an extra therapy appointment last week after I'd shared the news of Magnus's hiring. Roderick arranged for childcare so he could work continuous shifts for a while to make a good impression. Elizabeth made extra-large helpings for lunch and was running everyone's schedule to the minute. Lewa asked if she needed to start looking for another job to maintain her good standing on her citizenship quest. Only Oisin and Andrew seemed to be taking it in stride.

"How did it go with my favorite boy?" Damisi's voice sounded from just outside the gate. I glanced over and waved her inside. She dipped down and grabbed another brush from the bucket at my feet.

"He's a champ already."

She whispered in his ear and scratched his neck. "Is he ready for training?"

"We'll get him used to basic riding first before we introduce training. He won't get any cattle exposure for at least six months."

"Don't you want them to get used to cattle?"

"The best cutting horses are either skittish around cattle or want to dominate them. If they're indifferent, they probably won't make the best competitors."

She brushed along his neck while I brushed out the layer of light perspiration our short ride had caused. "He's a good'un."

I grinned at her. She didn't often slip into Scottish colloquialisms being a prestigious professor and all, but it was fun when she did. She was just as alluring when she mimicked her mom's Nigerian accent and sayings.

Rhona made her way out of the tack room with another set of grooming tools to tend to Jacobus. "Hey, Damisi. Have you met the new ranch manager?"

Damisi's smile dimmed a moment. "Hearn introduced us." Her gaze shifted between us. She also felt a bit precarious, seeing as the cottage was to be the ranch manager's residence. Hearn assured her she could live there as long as she wanted and he'd find other accommodations for the ranch manager. I wasn't sure she believed him. She probably thought his attitude would change if Magnus insisted.

"What did you think?" I couldn't help but ask.

Her head tilted as she considered her answer. "I wouldn't hire him to teach history, but he's not applying for that."

"You don't approve, but you don't know why," I interpreted her response.

"I was on the back foot. We met as Hearn was showing him the cottage grounds."

"The cottage is yours, Damisi. You don't have to worry about needing to find another place until you're ready."

Her eyes bored into mine. For a moment it looked like she wanted to make it a permanent arrangement. Wanted to make my living there with her permanent as well. It was a fleeting look, as fleeting as my hope that I hadn't misread it. "Hearn's said, and Magnus didn't look impressed anyway. He'll probably take Hearn up on staying in the castle. It comes with a staff to do everything for him."

"Nothing has to change," I tried to assure both of them.

Their reactions were similar. Rhona hoped I was speaking the truth but would keep her guard up just in case. Damisi looked doubtful but hopeful for something I couldn't discern. Hopeful, I'd change my mind, perhaps? Or wishful thinking on my part.

CHAPTER 26

I WAS SCRAPING my boots by the side door when I heard Damisi's voice from inside.

"...fun fling, that's all. We have nothing in common, Mama."

"You most certainly do. You are both loyal and passionate and hardworking. You do not take guff from anyone. Your families mean a lot to you both. All the important things."

"What about work? You know what demands come with my position. The politics and social mixers and how Gina messed with that."

"That woman! She was wrong for you on every level. Never took your feelings into consideration. Always orchestrating things. That is not what I am seeing here. This one is secure enough to defer to your feelings. She reminds me of your father in that way."

"So, no worries with Nora, then?"

My pounding heart wanted to hear Eni's response to Damisi's facetious statement. I hoped to hear more encouragement because she always took her mom's advice to heart. Maybe with enough people pushing her to give us a chance at something more than a fling, she'd be open to it. But eavesdropping wasn't cool. My hand reached for the door to shut it harder than necessary to announce my arrival. Both voices stopped and waited until I finished hanging my hat, dropping my boots, and washing my hands.

"Nora," Eni greeted when I walked into the living room.

"Hello, Eni. Are you here for an evening ride?"

She'd been coming by once a week. The horses and Damisi pushed away the stresses from her workday. "Dinner, but I will not say no to a ride afterward." Her eyes flicked to her daughter. She always coaxed her into joining us for a ride. If Damisi was up for it tonight, I'd try her on Inky. He was a little stubborn when training with the mechanical bull, but he loved trail rides and he definitely loved Damisi. It should be a fun evening.

"Wonderful," I said to her and turned to Damisi. Her face was flushed, probably worried I'd overheard their conversation. "Good day?"

"So far."

"It's only going to get better. Dinner with your mom and a horseback ride. What more could you need?"

They shared a look I couldn't read. I'd been getting better at reading Damisi, but there were still so many mysterious expressions. Like when she looked at me after climaxing. I'd swear it was pure affection and longing, but then she'd straighten up and walk away, distancing herself as if she couldn't stand even one more second in my presence. A few days later, she'd come back for more. Talk about confusing.

My cell rang as Eni was discussing our meal prep options. I excused myself and checked the display, surprised to see the homestead number. My mother had taken to emailing me or Skyping once in a while, but this was the landline at home.

"Hi, Mom, how are you?"

"Not well, honey. Your father's had another heart attack. You need to come home."

My pulse started pounding hard in my ears. The first time my mom called with this news it seemed unbelievable. At fifty-nine and lean, he wouldn't be the first candidate to come to mind for a heart attack. Yet his diet and stress and blood pressure had combined to waylay him before his time. He'd made it through with lots of recuperation and what I thought was a good change to his diet and workload, but apparently, it wasn't good enough. A second heart attack within a year?

"Is he...how is he?"

"He collapsed at work."

"I thought he was taking things easier, eating better, letting others take care of stressful situations?"

"I don't know how it happened, honey. I just know he needs you back here."

I swallowed hard. This wasn't like last time when I placed a note on the classroom door to let my students know that our class was cancelled and drove a few miles to the hospital. This would take a lot more effort, leaving my post early, leaving my boss without a fully formed takeover team, but it had to be done.

"Of course. I'll get on the first flight out. Tell him I love him, and I'll be there soon."

"I will, sweetie. Thank you. See you soon."

"Nora?" Damisi's concerned voice broke through to my racing mind. "Is everything all right?"

"My father had another heart attack. I have to go see him."

"Oh, dear." Eni came forward and slipped her arms around me. "Is he in surgery?"

My head shook. I didn't ask. How could I not have asked? "I don't know. He collapsed at work. I didn't ask if surgery was necessary."

"What can we do to help?" Damisi reached to grasp my hand. Her other hand cupped over the top of my wrist, expressing an unspoken urgency. My devastation was hers in this moment. Her concern made me feel less panicky.

"I...I'm not sure. I have to get home." My head shook again. What did I need to do? I should, what? Call Hearn, pack, get a flight?

"Of course. Why don't you go pack a bag, and I'll check flights for you?"

A breath heaved out as some sort of a plan was formed. "Thank you."

"Don't worry, we'll get you sorted." Damisi let go of my hand and moved next to me to wrap an arm around my shoulders.

After taking a moment to savor her reassurance, I headed to my room and stood in front of my closet. My original plan was to leave in three weeks if Magnus felt ready to take over. Home in time to help with the hay harvest and the final carrot harvest of the fall. I could even start back at school for the late eight-week session of the fall semester if I wanted. Going early would leave Magnus in a scramble to take over, but with Oisin, Paisley, and Rhona for guidance, he'd be covered. The other employees would be a bonus help, but those three would be the key to his success. It wasn't the way I wanted to leave, but it didn't make a lot of sense for me to go home and come back for a week or two before leaving again.

Dread filled my stomach. It couldn't be avoided. I needed to be there for my dad, and I needed to be here for the ranch and Kenzi, Rhona, and Hearn. And for Damisi. Well, I didn't need to be here for Damisi, but I wanted to be here for her. Wanted to spend as much time as possible with her. Even if she truly thought it was nothing more than a fling. My heart was here and would likely stay here for a long while. I wouldn't meet anyone like Damisi again in my life. She was such a strong pull to stay, and yet, my family really needed me. I'd never been able to turn my back on that.

"You've got some options. Which is most important, airports, travel time, price, or all three?" Damisi was looking down at her iPad when she walked into my room. She looked up and saw me frozen in front of my closet with nothing packed yet. In the next second, she moved into my space and put her arms around me. A long, tight hug that felt like pure bliss. Today she smelled of caramel and vanilla, and as always, she felt strong and soft and perfect. "It's going to be okay. You said your dad was strong. Your mum would have told you to worry otherwise, wouldn't she?"

I soaked up the warmth of her embrace, wishing not for the first time I could look forward to this for many days to come. Years, even, but that wouldn't happen. She thought I was a frivolous fling, and I was getting on a plane tomorrow.

"I'll give Hearn a bell. I'm sure he can whip up a private flight for you or let you use his plane."

"No." I reluctantly stepped back from her embrace. "No. I'm already leaving him in the lurch. I don't need to add an outrageously expensive chartered flight on top of it."

She gave a careful smile. "I don't know anyone else who would give a billionaire that kind of consideration." Her hand reached up, fingers caressing my cheek. "He would want to help."

"Please don't. I feel like I'm ducking out on my responsibilities already."

"If you're sure. Are you ready to look at your flight options?" She gave me a hesitant smile. Her hands grabbed for the iPad. She tapped the screen and scrolled to the first option. "Edinburgh to Pocatello has two stops and is more expensive than two stops from Glasgow to Idaho Falls."

"Same flight duration?"

"Hour less and 200 quid cheaper."

"Let's do that one." Anything to shorten the travel duration and lower the cost of a next day flight. "Do you mind?" I gestured to her iPad. After a few taps and entering my credit card, I had the flight booked. A couple hours in the morning to get things settled, or as much as they could be, before going back home and hoping my dad's health wasn't as precarious as it was last time.

"Tea is on, lovelies." Eni's face popped around the doorframe.

"You didn't have to do that." My throat tightened at how they'd both immediately gone into caregiving mode. As if leaving wouldn't be hard enough, I didn't need my remaining time with them to be all heartwarming. It would make missing Damisi that much more intense.

"I did. You have a lot on your mind. We will help any way we can." Eni's fingers brushed through my hair.

"Aye, anything you need." Damisi gave me a comforting smile.

We sat down to dinner. My head was barely present, thinking about my dad and everything still needing to be done. I'd have just enough time to prep Magnus and say goodbye to everyone else.

Their chatter kept me calm as I ran through my checklist. Write up procedures, authorize timesheets, pack, give last minute instructions for Rhona to help Kenzi until her coach joined her full-time next week, ride my mare one last time, maybe see if Zoey could come for a short visit, drop in on Ainsley and the babies for a quick baby squeeze, get a ride to the airport, and try not to weep openly when saying goodbye to Damisi.

CHAPTER 27

IT FELT GOOD to be back. Not as good as the kiss I'd shared with Damisi before leaving, but familiar. And a relief to finally be here instead of on the endless hamster wheel of security checks, boarding passes, customs lines, and interminable flights.

"You okay?" Sayen asked as we stepped out of her car in front of my house.

"Yeah, just need to see my dad."

"I called Nolan, but he was pretty tight-lipped."

"Same with me." I'd texted my brothers on the layovers. They both sounded happy about my return, but neither mentioned Dad's health status. "It makes me wonder if things are worse than they're letting on."

"Don't think that way. Good thoughts only." Sayen reached over and rubbed a calming circle on my back. "Want me to drive you to the hospital?"

"I'll drop my bags and make a call first." When we walked through my front door, I was surprised at how much it didn't immediately comfort me. Sayen had been living here since I left and her mom stayed with her for six weeks while some construction was going on near her home. They hadn't changed anything, but Melanie's lavender lotion scent was prevalent and Sayen's laptop was on the dining room table, her boots and jacket were also on display.

Going into my room, I noticed the scent of a recently scrubbed bathroom and furniture polish. Sayen had been staying in here while her mom crashed at the house so they wouldn't have to share the bathroom upstairs. Knowing this, I again felt out of place. It would take a while to ease back in after more than five months away, but I'd get there.

I fished out my phone and started dialing before I realized it still flashed my UK number. Plucking out the sim card, I replaced it with the US one and called over to my parents' house. "Hi, Mom. I'm back. How's Dad?"

"Oh, honey. We're so glad you're back." The relief was evident in her tone.

"What room are you in?"

"Room?"

"At the hospital, Mom."

"Come to the house, sweetie. We all want to see you."

"I want to see Dad."

"Just come to the house."

My heart was beating really hard now. If Mom kept deflecting, it had to be bad news she was going to deliver. I no longer wanted to go over there, but I didn't have a choice. "Okay."

"News?" Sayen asked when I went to grab the keys to my truck.

"She wants me to come over to the house. Won't tell me what room he's in."

Her face fell. She knew almost everything about the complicated relationship with my father, but she also knew how much losing him would mean. "It doesn't have to mean anything bad."

I crossed my fingers in hope she was right. Outside, I fired up my truck, noting the difference in height between my full-sized, heavy duty truck and the pickup in Bathgate. My left foot stomped to the floorboard in a practiced motion, seeking a clutch that wasn't in this truck. I didn't think it possible, but I actually missed the smaller pickup and not just for the better fuel efficiency. Finally, I got the truck moving and out onto the road, swerving to get into the right lane. It would probably take a few more tries before it became habit again.

Nothing had changed on the route to my parents' place. The Portneuf River was running high this early in the season, but otherwise, no new construction or additions to the homes along the way out to their ranch.

As I turned into the driveway, passing under the log entryway with the wood carved Cleary Equines sign, the butterflies returned. I'd planned to come back under different circumstances, having successfully launched a fully formed horse training and breeding business. Instead, I'd left it at ninety-five percent done. Close, but not good enough. After things settled here, I planned to make sure everything was settled back there.

"Nora!" My mom threw open the front door and came down the two steps from the porch of their sprawling ranch house and into my arms. "Thank you for coming back so quickly."

"Of course, how's Dad?"

"Come inside." She slipped her arm around my waist and got us moving. I wanted to protest, to demand she tell me about Dad, get us in a car to the hospital, but I followed her inside.

"Hey, Nor," Nolan greeted as he walked out of the kitchen eating a sandwich. He didn't live in the main house anymore, but he took almost all his meals there, and of course, Mom still did his laundry. "Glad you're back." Casually, he took another bite.

"Nolan." I gave him a one-armed hug so as not to smash his precious sandwich. "How's Dad?" I asked for the last time.

He swiveled and left without a word. A lump formed in my throat. Mom barely glanced at him. She was used to his unpredictable behavior. She focused on me, patted my arm, and tugged me into the living room. I jerked to a halt at the sight of Dad sitting in his recliner.

"Dad!" I rushed over and gently wrapped my arms around him. "How are you feeling? Why aren't you still in the hospital?"

"It's good you're back, Nora." His grumbly voice sounded more hoarse than normal. He was looking pale but otherwise well enough.

"What did the doctors say?"

"Just a scare." Dad waved off my concern.

I sat back on my heels. Just a scare? "A scare? That doesn't sound like a medical diagnosis." My eyes went to Mom first and back to Dad. "What exactly happened?"

"Your father collapsed at work. His heart was beating out of his chest. We were all terrified." Mom reached to grip his hand.

I slid onto the sofa and absorbed what she said, or what she didn't say. "And what did the doctors say?"

"Len said it was lucky we had him lie back and take aspirin so quickly, or he might have died."

Len, the family doctor, was in no way a heart specialist. He hadn't even been on the team of doctors caring for him after his heart attack. A good enough family doctor, but not the first call for someone possibly going through a second heart attack in less than a year.

"Did Len consult with your cardiologist?"

"Dad's blood pressure decreased and his heart rate came down," Mom reported.

That didn't answer my question, but the repeated deflections were starting to make sense. "I see. So, a scare?"

They nodded their heads. Dad cleared his throat. "I'm going to need to take a step back like last time. We could use your help at the ranch."

The realization of what they'd done settled over me. Using his condition to get me to come back early was conniving, only more despicable. It enraged me that I was too practical to get a flight back to the UK for the short period before I was due back at work for the U of I. I should storm out right now. I really should, but I wouldn't, and they knew it. And worse, they had no shame about it.

Breath pushed through my lips to prevent me from saying something I'd regret. They were the people who raised me and taught me and loved me. I had to keep that in mind, or I'd scream into a pillow until my voice hurt. For now, I went with a polite but insincere offer. "Sure, I'll lend a hand if something urgent comes up the boys can't handle, but I'll be back teaching soon. That will be my priority."

They glanced at each other, obviously weighing their options. "Since you're here, you could sit in on a client meeting with Niall today."

Today? After staying up most of the night to tie up all the loose ends in Bathgate and a full day of travel? Did they really have no consideration for me at all? Stupid question, their actions today proved they didn't.

"Big sale," Dad continued, checking his watch. "Could set us up for the year. Niall could use your support."

"I don't know how much use I'll be. I'm pretty exhausted from all the travel."

"Just sit in, sweetie. You'll want to say hello to Niall anyway," Mom encouraged.

I wanted to laugh in their faces. I wanted to yell and rage at them. They were never going to change. Getting angry about it would only hurt me. I'd been gullible enough to fall for their deception, and now I had to make the best of it. "All right." Because there was really no other answer I could give them.

"Good." Dad brushed a hand through the air toward the door. "Head over to the office. Say hi to Niall, and he'll fill you in on the meeting."

My stare bounced between them for a long moment to solidify this exchange in my mind. They may be my family, but I wanted to remember how they made me feel so I'd never backslide into being manipulated again. They were probably thinking I understood and accepted what they'd done to get me back here, but I could feel the endless tug of family obligation snap apart. If a catastrophe occurred, I'd be there for them, but I no longer felt obligated to bend to their will.

"Yes, sir," I murmured when their expressions showed nothing but relief to have me back. My head shook in resignation. They'd coordinated this whole series of events, and nothing I could do would change it or them. Like with the extra chores and the double standard, I just had to learn to live with it or I'd be angry for the rest of my life.

Outside, I headed down the sweeping driveway and across the stable yards to the original house on the property, which now served as the ranch office. I'd spent many hours in that office, learning the business from the ground up. Almost as much time as I spent in the barn and working with horses outside.

"Hey, sis. You back?" Niall asked the obvious as I walked into the office. He seemed to stand taller now, and his face sported whiskers that aged him five years. They were a lighter shade than his dark brown hair, making it seem as if he dyed one or the other.

"Doing okay?" I gave him a brief hug. It was good to see him, even if he looked far more tired than ever before.

"Yep. So far. Did Dad ask you to come back?"

"Mom said he had a heart attack and gave me the impression he might die. I got on the first flight back."

He glanced away with a regretful look that had been missing from my parents' faces. He either knew beforehand or learned about their plan sometime over the past day and wasn't happy about it. "Not my idea."

Well, well, my little brother was growing up. "Figured. How's the ranch?"

"Good, yeah. Had a few workers flake on me and some of those clients you set up didn't like that you weren't around." Niall had a way of twisting everything into something that suited his needs. It could be charming at times and usually made him pretty upbeat. He also suffered from delusions of grandeur as a result.

"Dad asked me to sit in on your meeting, but it's up to you."

"Are you back?"

I studied him, wondering if he knew what he was asking. If he understood it. "I'm not, Niall. Do you get why?"

He shrugged and looked away. "We could run this place together."

For the first time, I didn't feel like he was just saying what I wanted to hear to get me to do whatever he needed. "That's not what Dad wants. It's not even what you want. Maybe temporarily, but soon, you'll need full authority."

His hands came up. "Fair enough. I miss having you here, though."

I punched his shoulder lightly. "You miss me doing all the jobs you hate doing."

"That too." His head tipped toward the space we'd set up as a conference area. "Sit in on the meeting?"

"Can't say I'll be much help."

"Dad wants it, so we might as well." He was as trapped by Dad's expectations as I used to be. His eyes widened as he glanced over my shoulder at the door. A smile tugged at his lips, slightly smirky, sort of smug, but a lot more sincere than usual. "Welcome to Cleary Equines."

I turned and came face to face with one of the clients I'd set up when I was in charge. A trainer on the cutting circuit. We'd become friendly during the peak of my competition days. When I took over running the ranch, she'd been one of my first sales calls. She was technically competition, but she was also in need of good cutting horses.

"Hey, Nora. How ya been?" She hugged me hello.

"Good, you?" I glanced over at Niall, wondering why he failed to tell me this meeting was with Colleen.

"Ladies, we're this way." Niall gestured us toward the conference table.

Colleen's eyes narrowed. Yeah, she caught his tone as well. When it came to women, whether in business or not, he always acted like he was on the prowl.

"It's good you're back," Colleen told me under her breath as we took our seats.

I jerked forward, surprised. Then, after thinking about it, not surprised. Dad had used me as his main marketing tool from the moment I landed my first championship on the circuit. It would make sense for Niall to dangle me as an incentive to clients I'd brought in. If I told her I wouldn't be working here any longer, she'd likely take her business elsewhere. Could I do that to Niall?

On one hand, my parents had manipulated my early return so I'd be here for this meeting. On the other, Niall was in over his head with this meeting and many others he'd have to go through before it came more naturally to him. If I wasn't on the end of a twenty-plus hour travel day, I might give this more effort, but it was no longer my responsibility.

"I'm not with Cleary Equines anymore."

"Excuse me?" She directed her confused stare from me to Niall. "I was under the impression I'd be dealing with you from now on." Her glare sharpened on him.

"Nora's trained everyone who works here, including me. You'll be in good hands."

She snapped her head around to look at me. Yeah, she'd heard the smirk in his voice, too. A slight innuendo, a cocky assurance. It could work in a bar, but not in a business meeting when he'd already angered her enough to insist I be part of this deal. "If you don't work here anymore, why are you at this meeting?"

"My parents asked me to sit in. I didn't know you were the client. I wasn't even in the US eight hours ago."

She leaned forward. "I wondered why I didn't see you at any of the summer competitions. Where were you?"

"Working at a new outfit in Scotland."

"That's great news. I'm starting something in Germany next spring. Hoping to get in on the European tour over the summer. Did you have a peek while you were there?"

"I rode in a few competitions. My boss's niece wants to start competing. Had to make sure the horses were ready."

"What have you got over there?"

"Hey, now, wait a minute." Niall caught the turn to this meeting.

If I hadn't already been punchy from the manipulation to get me here and the long travel day, I probably would have discouraged any further questions. "Quarter horses, cutting horses."

"Still in contact?" Her brow lifted when I nodded. "Let's talk soon." She stood to shake my hand and gave Niall a wave.

"But...don't you want to look at the horses you bought?" Niall must have taken some lessons on trying to close a deal while I was gone. Unfortunately, he skipped a few steps and went straight to the last.

"After you insulted me a couple of months ago, I agreed to give you a second chance if Nora was involved. She's not, so I'm out of here." She looked at me. "Give me a call. We'll work something out for my operation in Germany."

I tipped my head in acknowledgement as she walked out the door.

"Way to steal that sale, Nor. Don't you care about your family farm?" He was more bewildered than angry. Having not been in the house when I found out about our parents' deception, he hadn't grasped the extent of my resolve to step away completely. He still thought I'd be a reliable safety net for him where this business was concerned.

"It's not my family farm, Niall. Dad made that clear. It's time for you to step up and run this ranch on your own. Stop relying on him and start respecting your customers. It's easy once you step fully into the role."

He shook his head and blew out a world-weary breath. "Dad's not going to be happy."

"He gave you the reins. He doesn't get to be unhappy with the way you run things." I hugged him briefly. "Come out to the house for dinner this week?"

He grinned, almost as if he'd already brushed off the loss of a good client. "Free dinner? Count me in."

I sketched a wave and walked outside. I didn't bother going back up to the family home as they would expect. Being dead tired made me a little cranky. Being manipulated made me a little pissed off. Best not to confront them. Nothing good would come of it.

CHAPTER 28

THE DEPARTMENT CHAIR couldn't stop looking at my hair. It was a shocking difference from the last time he saw me, true, but really, he couldn't get over it? He'd been in academia too long, his agriculture roots long forgotten. Like me, he'd grown up on a farm, but once he went to college, he left it behind. Twenty-five years since acquiring his PhD, things had changed in the industry, but he had tenure and he was a good manager of academics. He'd always been fair to me and was very sympathetic when I had to take a leave of absence for my dad's heart attack.

"It's good you're back. We're considering increasing the number of AgriBiz classes we offer next year."

I tilted my head, contemplating what that would mean to my schedule. Adding more courses would take away training time with my horses, but I could handle more if I had to.

"Your replacement is quite good. We're very happy with him, so you'll be splitting the courses next semester, two each."

"Two?" That would drop me to part-time status and cut my salary and benefits.

"Sorry, Nora, but you're not tenured. We can't just drop Gus because you've come back. We made it clear you wouldn't have a guaranteed spot if you took a leave."

I'd recommended my replacement. Gus ran a profitable wheat, alfalfa, and barley operation with lots of employees and seasonal management. It gave him excellent knowledge to share with students in the agriculture school. It didn't give him an edge over someone like me running both a ranch and farming operation or someone with undergrad and graduate degrees in Agriculture Business. Lowering costs must be more important than having the most qualified teachers. Two part-time lecturers were less expensive than one full-time lecturer with full benefits.

"I understand." I didn't like it, but I understood. One more disappointment since returning home.

On my way back, I spotted Gus on the road coming toward me. My fingers lifted off the steering wheel in a standard acknowledgement wave. We'd exchanged goods and services over the years, winter hay and alfalfa for a cover from my stallion. He didn't compete, but a well-bred quarter horse would make a damn good ranch horse for him. When I needed a replacement at the school, he was the only one I could think of with the time and interest. I couldn't have known the university would look to cut back in a department that has been growing steadily since it first opened.

My mom's SUV was the next vehicle I recognized as I was turning into my drive. She had another friend farther down the road, but she was likely here to see me. Missed Sunday dinners, unreturned calls, and no response to her voicemail expressing disappointment about the outcome of the sales meeting with Niall must have prompted this visit. Dad's response was to leave a message to come check out their newest filly. He almost tempted me with the prospect of a newborn horse. I always wanted to see the newborns, but I resisted this time. Niall and Nolan weren't choosing sides, which I appreciated.

My foot barely plunked down on the running board of my truck before Mom's car came to a halt beside my truck. I met her at the front of her vehicle. "Hi, Mom. How are you?"

"Where have you been?"

"Just got back from a meeting at the U."

"Not just now," she blew out a frustrated breath and gestured us inside. When she spotted Sayen in the kitchen, she stopped. "Oh, hello, Sayen. Don't you look lovely. Going out?"

Sayen didn't need a PhD in reading tones to know my mother wanted her gone so she could talk to me alone. Her gaze cut to mine, and I nodded my head. She greeted my mom with a squeeze on the shoulder and told us she had work to do in the barn. We'd cut her lunch short, but she wouldn't mind.

"Where have you been since you've been back? We've missed you at the house and for Sunday dinners."

"Busy trying to make up for the lost wages and the last-minute airfare to come home early. You know, because my father had a heart attack and was in critical condition in the hospital." I thought I'd worked through my frustration but apparently not. Sass had never been my style and certainly never with my parents. I still had a hard time believing they thought things would return to normal for us. Nothing around here felt normal anymore.

Her eyes narrowed, but she had the grace to look a touch embarrassed. "I never said critical."

"You implied it, Mom. You gave me the impression he could be dying, when really, he'd just overworked himself. All so I'd be here to try to salvage a sale squandered by Niall."

"That's not entirely accurate."

"Feels pretty accurate."

"And you stealing that sale? Would that be accurate as well?"

"I didn't steal anything, and Niall knows that. I doubt he told you otherwise." Surprisingly, my relationship with Niall had only strengthened since getting back. Now that I was no longer his boss on the ranch, no longer the older sister organizing things in the family, no longer trying to prove myself to my parents, he didn't sulk or become petty anymore. He was also open to some of my suggestions about how to deal with clients, especially female clients.

"It's not been the same, honey. Your dad and I don't understand what happened to you in Scotland. You're like a different person now. Even more so than when you returned from grad school."

During college, I'd been able to come home once a month. The drive from WSU wasn't too bad, but grad school at UC Davis kept me away from home for two years. Concentrating only on my needs changed my outlook, and the family spotted it immediately. This trip to Scotland hadn't just changed my outlook, it changed me.

"A lot happened, Mom. I ran a ranching operation the way I wanted with no interference. My team was amazing to work with, and I made some great friends. I also met someone special, but I left all of that because I was manipulated by my parents. So, sorry if I'm not the compliant girl you're used to anymore, but this is me now."

Her eyes blinked repeatedly as she processed everything. "We didn't manipulate you."

My hands went up to stop any further protest. "I'm not going to argue anymore. I feel like you manipulated me whether you believe it or not." I paused to let that be the end of the topic. I didn't want to keep having this discussion every time I saw them and didn't immediately jump to do what they asked. "I'm having the boys to dinner on Wednesday night. If you and Dad want to join them, you'd be welcome."

"Not Sunday at home?"

"No, ma'am."

She sat back against the sofa arm, deflated. "I love you, honey."

"I love you, too. I just have to live my life the way I want to now." I reached for her hand. "Think about coming to dinner on Wednesday, Mom. I'd love to see you both."

"I will." She stood and wrapped me in a hug. "I only want the best for you."

"I appreciate that." I walked her back to her car and watched her drive away.

Over in the barn, Sayen was mucking out stalls that we'd already mucked out today. She looked up when I walked in. "How'd it go?"

"She's still disappointed, but I think she's starting to get it." I grabbed a shovel and started scooping the shavings into an empty wheelbarrow. "Let's scrub and disinfect the stalls while the weather is still warm."

"I can do that tomorrow if you've got to get something else done before you go back to the U."

"That's delayed till Spring semester. They like Gus, so we'll be splitting the classes."

"What the hell? You were the one to bring those classes to the campus."

The agriculture department at this branch campus didn't include business classes. I pitched offering some classes as electives in the department that would include a web feed to the main campus in Moscow for students there as well.

"I know, but if they can get two teachers for less than the price of one, they're going to go for it."

"Not a lot going your way since you got back, is there?" Her hand came down to clasp my shoulder in sympathy.

I shook my head and scoffed. Actually, no longer feeling that massive family pressure gave me a sense of freedom I'd never felt before. Except maybe for that last month in Scotland when my future, so set before, was suddenly up in the air.

CHAPTER 29

THE TRIP TO Wyoming for an auction went well. I bid on a few horses for Hearn and another mare for myself. After they were trained up, they'd be included in the sale to Colleen's new outfit in Germany next spring. It was my last obligation to him, and I'd been dragging my heels to prolong our necessary contact. I'd spoken with him a few times since leaving, promising to find those extra horses for him, but he was mostly interested in my dad's health. After learning about my parents' fake-out, he was mostly interested in how I was readjusting. The truth: not well.

The bitterness of being called back coupled with the fear of losing my dad, only to find out he was perfectly fine still hadn't dissipated. The loss of my status at the university didn't help. Sure, I'd be back at the start of the new semester, teaching some of my standard classes, but not all of them. With my absence from campus, work friends had drifted away. The competition season was mostly over and my friends from the circuit were scattered around the country. If not for my brothers and Sayen's family, I'd probably spend full days without speaking to anyone. The auction trip was a good way to shake off some cobwebs.

Making dinner soothed some of my inexplicable jitters. After three weeks back home, I still didn't feel completely settled. I knew it would take a while, but not having to work at the university or at the family ranch left me with more time than I was used to. For tonight, I'd take extra time trying a new recipe for dinner. After, I'd see if Sayen wanted to invite her cousin's family over for a ride. Five-year-old Jared was always entertaining and he loved the horses.

When the front door opened, I called out to Sayen, "Did Aaron drool all over you again?" The feed store assistant manager would follow her around the store constantly trying to chat her up. He'd ignore the other customers whenever she came in. It was pretty funny to witness but even better to tease her about.

"No drool involved." The lilting accent caused flutters to erupt in my stomach.

I whipped around to face Damisi who was somehow standing in my living room. She looked as gorgeous as ever in jeans and a peasant top. Her creamy almond skin glowed with a hint of perspiration from the still warm October evening. Barely-there makeup looked just as good as her go-to-work makeup. Her beautiful mouth spread into a smile, eyes glittering with mischievous happiness.

My heart skipped into a rhythmic thumping. Everything I'd been pushing down and locking inside rose to the surface. I clamped my mouth shut; too afraid I'd blurt something to scare her away.

"Surprise," she said softly, advancing toward me with open arms. "Hope you don't mind."

I stepped into her arms and hugged her tight. She settled against me perfectly. Her lips brushed my cheek. I longed to capture them with my own but refrained since she'd gone for a hello hug instead of a hello kiss. "Not at all. Great to see you."

"I was hoping to catch you dancing naked in the kitchen, but alas, disappointment."

I laughed, leaning back and watching her beautiful face display so much more than she ever spoke. She was just as happy to see me, just as excited, and just as aroused. That should please me, but I wanted so much more from her and for her.

"Not to sound displeased, but how are you here? No classes this week?"

"Ainsley is covering. She's ecstatic to be back on campus. As much as she loves maternity leave, she misses teaching." She shrugged like it was no big deal to turn over her classes to Ainsley. "Hearn has a tech conference in Seattle. He came over on his plane and offered seats to anyone interested. Zoey, Skye, the kids, and I hitched a ride."

"You took an international flight with babies?"

She laughed and my heart skipped a beat. I'd missed that sound. "It was an adventure, but I completely understand Skye wanting to take the trip. Her mom used all her time off this year to come over and help them with the newborns. She'd have to wait another year before she could see her grandkids. They got off the plane in New York, and Hearn dropped me in Idaho Falls. He and Zoey are continuing on to Seattle."

"Because you missed me?" I teased.

"Because you misled me," she countered and gripped my arms, scowling beautifully. "You didn't tell me when you left that you were leaving."

I tried not to laugh at her illogical statement. "But I did."

"Not really. You must have known I thought you were coming back to finish your term at the stables."

I gave a slow nod. Yes, deep down I realized she thought I'd be returning for a few weeks because that was always the plan. But so many factors played into it. After the sham to get me here, it felt like the wind had been knocked out of me. I could have returned, but for what? To have to say goodbye again to those wonderful friends and this amazing woman in a matter of weeks? There'd be no point.

"I'm glad you're here. How long can you stay?"

She glanced back to where her bag sat just inside the front door. A slight blush tinted her cheeks. "A few days. I haven't booked a hotel yet. I wasn't sure..."

"Don't be silly. You'll stay here." Even as much as having her in the guestroom upstairs would be painfully tempting, I didn't want to miss out on a second of her visit. "I assume Sayen's unplanned trip to the feed store was to grab you at the airport? Is she out in the barn or did she skip out?"

"The barn, I think. She thought you'd enjoy the surprise."

I reached for her hand, not able to keep from touching her for another moment. "She was right. Are you tired or hungry?"

"Both, but," she paused and glanced through the big windows in the living room. "I don't suppose there's enough light left tonight for a proper tour of your place. It looks much different than the stables at home."

"Well, yes, a billionaire can build a dream ranch. Peons must make do with what we can afford and build out over time. We'll take a tour tomorrow. Have a seat. I'm making a curry. Let me call Sayen in." I left before I pulled her into my arms and kissed her senseless. She didn't seem open to that. This was a surprise visit with a friend, nothing more.

Outside I spotted Sayen lurking near the barn. I waved her over and her smile grew wider as she approached. "I picked up when she called the house to find out if you'd be in town this week. I suggested she surprise you. Was that cool?"

"Sure. It's good to see her."

"Even if it breaks your heart a little more?"

I studied her. She wasn't immune to romantic feelings; she just didn't feel the need to engage in them. "How did you know?" I hadn't told her I'd fallen for Damisi. I hadn't even admitted it to myself.

"Because you weren't that angry with your parents for what they did. You were just resigned. If your heart hadn't already been broken by someone else, you would have been much more upset with them."

I grabbed her for a hug. She understood me so well. "Dinner is ready."

"I can get something later."

"No, eat with us. We'll ease into whatever she has in mind for this visit."

Her brow furrowed. "What do you mean?"

Admitting this might make me look like a chump, but only a best friend wouldn't judge. "One part of my heartbreak is because she was the one who decided if and when. I could only wait and hope." I brushed a hand through the air. "Pathetic, I know." Especially for someone used to being in the driver's seat with relationships.

Sayen gave that some consideration. "Not really. She's a cautious thinker. You're a daring thinker. She'd need to weigh consequences every time. You weigh consequences once and handle the risk thereafter."

"You should write a book on this crap."

"I'd make enough to gas up the truck."

We laughed and headed back in to join my unexpected guest.

CHAPTER 30

"IT'S GORGEOUS, DIFFERENT, but most definitely gorgeous," Damisi exclaimed when she was safely back on the ground after our tour of my property on horseback.

We'd spent the morning on a driving tour of the area. Vacation Damisi was almost jaunty. She'd relished every minute of both the driving tour and the afternoon horseback tour. I was aware I'd missed her before she arrived, but spending the day together only highlighted how much.

"Smaller, that's for sure," I qualified. I had just over thirty acres compared to Hearn's hundreds.

"And dry or less verdant?"

"High desert is the term you're looking for. Sagebrush, sandy and rocky soil, and ground cover where grass isn't purposely planted."

"I like that you plant your own hay and carrots."

"I'd planned to do the same in Bathgate if I knew whoever took over for me could handle farming duties." It didn't matter that Hearn had nearly unlimited resources. My goal for the stables was to become sustainable and profitable. Growing crops we'd need for the horses would go a long way toward lowering our costs. Something else I didn't have time to put into place before I left.

"From what I've seen he can barely handle half the horses, let alone anything else."

My head came around. "I haven't had a chance to check in with anyone in a week. Has something happened?"

"You could say that."

I handed her a brush and to work on Sunbringer. "What's happened?" And why didn't Paisley or Oisin let me know? We'd had weekly Skype calls since I left. Rhona was off on a school field trip, so I hadn't expected any word from her till next week.

"Things were okay for a couple of weeks, but then he sacked Roderick when he wouldn't give up his split day schedule." She glanced over and took note of my confused stare. "Apparently, Paisley wasn't happy about that and had an over-the-top reaction which got her fired."

That couldn't be right. Paisley was almost always composed. She'd had two uncharacteristic responses to loud noises in the five months we worked together. She'd been quick to anger and jumpy on both occasions, certainly not something that would warrant firing. Especially not since she'd been diagnosed and her employer was aware of the diagnosis.

"When he kicked Rhona out, Oisin almost quit," Damisi continued unloading more and more shocking news.

"He what?" My voice rose high enough to startle the horses. A pounding started in my ears, making it difficult to keep a clear head.

"He caught a friend of Rhona's leaving her room one morning and used that as an excuse to fire her." She gave a mirthless laugh. "Of course, this was after he'd already moved her to the bunkbed room so he could move his girlfriend into Rhona's larger suite in the bunkhouse."

My head shook comically hard, as if trying to toss aside her bad news and clear the pounding in my ears. "You're joking, right?"

"Not joking." Her mouth drew into a serious line. "I think he started resenting not having much to do with the success of the place. Everyone kept talking about you. When Hearn informed him of the sale of horses you made, Magnus wasn't happy you were still making a mark on the stables."

I leaned back against the nearest stall door, sucking in air. Rhona, vulnerable young person, out on her own again, not to mention she loved those horses as much as I did. Paisley looking for another job and having to share her medical status with potential employers. Roderick taking on more part-time jobs so he could be around for his kids every day after preschool. This was worse than the disappointment I felt after learning my parents had lied to get me home early.

"Where is Rhona staying?" That was my first concern. She'd been couch surfing when she came to live at the stables. She'd be covered on this week's school trip, but afterward, she wouldn't have her space in the bunkhouse.

"Elizabeth's. She's also furious and wants to quit, but she needs the job." Damisi stepped closer and laid a comforting hand on my shoulder. Her expression told me she understood how this news was affecting me. "I didn't mean to ruin your day, but I thought you'd want to know."

"It's a lot to process. I feel pretty horrible." Worse than horrible. I'd picked the guy. Worked side by side with him for a week, and he never once showed any kind of bruised ego. Why would he risk tearing everything down? Especially with a boss who was so thrilled with the way things were going?

"It's not your fault."

"I let those people down by rushing through the hiring and training of my replacement. I might have noticed some of these warning signs if I'd trained him longer." No one could hide an enormous ego for that long.

"You can't blame yourself."

"There's no one else to blame. I'm sick about them losing their jobs." More than sick. Something had to be done. "Is Hearn all right with Magnus's decisions?"

"He is not."

I shot her a suspicious look. "So, that's why you're here? To tell me how everything I put in place has been torn down and get me to come back to find someone more suitable?"

Her eyes searched mine. She took a long time to contemplate her response. "I'm not here to convince you to come back and fix everything. Hearn is going to stop by on our way home to do that."

Even the thought of seeing Hearn soon didn't lift my spirits much. Despair knotted my stomach. The one good thing I'd done with my life in the past year was slowly disintegrating.

"I don't want you to come back for the ranch," Damisi drew my attention back.

My posture slumped, disappointment weighing me down. Even if Hearn did ask me to come back, apparently, Damisi wasn't fond of the idea. "Oh."

She brought her hand up in slow motion until it cupped my face. Her eyes closed briefly at the contact, as if the touch brought her relief. "I want you to come back for me. For what we can be together."

My heart started into a steady gallop. I swallowed hard, eyes tracing every feature of her gorgeous face. For months she'd avoided anything intimate to pass between us. Sure, we'd had sex, lots of sex, great sex, but to her it was only sex. Sex with a casual fling. Was that what she was suggesting now? More no-strings sex for as long as I needed to get things back in order at the estate? Except the heartful tone she was using didn't speak to casual. Nor did her taking time off from work and giving her classes to someone she feared had a better academic reputation than she. Traveling impulsively to see me was further proof she couldn't just be here to preserve a casual fling.

"For us?" I needed clarification.

"Aye, for us. I've missed you." Her fingers feathered over my jaw. "Everything about you. Even the tacky laundry line drying your dungarees every week."

"Hey, I did that for you," I exclaimed in mock indignation. "Jeans take forever to dry in that washer-dryer combo thingy. You'd never get to use it if I kept it busy drying my jeans."

"I know. It's why I asked Hearn to replace it with separate washer and dryer units. No more tacky laundry lines ... if you come back."

She looked completely serious. Looked completely invested, too. As much as her words and caressing fingers and longing looks were making my heartbeat race to the point of dizziness, this seemed so out of character. Why would her mind change about me in three weeks when it hadn't for the few months we were together? Then, it hit me.

"Zoey told you about my real job, right? Told you this cowgirl thing is my part-time gig?"

She stepped back and dropped her hand. "What are you talking about? What do you mean this is part-time?"

"Zoey didn't tell you I teach at the university?"

"No, she did not." Her eyes bored into mine, annoyance very evident. "And neither did you, Cowgirl. Are you telling me you're a professor?"

"A lecturer. Master's only, no PhD, and because of the sabbatical I took, it's no longer my full-time gig either. They're cutting my lecture hours to save money."

"You work at a university?"

I lifted my chin at her disbelieving tone. "I do. I took a year off to help after my dad's heart attack."

She shook her head and blinked. Even confused she looked beautiful. "There are so many things I want to ask."

"Makes me more respectable, don't you think?" I was only partially kidding. She had issues with status which had been ground into her by her deceptive ex.

"You are respectable, respectful, and highly regarded by everyone you meet," she said sincerely.

"And yet, I was never more than a fling for you."

Her hand pressed against her stomach as she let out a long breath. "I was an idiot."

I laughed at the statement's certain delivery. "No one would ever accuse you of doing a stupid thing, let alone being an idiot."

"I must be to have let you leave."

"Where is this coming from?" I had to know even if my heart was screaming at me to just shut up and believe her. "The day before I left you were telling your mom we had nothing in common and I was a fling."

She gave me a suspicious look. "You heard that, did you?"

"I wasn't eavesdropping. I walked into the house just as you made your declaration. Then I got my mom's call and didn't bother talking to you about it."

She nodded and flicked her eyes about as if searching for a response. After a moment, she let out a sigh. "I was trying to convince myself. Protect myself for when you left because this is your home." Her arm waved in a half circle around us. "This lovely place is your home. As much as I was hoping you'd come to love the estate, I can see this is your home."

I glanced about, seeing my ranch through her eyes. Small ranch house that could use some updating, eight-stall barn with a new roof and windows but in need of more, two training corrals to the side and a pasture beyond bordered by wood rail put in when the ranch house was built years ago. The fencing needed to be replaced, which was next on my list, and a storage shed for the hay harvest, and a new tractor and the list went on and on. My earnings from Scotland would cover a lot on the list, but it would never be as slick as my father's ranch, nor as extraordinary as Hearn's stables. It had been my home for four years, slowly becoming more my style, but the family ranch felt more my home than this place, and that would never be mine.

"It's nice, but it's never been more than a place to sleep and earn a little extra."

Her eyes zipped back to mine, hope and something else making them shine. "Because you wanted your family's ranch?"

"Yes, and I teach."

"And now?"

"Now, I have a part-time teaching gig and this, which isn't a big enough operation for both Sayen and me full-time."

That beautiful mouth of hers smiled, and I ached to lean in and kiss it. "Or you could run Hearn's stables, and there has to be a uni nearby with an agriculture department in need of good lecturers."

"Because Magnus tore down what I built there and my employees need me back?"

"Because the place is falling apart without you, and I need you back."

"Do you really?" I couldn't stop the incredulity from entering my tone. Never had she expressed anything more than fondness for me and that was only after great sex.

She grasped my shirt and pulled me close with fire in her eyes. "I'm mad for you."

A sound left my throat, surprise and happiness. My heart thumped against the fists she had gripping my shirt. I gazed into her eyes and down to her lips.

"Entirely," she whispered before leaning in to kiss me.

My head grew fuzzy, and my heart pounded ferociously. I grasped her hips as my lips nipped and slid against hers. She felt amazing, and I felt giddy. I pulled back before our kiss led to shedding clothes as it usually did. "I've been falling for you since you first screamed at me."

She grinned and touched my face. "I know."

I laughed at her brash pronouncement. "It helped that you were naked."

She shoved me and I stumbled back a step, laughing harder. "You're never boring."

My eyes brightened. I was boring, though. My life revolved around taking care of horses and the land and teaching others to do the same. Up early, work hard, make dinner, go to sleep, and do it all over again the next day. Boring. But apparently, she didn't think of me that way. I couldn't ask for more in someone to love.

"Don't make a decision today. It's a lot to think about, and Hearn will be here in a couple of days to make his pitch. I just needed..." she paused searching for the right words.

"To express your undying love?" I teased and got another shove. "Too soon?"

"You make me want to smack and kiss you at the same time. How is that possible?"

"I'm special?"

Her hand cupped my face as she stepped close. Her scent and heat washed over me. In as certain a tone as I'd ever heard her use, she agreed, "You are."

CHAPTER 31

MY FINGERS SKIMMED over smooth, warm skin. I hadn't stopped touching her all night, even in sleep. It felt so glorious to make love with her in a bed with lots of space to maneuver. Once exhausted, she'd snuggled close and didn't let go. My heart felt as if it might burst from an overflow of love. What a difference a night could make.

"This is a pleasant way to wake up." Her husky morning voice made me shiver.

"There's that word again." She really couldn't come up with a more enthusiastic descriptor for how marvelous this morning was?

Her soft chuckle prompted me to roll her over and pin her beneath me. She hissed as our bodies slid together. I bit my lip when she slotted a thigh between my legs.

"You'll have to get used to British reserve if you're coming back with me."

I pushed up onto my palms to study her. We'd declared our feelings for each other yesterday and spent the night making love for the first time. When she'd asked me to return for what we could be together, my heart soared. In the daylight, I was still certain of my feelings for her, but was she?

"What would I be coming back to? More of the same casual hookups?"

Her fingers traced my cheekbones. She searched my eyes. "Is that what you want?"

"This is what I want. What I've wanted for so long with you."

"I would say we could have had this all summer, but it's not true."

A chill skittered down my spine. Was she having second thoughts about asking me to come back for her?

"It took you leaving and time to analyze the ache I felt as it expanded into all areas of my life. Without that absence, it might have taken months or years for me to comprehend how deeply you've invaded my life."

Unable to speak, I leaned down and captured her mouth in a kiss that said a lot more than good morning. Her hands skated down my back and squeezed my ass. I lurched and started rocking against her. I was deliciously sore but swollen and needy again. Her hips rose off the bed to meet my thrusts. Puffs of air pushed against my lips as she fought her impending orgasm. She liked delayed gratification, but I wasn't going to give it to her this morning. She needed to give in because I wouldn't last.

"Oh, aye," she groaned as her climax shuddered through her.

"Yes, yes," I moaned, joining her in bliss.

My head dropped onto her shoulder as I slid to the side. She wriggled her arm under me and pulled me closer. I could feel her heart beat against my chest. Her breathing slowed as she faced me and kissed my forehead.

"Do you need more convincing about how things will be between us?"

I grinned. "I'll take all the convincing you want to give."

"Greedy." She patted my behind. "Come on, there are horses to visit." She pressed a kiss to my mouth and rolled out of bed.

I would have protested if her nude body hadn't robbed me of speech. I'd seen most of her naked over the last few months but never completely disrobed in full light. Not since the first time I stumbled upon her in the cottage.

She glanced over her shoulder at me as she walked toward the bathroom. "Yes?"

It was a loaded question. Was I going to join her? Did I like what I was seeing? Would I follow her off a cliff? I popped out of bed and reached for her beckoning hand. "Yes, ma'am."

She laughed at my eagerness but her progress halted as her eyes took in every inch of my nudity. I gave her the same look she'd given me and received a playful shove for my mock cockiness. I gathered her up in my arms and captured her lips, then started walking her backwards to the bathroom.

After a great deal of fun in the shower, we finished getting ready and had a quick breakfast. She was keen for another ride today. I smiled at the influence I'd had on her regarding horses. Sayen was already in the barn when we got there. I should have felt guilty that she'd decided to stay over at her mom's last night to give us some privacy, but I couldn't be bothered. I was in love and Sayen wouldn't feel put out.

"Good morning, Sayen," Damisi greeted, giving her shoulder a squeeze. "What can we do to help?"

"Hey, Damisi." Sayen smiled at her and flicked her eyes to me. With the quick eye-flick, she could tell how our night and morning had gone. "I've got everything covered. You should give Inkswept a try while Nora puts in some work with her newest horse."

"An hour or two and then we'll explore the town a little more," I assured Damisi and turned to Sayen. "Can Melanie meet us for lunch or dinner today?"

"She's up for either. Are you going to take Damisi over to the ranch?"

I looked to Damisi to gauge her interest. She didn't seem anxious about it, but it was one thing to declare love for someone one day, then meet her entire family the next. Considering I was still trying to fortify the new boundaries I'd set with them, it might not be the smartest idea to descend on their homestead all giddy about the woman with me.

"I'd love to see your family ranch and meet your father and other brother if they're around." Damisi's curiosity was beating out her anxiety about "meeting the family."

Sayen's brow lifted as she turned to me with a smile. "Sounds like a plan."

Damisi reached to scratch Salander's neck while Sayen led Inkswept out of her stall to be saddled. "He's very noble looking, isn't he?"

"That he is. You can try him tomorrow. South pasture for him today?" I asked Sayen who was keeping track of our pasture rotations.

"Yep. When you're done, I'll take the girls out to the west pasture."

I swung a saddle up onto Inkswept for Damisi and only had to make one adjustment to her technique. She'd gotten better at saddling in the three weeks I'd been gone.

Sayen haltered Salander and brought him outside. I set my hands and gave her a leg up. She would ride him out to the south pasture and let him graze for the day.

Damisi stared wide-eyed at her easy mount and glide away from the barn without a saddle. "Does she compete as well?"

"She's done some reining comps, but she prefers taking care of the horses."

"What about your brothers?"

"They've done some roping and tried cutting, but neither placed high enough."

She watched as I tightened the cinch on Starling's saddle. "You'll miss this." She glanced away and looked over the grounds.

I went to stand in front of her and tugged on her chin to look at me. "I will, but not as much as I've been missing you these last few weeks." I leaned in for a soft kiss.

Her arms came around my waist and squeezed me tight. "I'm very happy to hear that. I know it's a lot to ask of someone. Walking away from everything she's known for someone who..." she paused, searching for the right description.

"Needed time to work through these enormous feelings? It is a big ask, but these feelings don't happen every day. For me, they haven't happened for thirty-two years. I'm not walking away from all I've known. I'm running to something and someone I've always wanted."

Her chest expanded and the exhale blew across my forehead. Soft lips traced across my face to my mouth. "My sweet cowgirl."

"My sexy professor." I kissed her back.

CHAPTER 32

"AM I MAKING a huge mistake?"

My question stopped Sayen mid-rise from the sofa where we sat. She had been on her way to get another cup of coffee but now sank back onto the cushions and faced me. Her hand landed on the partnership papers we were going through on the coffee table.

"Do you feel like you are?" She was always so diplomatic, learned after years of holding her tongue when we worked together at the family ranch. She saw the situation for what it was from the beginning, but I'd held out hope until the final decision was made in favor of the boys. She never once said, "I told you so." She'd hoped right along with me, but she was more pragmatic than I was.

"I don't, but I feel like I should. This ranch is what I've always wanted. The teaching position, you, your mom, your cousin and her son, my brothers and parents. I shouldn't feel so okay with just walking away."

"It's easy when it's right. Scotland suits you. We could see that as soon as we stepped out of the car. You built that place. It might not have been your money, but you poured your soul into it. Hearn is a good guy and knows when to let experts do the work he's hired them to do. Your workers are a great bunch, and that woman of yours is pretty amazing."

My face split into a smile. That woman of mine. It was still so new and seemed not entirely settled, but we'd spent three days unlike any of the others we'd spent together. There was an air of intimacy that we'd purposely never allowed before. A confidence as well. She'd asked me to come back to her, not the ranch, to her. I'd stopped holding back my emotions, and she was being more effusive. I'd shown her around the area and let the idea of a life with her settle in. It felt exhilarating.

Hearn had flown over to talk to me in person yesterday. His offer was even better than my original. A profit-sharing arrangement on all aspects of the business and competitions would make me as good as a partial owner. He had plans to build out the estate and wanted me in charge of that as well. It was too good to pass up. With Paisley, Roderick, and Rhona being hired back and the promised total control over the ranch, it was everything I'd worked my whole life for. Add in my relationship with Damisi—beguiling, no longer reserved Damisi—how could I pass it up?

The partnership papers waited to be signed. After a brief discussion, we decided Sayen would no longer be an employee. She'd be taking care of this ranch and helping to pay the mortgage while she lived here. Her mom was thinking of moving in permanently to help out in her off hours. We'd keep it small, three mares and a stallion, we'd split the profit from my stallion's cover charges, competition winnings, and any foals from my new mare. They'd keep the profits from their own foals. Sayen would continue to train the horses to compete, which would bring in a higher price for each sale. I'd continue to do some marketing and competing stateside when I was here, but basically, the operation would be mostly Sayen's. In the future, if she decided to do something else somewhere else, I'd consider selling the property. She seemed happy with the arrangement, and I knew the horses and property would be well cared for. With Melanie in residence, they'd live very comfortably, even in those hard winter months without competitions or breeding activities to supplement their income.

Last night, Damisi had flown to San Francisco with Hearn. He was speaking at an investor symposium, and she was going to visit her father's sister who lived in the Bay Area. Their flight back to Scotland was the day after tomorrow. They hoped I'd join them but weren't putting any pressure on me to make the decision so quickly. Hearn was giving me time to contemplate his offer of employment. Damisi was giving me space to make a decision that would affect the rest of our lives. That was my commitment level. She owned my heart. I'd left it behind when I came back to Idaho. With time, I hoped it would airmail itself back to me to be used with someone else, but I wasn't sure. Now, I'd get to claim it again, along with a wonderful woman. I should be more nervous, but all I felt was excitement. As much as I hadn't wanted Damisi to give me this thinking-time apart when we'd only had a few days back together, I was now grateful to have it. It was easy to say "yes" in the moment when a beautiful woman crosses continents to entice me back. It was better to say "yes" after some contemplation away from the allure of said beautiful woman. We could both be sure of my answer this way.

"Tell your parents first," Sayen suggested. "Don't sign until they know. You're in love and you've got your ideal ranch waiting for you in Scotland, but you're not finished here. Your parents and the carrot they dangled all your life was always your purpose. It may take time to adjust that mindset."

"You're right." I checked my watch. Mom would be getting dinner started and Dad, if he was following doctors' orders, would be in his study going over paperwork instead of out on the ranch working with horses.

On the drive over, I rehearsed what I'd say. When they came for dinner the other night, they might have guessed. We didn't hide that we were more than friends, a change from how my mother had seen us together back in Scotland. Nolan had likely told them I wasn't getting my regular teaching position back because he loved to gossip. And since I was no longer working at the ranch, they knew things had changed for me. They were hoping I'd relent and take my usual role on the ranch to work with Niall, but seeing me with Damisi made them unsure.

"Hi, honey," Mom greeted when I stepped into the house. "Did Damisi leave already?"

"She went to visit her aunt in San Francisco." I hugged her hello. "Where's Dad. I want to talk to you both."

"Oh, well, he's probably over at the ranch office."

"I thought he was supposed to be taking it easy? Niall is never going to succeed if Dad doesn't let him do what he's been hired to do."

"You know your father."

"You've got to be firm with him. The boys need him, you need him. He's not taking care of himself, so you all have to."

"Not you?"

My head shook as I sighed. "I think you know why I'm here."

She pushed out a shaky breath. "I was afraid you'd say that. I didn't understand before when you left. I thought you were hurt and punishing us. After seeing what you've built there, listening to Damisi tell us all you've done, I understand now. And she's lovely."

For as much as they stuck to tradition, they'd never had a problem with my sexuality. They treated any woman I was dating the same way they treated my brothers' girlfriends.

They hoped I'd find love and have a family. They just assumed the men in my family or hers would have to help support us.

"I never wanted to leave here, but I'm glad I did. This is best for the boys and me. They'll step up and you've got to get Dad to step back. We all need him."

"We'll make him understand. It will be harder without you here, but I can see how much you need to be free."

I leaned in and wrapped my arms around her. Over the past few weeks, my brothers had come a long way in modernizing their viewpoint. My mother may never get there, but it did feel like she finally understood how much they'd been holding me back.

CHAPTER 33

EXHAUSTED, I ALMOST didn't want to walk down to the barn to greet everyone and see the horses. An overnight flight from New York to Edinburgh would have been tiring enough, but Skye's baby girl insisted on having someone walk her up and down the aisle for many hours of the flight. Skye was a zombie after having cared for the kids on her own for a week, despite the help of her mom and best friend, so we all took turns keeping Isla happy. Tavish was content to sit on the floor and play with his blocks and sleep. Isla's hands gripped our fingers as her little legs staggered through the aisle to visit everyone seated and pat her brother's head on each lap. At seven months, she seemed to want to skip crawling altogether and go straight to walking. It was entertaining and kept my mind off not feeling guilty for walking away from a life I thought I'd always wanted.

At the airport, Gresham, Celia, and Ainsley stood together waiting for us to deboard. Ainsley looked antsy enough to race up the stairs and find her babies, but she waited patiently for us to bring them to her. Ainsley kissed Skye and grabbed Tavish for a cuddle in the same motion. I turned Isla in my arms and waited for Ainsley to reach a hand out for the second baby cuddle.

With one arm draped around Zoey, Celia dragged me into a hug as soon as Isla was safely in her mother's arms. "I'm so glad you're back. She's been unbearable since you left." Her head tipped toward Damisi.

"Right enough," Hearn agreed.

"Hey now," Damisi protested with a grin. "She missed the horses most."

I looped an arm around her waist, still marveling that I could do that any time I wanted now. Within reason, of course. She didn't magically become sickeningly affectionate overnight. "I missed everyone and everything." Turning to whisper in her ear, I admitted, "You most of all."

"Shall I get the car seats situated, Ainsley?" Zoey's dad was lugging both seats from the plane. He'd made the trip back with us for a vacation stay with his daughter and Celia.

"Thanks, Priam." Ainsley looked up from staring at the babies she'd missed over the last week. "Sorry, Nora, I've been caught up. It's wonderful to have you back."

"Great to see you again. Love your kids. Isla had us entertained the whole way back."

Groans sounded from the other passengers, but laughter overrode the groans. Gresham approached and shook my hand with a bright smile and grabbed two of my bags from the pile the attendant had offloaded.

"How'd the classes go?" Damisi asked Ainsley.

"I loved them," she breathed out, looking equal parts guilty and joyful. "Let me know if you need me to sub again before the semester ends. I'd even take over office hours."

"Missing it, hon?" Skye asked, her expression matching her wife's.

"Not enough to give up the rest of my maternity leave." She kissed the babies' heads.

We started toward the cars. Zoey, her dad, Gresham, and I all loaded the various bags into the cars while Damisi got the download from Ainsley about the week of classes she missed and Hearn, Celia, and Skye settled the babies into the car seats. Soon enough we were loaded and saying goodbye.

Gresham had us back at the estate in fifteen minutes. We passed the partially hidden parking lot teeming with visitor cars, and a shuttle bus followed us up the drive. This was the last full weekend before winter hours would limit the tours of the estate.

I was dead tired, but Hearn asked all the ranch employees to come in today and it was already mid-morning. Once Hearn found out Magnus had fired three of the amazing employees who'd built up the ranch, he fired Magnus and hired the employees back, promising to find someone decent to take over. He didn't tell them it was me.

Gresham pulled the car to a halt in front of the cottage. Damisi groaned with relief. I wanted to do the same, but the excitement of seeing everyone and the horses again made me bound out of the car. I reached back to pull Damisi with me. She smiled and gripped my chin. Her mouth closed over mine for a luxurious kiss.

"Skedaddle. I know you're exited. I'll get your bags inside." She patted my arm. "We'll be using my room, by the way, but if you're getting up before the sun as per usual, you can keep showering in your old bathroom downstairs."

I laughed at her exaggeration of my morning wake-up time. I would alter whatever she wanted if she kept kissing me like that. "I finally get to see your secret lair?"

Her lips brushed against my ear as she whispered, "You'll get to see anything you fancy, my darling."

The promise of her words made me shiver. I leaned in for another kiss. We broke apart when Gresham and Hearn came back from lugging my bags up to the front door. I sketched a wave at them, and darted off toward the stables. Small signs showed that the property had been neglected for a couple of weeks. Roderick, Paisley, and Rhona had been given the two weeks between being fired and my return as paid vacation. The others weren't enough to keep the grounds pristine as Magnus had apparently fired all the part-time helpers and tried to bring in people he knew. I'd have to see about getting some of those part-timers back.

"No way. You're back!" Rhona cried out from inside the barn and rushed toward me. In the next instant, she crashed into me, hugging hard. "You're back," she repeated much softer this time.

I was so glad Hearn decided to surprise everyone. The hug was even more proof I'd made the right decision in coming back. "Good to see you, too."

"Oi, Nora," Oisin called out with a huge smile on his face. "Our savior."

Paisley, Roderick, Lewa, and Josie followed him out of the barn. Elizabeth and Andrew surfaced from the entrance closest to the office. Their exuberance chased away any lingering doubts about leaving behind everything I'd ever known.

"Are you back?" Paisley asked.

"I shouldn't have left." I shook my head and corrected, "Well, I had to leave, but I shouldn't have stayed away. I'm very sorry for what you went through with that asswipe. If you'll give me another chance, we'll make things right again."

"You're here to stay?" Oisin wanted to confirm.

"I am, and after talking with Hearn, we have plans for the grounds. Paisley and Roderick, I'd like to use your construction and project management skills a lot more. New buildings, another wing to the barn for more horses, a riding arena, and a few homes for the employees. Rhona and Lewa, I'll lean heavily on you for horse care. Oisin and Andrew, you're my all-around guys, always willing to jump from task to task. We'll need that all day every day. Elizabeth, keeping everyone scheduled and fed is key to how this place can run successfully. Josie, I appreciate you stepping in while we sorted through this mess. Having you stay on as Kenzi's coach will be a big load off my shoulders."

Oisin shook his head and repeated, "You're really back?"

"To stay. I've found happiness here. Something I didn't realize I was missing, and you all are a large part of that. I'm hoping you'll want to stay on."

Oisin grabbed me in a hug, lifting me off the ground with a gleeful shout. "We're in. Right, mates?"

"Wouldn't be anywhere else," Elizabeth agreed.

After more shared anecdotes of the goings on while I was gone, the non-weekend crew were on their way home, leaving Andrew, Lewa, and Rhona to get back to their regular duties. I spent extra time with Angelou, Subi, and Inky before going to tally up everything we'd need to start working on after the weekend.

"Are you happy?" Damisi's voice called out to me as she approached the corral where most of the horses were stretching their legs.

I turned back and caught my breath. She'd showered and changed into the jeans she normally wore for riding. Her curly locks were spilling over her shoulders, face free of makeup, and she'd never looked more beautiful. "So happy."

"I know you missed these horses."

"I missed you and the horses."

"But mostly the horses, right?"

I pulled her to me. She was too tempting for her own good. "Mostly you, and you know it."

"Figured," she agreed smugly. Her eyes drifted to Inky as they so often did whenever she came to the stable grounds.

"You missed Inky while you were away. I'll turn you into a cowgirl, yet."

"Since you're also a professor, it only seems appropriate."

"Not a professor."

"Close enough, Cowgirl." She glanced over at the corral again. "I did miss Inky this week."

"Good, because he's yours now."

Her head whipped around. "What?"

"Hearn let me choose a horse as part of my signing bonus. The stables get ten percent of any winnings and cover charges if he becomes a champion, but otherwise, he's yours."

"But..." Her brow furrowed. "That makes him yours."

"Grand gesture, here, Damisi. Let me have my moment." My heart was beating fast. This wasn't exactly an engagement ring, but it was close. Giving her a horse brought her wholly into my world. Moving to Scotland put me in hers. "You adore Inky, and you need a horse if you're going to be a cowgirl."

"So do you." She was resisting verbally but looking over at Inky with wonder in her expression.

"I have a horse in Idaho. Two actually, and I'll see them whenever I visit. By the time Inky is ready to compete, you'll be an expert and might even give it a go."

"Ha! Listen, Cowgirl, I'd do just about anything for you, but you'll stick to the competitions and I'll stick to petting the horses."

"We'll see about that."

She leaned in and planted a kiss on my lips. "You'll see things my way. You usually do."

EPILOGUE

THE STABLES WERE a welcome sight after a few weeks away. Not that I hadn't enjoyed all the sights on my honeymoon, but it was nice to be home.

In the corral, Kenzi was training with Josie on Subi. It took a lot of training for both of them before they were ready to start competing, but they'd managed several competitions so far and a few good placements on the leaderboard. Oisin and Rhona were leading Inky to the outside bathing station in anticipation of Damisi's return. She'd be down to ride him as soon as she settled in. He and I had a competition in two weeks. His winnings and stud fees over the years paid for our wedding and honeymoon. Damisi insisted he belonged to both of us. It might have taken her years to trust in my desire to be her spouse, but she'd insisted on sharing what could become a million-dollar asset from the start.

In the distance, I could hear construction noise where Paisley and Roderick would be directing the framers on the second housing development on the far corner of the estate. The first was now home to some of the staff members at the castle, including Gresham. The second development would offer cottages for the members of my crew who hadn't already relocated to homes they'd purchased in Bathgate.

"Nora!" two excited voices called out at the same time.

I turned to the familiar sight of Zoey walking up the side road pulling a wagon cart with Ainsley and Skye's kids inside. She frequently came out to the estate to explore the grounds or go for a ride. She'd often stop off at the neighbors' home and see if she could give the moms a break and take the kids with her. She waved and plucked the kids out of the wagon.

"My favorite kiddies." I widened my arms as they raced toward me. I scooped them up in each arm, twirling and bouncing as they giggled. Isla's blond hair was as wild as Ainsley's, curly and frizzy and beautiful. Tavish's locks were slightly darker and much shorter.

"Missed you," Tavish said and smacked a kiss on my cheek. He was the more affectionate of the two, but when Isla chose to give hugs, she was just as sweet.

"Missed you both. You, too, Zoey." Their little arms reached to pull her into our hug. She laughed and stepped up to encircle us as a unit. "Are you here to look at the horsies?"

"Horsies!" the kids cried. I set them down but held on until enough eyes and hands were available for the usual zone defense we employed whenever the kids were at the stables.

"Nora's back!" Kenzi exclaimed as she heard the kids' excitement.

Oisin and Rhona left Inky's bath and came toward us as Kenzi slipped off the horse and joined them. Elizabeth poked her head out of the office and smiled. She ducked back inside, probably to call Paisley and Roderick before coming to join us.

"Hey, everybody." My tone was more mellow than ever.

The honeymoon had been amazing for so many reasons. First and foremost, I married the love of my life, but also, it allowed me to step back and focus on something other than ranching. Sure, I'd had far more balance in my life over the past three years, guest lecturing for Agatha's vet students, competing, hanging out with friends, babysitting for Ainsley and Skye, and spending time with my new family. Damisi and her mother were everything to me, and we gathered our friends close whenever we had time. My employees had become like family as well. The honeymoon gave me time to realize my work wasn't the most important thing in my life anymore. My employees were as capable as Sayen had always been, and I could focus on much more than work or my competitions.

"How was it?" Elizabeth asked and reached to pick up Tavish.

"Glorious." We'd traveled first to northwestern Scotland for Damisi's research, then to Florence and Rome for a museum crawl and to the Spanish coast for some sunny beach time, and finally, to Nigeria so Damisi could show me where she'd spent some time in the summers of her youth. It wasn't what I would have planned as my ideal honeymoon. I'd have gone straight to the Spanish coast to chill on the beach, but I married a historian and I loved to learn, so it turned out even better than I could have planned.

"As it should be," Elizabeth agreed.

"Welcome back," Oisin said. Over the years, he'd eased into the cowboy life. He especially loved traveling and staying with the horses during the competition season. He'd also entered some reining competitions with a horse that didn't take well to cattle. At the ranch, he was my second-in-command. "Everything's running smoothly."

I nodded at him and looked to Paisley, who was the project manager for all the construction on the estate. She shot me a thumbs up as she turned to chase after Isla, who took off toward the corral. A glance at Elizabeth told me everything was on schedule. Rhona's calm expression let me know the horses were all happy and healthy. A feeling of bliss settled over me. I hadn't really been worried, but it felt good to know that I could leave work at work and concentrate on home when I was home. Kids were next on the list for our lives together. I'd need a lot of home time once we had a baby.

After checking on all the horses, I made my way back to the cottage. Hearn and his wife, Agatha, were coming toward me, their baby boy in Agatha's arms. Hearn hadn't wasted much time locking Agatha in as his wife. I couldn't be more pleased for them, even if I envied how quickly they'd gotten married when it took me three years to convince Damisi I wouldn't be like her moronic ex and change my mind as soon as we were married.

"Welcome back, Nora," Hearn called out. "Just had a chat to Damisi. Sounds like you had a grand time."

"We did, and thank you again for letting us use the castle for the wedding. It was very generous." A vision of Damisi walking down the elegantly decorated aisle in the castle's great hall filled my head. I'd blurted out how incredible she looked as soon as her mom guided her hand into mine. The small gathering chuckled at my exclamation, but I barely heard them. My entire focus was on my beautiful bride.

"Such a fun wedding and reception. We can't wait to hear more about your honeymoon travels." Agatha brought me back from the wedding recall.

"Absolutely," I agreed and reached out. "Now, gimme that baby."

They laughed as they handed over little Callum. At six months he was almost as big as Tavish had been on his first birthday and just as sweet. Hearn and Agatha were splitting their family leave so Agatha could start back for the fall semester. Hearn had relocated his company headquarters to

Edinburgh a couple years ago. They spent their weekends at the castle and weekdays at Agatha's house in the city. Once Callum came along, they extended their weekend time at the castle. I had a feeling I'd be seeing a lot of Hearn and Callum at the stables over the next six months.

"Zoey's at the barn with the sibs. You know how much Tavs loves Cal."

"We really just wanted to welcome you back, but the kids are always fun to see. Damisi agreed to dinner later this week. We'll get Kenzi to babysit and go out somewhere nice, what do you say?" Hearn took Callum back and snuggled him into a one-armed cradle.

"Sounds good. See you both then."

Entering the cottage through the side door, I kicked off my boots. Music played from the speakers in the living room. Damisi was singing along, bringing a smile to my face. The number of times I'd walked into the house to hear music and Damisi's soft voice following along were too numerous to count, but it always brought up the first time. Her shock, flare of outrage, and gorgeous flash of nakedness always popped to mind.

Damisi was walking toward the kitchen as I came up behind her and slid my arms around her waist. She startled only for a moment, then leaned back against me. "That was a quick check."

"I'm still on our honeymoon."

She turned in my arms and lifted her face, waiting. She liked making me work for her affection, and it made her that much more tempting. I leaned down and planted my lips on hers. Her arms tightened around me as her mouth fused with mine.

"How long will this honeymoon last?" She was slightly breathless when she ended the kiss.

"If I have any say in the matter, the rest of our lives."

"You are such a sweetheart. Who knew my cowgirl would be so sweet?"

"Only for you, Professor."

"I've had about a million calls since you went off to play with your ranch."

I laughed and pulled back. "Everyone says hello by the way. Elizabeth wants to cook us dinner for tonight so we can extend our relaxation. Rhona would like some help choosing her classes for the fall semester. Oh, and Zoey and the kids are at the barn if you wanted to say hi."

"Celia invited us for dinner this week. She sounded excited but wouldn't spill. Maybe they received final approval for adoption." She pointed a commanding finger at me. "Act surprised when they tell us."

I laughed at the command and felt giddy with excitement for our friends. They'd been wanting to adopt for years but had to wait for Zoey's citizenship to come through. If this was the news they'd be sharing, I wouldn't have to act at all. Every reaction would be genuine.

"Yashika and Fin are having a dinner party next weekend. We're to bring your vegetarian lasagna to satisfy their veggie friends."

"I thought Yashika's actor friends didn't eat carbs?"

"You're the only one who knows how to make anything vegetarian tasty. They'll be made to eat it and like it." Her firm tone made me laugh.

"One look of complete surprise and one vegetarian lasagna, check and check."

"Mama is going to make an appearance tonight." Her brown eyes turned hesitant. She was nervous about her mom's frequent visits when my family was so far away.

"Your mom is welcome any time. You know I love her."

She pressed her forehead against mine. "Thank you, my darling. It means so much to me."

"Nothing has changed except now we legally belong together. Your mom included."

"She'll be happy to hear that." She leaned away and picked up a large envelope. "From Sayen." She watched me set it aside without bothering to open it. "Will that be the finalized sale of your ranch and business?"

I smiled reassuringly. "It's been Sayen's ranch since I left. We might have kept a partnership going and had a place to stay when we traveled, but it's been hers since I left. She'll be a good source for quarter horses in the future, and the guard dog training she's taken on is a good challenge for her."

"But it was your home, and now it's like you're breaking ties with it."

"You're my home, Damisi. You. You were brave enough to ask me to come back, and I've never been happier. This life here with you and working at the ranch are all I've ever wanted. If we're blessed with kids, all the better." I stared into her eyes with all the sincerity in my heart. "Sayen will always have a guestroom to host us, but it's not my home anymore."

"At some point, I will stop questioning that." Her eyes glistened with the start of happy tears.

"I'll always be here to remind you."

She wrapped her arms around me, sliding her hands up my sides. "I love you."

"You're mad for me," I mimicked her accent.

"You drive me mad, that's for certain." She gripped my shirt and planted a kiss on me. "I've usurped the laundry for today. It's your usual day, but now that we're married, I can do what I like. You can just shut your gob about it." Her own gob formed a dazzling smile.

"Yes, ma'am." I grinned back.

"Ma'am," she mocked my accent and looked like she would remind me she wasn't the "bloody queen."

"Now that we're married," I began, staring deep into her beautiful eyes. "You will forever be my queen."

Her tempting, so gorgeous mouth snapped closed and moved in for a soft kiss. When she tipped back, she smiled in that all-knowing way of hers. It finally looked like she was ready to believe we would last a lifetime together.

ABOUT THE AUTHOR

Lynn Galli lives in the Pacific Northwest where she actively avoids any news coverage on the putrid garbage dump of hellfire that is American politics. Her ultimate goal is to start a self-reliant cult where the words "hashtag," "winners," and "fake news" would cause immediate expulsion of its members. To maintain her sanity during election seasons, she regularly engages in her most cherished hobbies: collecting airplane sick bags, train surfing, cheese rolling, and competitive shin kicking. On the occasions when she surfaces from her despair at the downfall of society, she tries to create fictional worlds where its inhabitants are less likely to irrationally erect border walls, deny resources to the people who need them most, and consider reality television award-worthy.

Other Publications by Lynn Galli

SCOTTISH CHARM

One-Off (Book 1) – Weddings have never been Skye MacKinnon's thing. When she's put in charge of planning her friend's big event, she's less than thrilled. Finding out she'll have to work with the bane of her college existence, Ainsley Baird, may push her right over the edge. Knowing there's nothing she can do to change her circumstances or the company she'll have to keep, her only plan is to make it through the happy occasion without setting fire to the whole show or one person in particular.

Speak Low (Book 2) – With a unique view on legal marriage, Zoey Thais tends to have a fleeting relationship with relationships. It suits her chosen roving career path, even if she wishes she could find someone to put up with her quirks. Celia Munro is sensible about love, even if she wishes she had the courage to take a risk on a wanderer. Will the marriage cynic and the reluctant romantic set aside their ingrained hesitancy to take a chance on love?

So Well As You (Book 3) – From their first memorable meeting, Nora Cleary and Damisi Dalziel waver between civility and aggravation. Both have taken temporary postings nearby and must share a house belonging to Damisi's friend who is Nora's new boss. Will the forced cohabitation highlight their differences or give them the opportunity to grab onto something they've both been looking for?

Virginia Clan

At Last (Prequel) – Willa Lacey never thought acquiring five million in venture capital for her software startup would be easier than suppressing romantic feelings for a friend. Having never dealt with either situation, Willa finds herself torn between what she knows and what could be.

Wasted Heart (Book 1) – Attorney Austy Nunziata moves across the country to try to snap out of the cycle of pining for her married best friend. Despite knowing how pointless her feelings are, five months in the new city hasn't seemed to help. When she meets FBI agent, Elise Bridie, that task becomes a lot easier.

Imagining Reality (Book 2) – Changing a reputation can be the hardest thing anyone can do, even among her own friends. But Jessie Ximena has been making great strides over the past year to do just that. Will anyone, even her good friends, give her the benefit of the doubt when it comes to finding a forever love?

Blessed Twice (Book 3) – Briony Gatewood has considered herself a married woman for fifteen years even though she's spent the last three as a widow. Her friends have offered to help her get over the loss of her spouse with a series of blind dates, but only a quiet, enigmatic colleague can make Briony think about falling in love again.

Forevermore (Book 4) - M Desiderius never thought she could have a normal life filled with love. She gets all that and more when she marries Briony, including an amazing foster daughter named Olivia. Every wish she'd never allowed herself to voice became real. When someone from Olivia's past threatens M's newfound family, can she carry on in the face of loss or will it push her back into a life of solitude?

ASPEN FRIENDS

Mending Defects (Book 1) – Small town life for Glory Eiben has always been her ideal. With her rare congenital heart defect, keeping family and friends close by preserves her easygoing attitude. When Lena Coleridge moves in next door, life becomes anything but easy. Lena is a reluctant transplant and even more reluctant friend. Their growing friendship adds many layers to Glory's ideal.

Something So Grand (Book 2) – A designer for the wealthy, Vivian Yeats doesn't have time for relationships, yet she longs for romance. She's had to settle in the past when it comes to women but won't be doing that again. If romance is going to happen for her, it'll take someone special to turn her head. Natalie Harper, the new contractor on her jobsites, might just be the woman to make that happen.

Life Rewired (Book 3) – Two years ago, Molly Sokol decided she wanted to get serious about finding that special someone. She can picture her ideal woman easily: petite, feminine, excitable, adoring, and ultra-affectionate. When the opposite of all that comes along in the form of Falyn Shaw, Molly never thought they'd be anything more than friends. Being wrong has never felt so good.

OTHER ROMANCES

Uncommon Emotions – When someone spends her days ripping apart corporations, compartmentalization is key. Love doesn't factor into any decision for Joslyn Simonini. Meeting Raven Malvolio ruins the harmony that Joslyn has always felt. Finally, she's introduced to passion for the first time in her life.

Full Court Pressure – The pressure of being the first female basketball coach of a men's NCAA Division 1 team may pale in comparison to the pressure Graysen Viola feels in her unexpected love life.

Clichéd Love – As a journalist, Vega spends her days writing other people's stories. For her latest assignment, she's taking down LGBT love stories and worrying that her eyes might roll right out of their sockets during every mushy interview. Only the help of her new friend, Iris, who also believes romance stories are worth mocking, prevents her from finding ways to make her subjects mysteriously disappear to save her from having to listen to more clichés.

Out of Order – Lindsay St. James spends her days fixing political problems. No problem too taxing, no issue too complex to resolve for someone who dedicates herself to her career. When she stumbles into a judicial bribery scheme affecting her candidate, she has to rely on the help of the newest and most distracting member of the judiciary. For the first time, her personal interests are keeping her from focusing on her profession, and she doesn't seem all that bothered about it.

Winter Calling – As a human resources coordinator for a ski resort, Tru's biggest challenge is finding people to take a leisure job seriously. The new CFO fits that characterization a little too well according to Tru's colleagues. Renske's stoic demeanor makes them believe she's a cold, unfeeling android. Always willing to think the best of people, Tru sets out to discover if Renske is really as imperturbable as she seems.